*Also by:*

# C.M. EDDY, JR.

## EXIT INTO ETERNITY:
### TALES OF THE BIZARRE
### AND SUPERNATURAL

## THE GENTLEMAN
## FROM ANGELL STREET
### MEMORIES OF H.P. LOVECRAFT
*(With Muriel E. Eddy)*

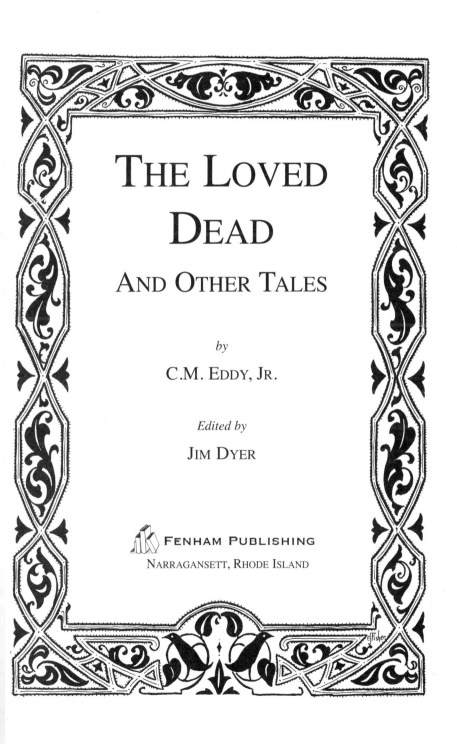

# THE LOVED
# DEAD

## AND OTHER TALES

*by*

C.M. EDDY, JR.

*Edited by*

JIM DYER

FENHAM PUBLISHING

NARRAGANSETT, RHODE ISLAND

Fenham Publishing
P.O. Box 767
Narragansett, RI  02882

First Fenham Publishing Trade Edition February 2008

10 9 8 7 6 5 4 3 2 1

These are works of fiction. While as in all fiction, the literary perceptions and insights are
based on experience, all names, characters, places and incidents are either products of the
author's imagination or are used fictitiously.

Cover Illustration by David Moen

Interior story heading artwork by Andrew Brosnatch
© 1924-1925 Popular Fiction Publishing Company

All stories reprinted by permission of the Eddy Family.

Interior story heading artwork reprinted by permission of Weird Tales LTD.

Library of Congress Control Number: 2008920985

ISBN 978-0-9701699-2-1

Cover Design and Book Layout: Lesa Nash

Printing and Binding: Regine Printing Inc., Providence, RI
Author Photograph: © Eddy Family. Used by permission

Printed in the United States of America

# Acknowledgements

THE LOVED DEAD   © 1924 Rural Publishing Corporation, © renewed C.M. Eddy, Jr.
Originally published in Weird Tales May-July 1924 - Written 1919

WITH WEAPONS OF STONE   © 1924 Popular Fiction Publishing Company,
© renewed C.M. Eddy, Jr.
Originally published in Weird Tales December 1924 - Written 1919

RED CAP OF THE MARA   © 1976 Fay A. Dyer and Ruth M. Eddy
Originally published in Fantasy Crossroads #8 May 1976 - Stygian Isle Press - Written 1922

AN ARBITER OF DESTINY   © 1977 Fay A. Dyer and Ruth M. Eddy
Originally published in Fantasy Crosswinds #1 January 1977 - Stygian Isle Press - Written 1918

THE CUR   © 1976 Fay A. Dyer and Ruth M. Eddy
Originally published in Erased From Exile – Stygian Isle Press, 1976 - Written 1923

THE BETTER CHOICE   © 1925 Popular Fiction Publishing Company,
© renewed C.M. Eddy, Jr.
Originally published in Weird Tales March 1925 - Written 1919

ASHES   © 1924 Rural Publishing Corporation, © renewed C.M. Eddy, Jr.
Originally published in Weird Tales March 1924 - Written 1919

ETERNA   © 1976 Fay A. Dyer and Ruth M. Eddy
Originally published in Terror Out of Time 1976 - Written 1915

ARHL-A OF THE CAVES
© 1925 Popular Fiction Publishing Company, © renewed C.M. Eddy, Jr.
Originally published in Weird Tales January 1925 – Written 1919

THE GHOST-EATER   © 1924 Rural Publishing Corporation, © renewed C.M. Eddy, Jr.
Originally published in Weird Tales April 1924 – Written 1922

DEAF, DUMB, AND BLIND   © 1925 Popular Fiction Publishing Company,
© renewed C.M. Eddy, Jr.
Originally published in Weird Tales April 1925 – Written 1922

SOULS & HEELS   © 1976 Fay A. Dyer and Ruth M. Eddy
Originally published in Erased From Exile – Stygian Isle Press, 1976 – Written 1919

SIGN OF THE DRAGON   © C.M. Eddy, Jr.
Originally published in Mystery Magazine September 1, 1919 issue #44 – Written 1918

# THE LOVED DEAD

# Introduction

C. M. Eddy, Jr. was an author best known for his horror and supernatural short stories. He began his career writing for a broad range of pulp fiction genres in the 1920's, including detective mystery and weird macabre. He is best remembered for his work in *Weird Tales* Magazine.

Clifford Martin Eddy, Jr. was born on January 18, 1896 and died at age 71 on November 21, 1967, living most of his life in Providence, Rhode Island. During his early years he was friend and confidant to both H.P. Lovecraft and Harry Houdini. He was a member of Lovecraft's inner circle of friends and authors, and a ghostwriter and investigator for Houdini.

As a youngster, Eddy was an avid reader and began to write at an early age. His interests were varied and included the occult, mysticism, mythology, as well as detective stories.

A composer of many songs, he wrote both lyrics and melodies. Some of his more widely circulated published compositions were "Dearest of All", "When We Met By The Blue Lagoon", "Underneath the Whispering Pine", "Sunset Hour", and

"Hello, Mister Sunshine (Goodbye, Mister Rain)".

Clifford met his wife Muriel though their mutual interest in creative writing. Following marriage in 1918 they continued their writing pursuits while raising a family of three children.

C.M. Eddy, Jr.'s first nationally published fiction was the featured cover story "Sign of the Dragon" in the September 1, 1919 issue of *Mystery Magazine*. This detective mystery story is reprinted here for the first time.

Along with "Sign of the Dragon" are a number of his stories from *Weird Tales* including "The Loved Dead", perhaps one of the most infamous stories from that time. It was originally written in 1919 as "Beloved" and submitted to various pulp magazines. But as one editor put it – no one in their right mind would ever publish that story in America and suggested it be published in France, referring to Grand-Guignol, the French theatre.

The story was submitted several years later to *Weird Tales* for publication. Editor Edwin Baird wrote in a January 1924 letter to Eddy, "I hardly know what to say about 'The Loved Dead'. The thing is so gruesome that even I, with my well known broad-minded editorial policy, am almost afraid to publish it." It was ultimately included in the first year anniversary issue, May/June/July of 1924.

Farnsworth Wright, who took over as editor of *Weird Tales* from Edwin Baird, wrote in a September 1924 letter, "The Richmond (Indiana) Parent Teachers' Association tried to get an injunction out against the further publication of Weird Tales because of 'The Loved Dead.' " The resultant publicity and the increase in sales helped the financially strapped magazine stave off bankruptcy and continue to publish.

Seven of C.M. Eddy's stories from *Weird Tales* are included in this volume. Story headings from four of these tales are reproduced from the original artwork created by Andrew Brosnatch. His illustrations were showcased on fifteen *Weird Tales* covers and he created the majority of the interior artwork from 1924 – 1926. Brosnatch also designed the logo for the Eyrie section of the magazine.

C.M. Eddy's most prolific period of short story writing was during the years 1919 through 1922 — the time the majority of this collection was produced. The original manuscripts were used for the texts in editing this book. Deciphering the yellowing, brittle handwritten pages was a task well worth the challenge and effort. These thirteen tales show C.M. Eddy's diversity and range as an author and storyteller.

It is a pleasure to present another volume from one of the original pulp authors, whose imaginative storylines and descriptive phrases allow you to be fully transported into the narrative.

*Jim Dyer*

# CONTENTS

The Loved Dead . . . . . . . . . . . . . . . . . . . . . . . . . . . . . . . . . . . . . . . . . . . 1

With Weapons of Stone . . . . . . . . . . . . . . . . . . . . . . . . . . . . . . . . . . . . . 16

Red Cap of the Mara . . . . . . . . . . . . . . . . . . . . . . . . . . . . . . . . . . . . . . . 29

An Arbiter of Destiny . . . . . . . . . . . . . . . . . . . . . . . . . . . . . . . . . . . . . . 46

The Cur . . . . . . . . . . . . . . . . . . . . . . . . . . . . . . . . . . . . . . . . . . . . . . . . . . 57

The Better Choice . . . . . . . . . . . . . . . . . . . . . . . . . . . . . . . . . . . . . . . . . 68

Ashes . . . . . . . . . . . . . . . . . . . . . . . . . . . . . . . . . . . . . . . . . . . . . . . . . . . . 82

Eterna . . . . . . . . . . . . . . . . . . . . . . . . . . . . . . . . . . . . . . . . . . . . . . . . . . . 95

Arhl-a of the Caves . . . . . . . . . . . . . . . . . . . . . . . . . . . . . . . . . . . . . . . 108

The Ghost-Eater . . . . . . . . . . . . . . . . . . . . . . . . . . . . . . . . . . . . . . . . . 122

Deaf, Dumb and Blind . . . . . . . . . . . . . . . . . . . . . . . . . . . . . . . . . . . . 136

Souls & Heels . . . . . . . . . . . . . . . . . . . . . . . . . . . . . . . . . . . . . . . . . . . 153

Sign of the Dragon . . . . . . . . . . . . . . . . . . . . . . . . . . . . . . . . . . . . . . . 176

# The Loved Dead

IT IS MIDNIGHT. Before dawn they will find me and take me to a black cell where I shall languish interminably, while insatiable desires gnaw at my vitals and wither up my heart, till at last I become with the dead that I love.

My seat is the fetid hollow of an aged grave; my desk is the back of a fallen tombstone worn smooth by devastating centuries; my light is that of the stars and a thin-edged moon, yet I can see as clearly as though it were midday. Around on every side, sepulchral sentinels guarding unkempt graves, the tilting, decrepit headstones lie half-hidden in masses of nauseous, rotting vegetation. Above the rest, silhouetted against the livid sky, an august monument lifts austere, tapering spire like the spectral chieftain of a lemurian horde. The air is heavy with the noxious odors of fungi and the scent of damp, mouldy earth, but to me it is the aroma of Elysium. It is still — terrifyingly still — with a silence whose very profundity bespeaks the solemn and the hideous. Could I choose my habitation it would be in the heart of some such city of putrefying flesh and crumbling bones; for their nearness sends ecstatic thrills through my soul, causing the stagnant blood to race through my veins and my torpid heart to pound with delirious joy— for the presence of death is life to me!

My early childhood was one long, prosaic and monotonous apathy. Strictly ascetic, wan, pallid, undersized, and subject to protracted spells of morbid moroseness, I was ostracized by the healthy, normal youngsters of my own age. They dubbed me a spoil-sport, and "old woman", because I had no interest in the rough, childish games played, or any stamina to participate in them, had I so desired.

Like all rural villages, Fenham had its quota of poison-tongued gossips. Their prying imaginations hailed my lethargic temperament as some abhorrent abnormality; they compared me with my parents and shook their heads in ominous doubt at the vast difference. Some of the more superstitious openly pronounced me a changeling while others who knew something of my ancestry called attention to the vague mysterious rumors concerning a great-great-grand uncle who had been burned at the stake as a necromancer.

Had I lived in some larger town, with greater opportunities for congenial companionship, perhaps I could have overcome this early tendency to be a recluse. As I reached my teens I grew even more sullen, morbid, and apathetic. My life lacked motivation. I seemed in the grip of something that dulled my senses, stunted my development, retarded my activities, and left me unaccountably dissatisfied.

I was sixteen when I attended my first funeral. A funeral in Fenham was a pre-eminent social event, for our town was noted for the longevity of its inhabitants. When, moreover, the funeral was that of such a well-known character as my grandfather, it was safe to assume that the townspeople would turn out en masse to pay due homage to his memory. Yet I did not view the approaching ceremony with even latent interest. Anything that tended to lift me out of my habitual inertia held for me only the promise of physical and mental disquietude. In deference to my parents' importunings, mainly to give myself relief from their caustic condemnations of what they chose to call my unfilial attitude, I agreed to accompany them.

There was nothing out of the ordinary about my grandfather's funeral unless it was the voluminous array of floral tributes; but this, remember, was my first initiation to the solemn rites of such an occasion. Something about the darkened room, the oblong coffin with its somber drapings, the banked masses of fragrant blooms, the dolorous manifestations of the assembled villagers, stirred me from any normal listlessness and arrested my attention. Roused from my momentary reverie by a nudge from my mother's sharp elbow, I followed her across the room to the casket where the body of my grandparent lay.

For the first time I was face to face with Death. I looked down upon the calm placid face lined with its multitudinous wrinkles, and saw nothing to cause so much of sorrow. Instead, it seemed to me that grandfather was immeasurably content, blandly satisfied. I felt swayed by some strange discordant sense of elation. So slowly, so stealthily had it crept over me, that I could scarcely define its coming. As I mentally review that portentous hour it seems that it must have originated with my first glimpse of that funeral scene, silently strengthening its grip with a subtle insidiousness. A baleful malignant influence that seemed to emanate from the corpse itself held me with magnetic fascination. My whole being seemed charged with some ecstatic electrifying force, and I felt my form straighten without conscious volition. My eyes were trying to burn beneath the closed lids of the dead man's and read some secret message they concealed. My heart gave a sudden leap of unholy glee, and pounded against my ribs with demoniacal force as if to free itself from the confining walls of my frail frame. Wild, wanton, soul-satisfying sensuality engulfed me. Once more the vigorous prod of a maternal elbow jarred me into activity. I had made my way to the sable-shrouded coffin with leaden tread; I walked away with new-found animation.

I accompanied the cortege to the cemetery, my whole physical being permeated with this mystic enlivening influence. It was as if I had quaffed deep draughts of some exotic elixir — some abominable concoction brewed from blasphemous formulae in the archives of Belial.

The townsfolk were so intent upon the ceremony that the radical change in my demeanor passed unnoticed by all save my father and my mother, but in the fortnight that followed, the village busybodies found fresh material for their vitriolic tongues in my altered bearing. At the end of the fortnight, however, the potency of the stimulus began to lose its effectiveness. Another day or two and I had completely reverted to my old-time languor, though not to the complete, and engulfing insipidity of the past. Before, there had been an utter lack of desire to emerge from the enervation; now vague and indefinable unrest disturbed me. Outwardly I had become myself again, and the scandal-mongers turned to some more engrossing subject. Had they even so much as dreamed the true cause of my exhilaration they would have shunned me as if I were a filthy, leprous thing. Had I visioned the execrable power behind my brief period of elation I would have locked myself forever from the rest of the world and spent my remaining years in penitent solitude.

Tragedy often runs in trilogies, hence despite the proverbial longevity of our townspeople the next five years brought the death of both parents. My mother went first, in an accident of the most unexpected nature; and so genuine was my grief that I was honestly surprised to find its poignancy mocked and contradicted by that almost forgotten feeling of supreme and diabolical ecstasy. Once more my heart leaped wildly within me, once more it pounded at trip-hammer speed and sent the hot blood coursing through my veins with meteoric fervor. I shook from my shoulders the harassing cloak of stagnation only to replace it with the infinitely more horrible burden of loathsome, unhallowed desire. I haunted the death-chamber where the body of my mother lay, my soul athirst for the devilish nectar that seemed to saturate the air of the darkened room. Every breath strengthened me, lifted me to towering heights of seraphic satisfaction. I knew, now, that it was but a sort of drugged delirium which must soon pass and leave me correspondingly weakened by its malign power, yet I could no more control my longing than I could untwist the Gordian knots in the already tangled skein of my destiny.

I knew, too, that through some strange satanic curse my life depended upon the dead for its motive force; that there was a singularity in my makeup which responded only to the awesome presence of some lifeless clod. A few days later, frantic for the bestial intoxicant on which the fullness of my existence depended, I interviewed Fenham's sole undertaker and talked him into taking me on as a sort of apprentice.

The shock of my mother's demise had visibly affected my father. I think that if I had broached the idea of such *outré* employment at any other time he would have been emphatic in his refusal. As it was he nodded acquiescence after a moment's sober thought. How little did I dream that he would be the object of my first practical lesson!

He, too, died suddenly; developing some hitherto unsuspected heart affliction. My octogenarian employer tried his best to dissuade me from the unthinkable task of embalming his body, nor did he detect the rapturous glint in my eyes as I finally won him over to my damnable point of view. I cannot hope to express the reprehensible, the unutterable thoughts that swept in tumultuous waves of passion through my racing heart as I labored over the lifeless clay. Unsurpassed love was the keynote of these concepts, a love greater — far greater — than any I had ever borne him while he was alive.

My father was not a rich man, but he had possessed enough of worldly goods to make him comfortably independent. As his sole heir I found myself in rather a paradoxical position. My early youth had totally failed to fit me for contact with the modern world, yet the primitive life of Fenham with its attendant isolation palled upon me. Indeed, the longevity of the inhabitants defeated my sole motive in arranging my indenture.

After settling the estate it proved an easy matter to secure my release and I headed for Bayboro, a city some fifty miles away.

Here my year of apprenticeship stood me in good stead. I had no trouble in establishing a favorable connection as an assistant with the Gresham Corporation, a concern that maintained the largest funeral parlors in the city. I even prevailed upon them to let me sleep upon the premises — for already the proximity-of the dead was becoming an obsession.

I applied myself to my task with unwonted zeal. No case was too gruesome for my impious sensibilities, and I soon became master at my chosen vocation. Every fresh corpse brought into the establishment meant a fulfilled promise of ungodly gladness, of irreverent gratification; a return of that rapturous tumult of the arteries which transformed my grisly task into one of beloved devotion — yet every carnal satiation exacted its toll. I came to dread the days that brought no dead for me to gloat over, and prayed to all the obscene gods of the nethermost abysses to bring swift, sure death upon the residents of the city.

Then came the nights when a skulking figure stole surreptitiously through the shadowy streets of the suburbs; pitch-dark nights when the midnight moon was obscured by heavy lowering clouds. It was a furtive figure that blended with the trees and cast fugitive glances over its shoulder; a figure bent on some malignant mission. After one of these prowlings the morning papers would scream to their sensation-mad clientele the details of some nightmare crime; column on column of lurid gloating over abominable atrocities; paragraph on paragraph of impossible solutions and extravagant, conflicting suspicions. Through it all I felt a supreme sense of security, for who would for a moment suspect an employee in an undertaking establishment, where Death was supposedly an everyday affair, of seeking surcease from unnameable urgings in the cold-blooded slaughter of his fellow-beings? I planned each crime with maniacal cunning, varying the manner of my murders so that no one would even dream that all were the work of one blood-stained pair of hands. The aftermath of each nocturnal venture was an ecstatic hour of pleasure, pernicious and unalloyed; a pleasure always heightened by the chance that its delicious source might later be assigned to my gloating administrations in the course of my regular occupation. Sometimes that double and ultimate pleasure did occur — O rare and delicious memory!

During long nights when I clung close to the shelter of my sanctuary, I was prompted by the mausoleum silence to devise new and unspeakable ways of lavishing my affections upon the dead that I loved — the dead that gave me life!

One morning Mr. Gresham came much earlier than usual — came to find me stretched out upon a cold slab deep in ghoulish

THE LOVED DEAD

slumber, my arms wrapped about the stark, stiff, naked body of a fetid corpse!

He roused me from my salacious dreams, his eyes filled with mingled detestation and pity. Gently but firmly he told me that I must go, that my nerves were unstrung, that I needed a long rest from the repellent tasks my vocation required, that my impressionable youth was too deeply affected by the dismal atmosphere of my environment. How little did he know of the demoniacal desires that spurred me on in my disgusting infirmities! I was wise enough to see that argument would only strengthen his belief in my potential madness--it was far better to leave than to invite discovery of the motive underlying my actions.

After this I dared not stay long in one place for fear some overt act would bare my secret to an unsympathetic world. I drifted from city to city, from town to town. I worked in morgues, around cemeteries, once in a crematory-anywhere that afforded me an opportunity to be near the dead that I so craved.

Then came the World War. I was one of the first to go across, one of the last to return. Four years of blood-red charnel Hell... sickening slime of rain–rotten trenches... deafening bursting of hysterical shells... monotonous droning of sardonic bullets... smoking frenzies of Phlegethon's fountains... stifling fumes of murderous gases... grotesque remnants of smashed and shredded bodies... four years of transcendent satisfaction.

In every wanderer there is a latent urge to return to the scenes of his childhood. A few months later found me making my way through the familiar byways of Fenham. Vacant dilapidated farm houses lined the adjacent roadsides, while the years had brought equal retrogression to the town itself. A mere handful of the houses were occupied, but among those was the one I had once called home. The tangled, weed-choked driveway, the broken window panes, the uncared-for acres that stretched behind, all bore mute confirmation of the tales that guarded inquiries had elicited-that it now sheltered a dissolute drunkard who eked out a meager existence from the chores his few neighbors gave him out of sympathy for the mistreated wife and undernourished child who shared his lot. All in all, the glamour surrounding my youthful environment was entirely dispelled; so, prompted by some errant foolhardy thought, I next turned my steps toward Bayboro.

Here, too, the years had brought changes, but in reverse order. The small city I remembered had almost doubled in size despite its wartime depopulation. Instinctively I sought my former place of employment, finding it still there but with an unfamiliar name and "Successor to" above the door, for the influenza epidemic had claimed Mr. Gresham, while the boys were overseas. Some fateful mood impelled me to ask for work. I referred to my tutelage under Mr. Gresham with some trepidation, but my fears were groundless-my late employer had carried the secret of my unethical conduct with him to the grave. An opportune vacancy insured my immediate re-installation.

Then came vagrant haunting memories of scarlet nights of impious pilgrimages, and an uncontrollable desire to renew those illicit joys. I cast caution to the winds and launched upon another series of damnable debaucheries. Once more the yellow sheets found welcome material in the devilish details of my crimes, comparing them to the red weeks of horror; that had appalled the city years before. Once more the police sent out their dragnet and drew into its enmeshing folds — nothing!

My thirst for the noxious nectar of the dead grew to a consuming fire, and I began to shorten the periods between my odious exploits. I realized that I was treading on dangerous ground, but demoniac desire gripped me in its torturing tentacles and urged me on.

All this time my mind was becoming more and more benumbed to any influence except the satiation of my insane longings. Little details vitally important to one bent on such evil escapades escaped me. Somehow, somewhere, I left a vague trace, an elusive clue behind — not enough to warrant my arrest, but sufficient to turn the tide of suspicion in my direction. I sensed this espionage, yet was helpless to stem the surging demand for more dead to quicken my enervated soul.

Then came the night when the shrill whistle of the police roused me from my fiendish gloating over the body of my latest victim, a gory razor still clutched tightly in my hand. With one dexterous motion I closed the blade and thrust it into the pocket of the coat I wore. Nightsticks beat a lusty tattoo upon the door. I crashed the window with a chair, thanking Fate I had chosen one of the cheaper tenement districts for my locale. I dropped into a dingy alley as blue-coated forms burst through the shattered door. Over shaky fences, through filthy back yards, past squalid ramshackle houses, down dimly-lighted narrow streets I fled.

I thought at once of the wooded marshes that lay beyond the city and stretched for half a hundred miles till they touched the outskirts of Fenham. If I could reach this goal I would be temporarily safe. Before dawn I was plunging headlong through the foreboding wasteland, stumbling over the rotting roots of half-dead trees whose naked branches stretched out like grotesque arms striving to encumber me with mocking embraces.

The imps of the nefarious gods to whom I offered my idolatrous prayers must have guided my footsteps through that menacing morass. A week later-wan, bedraggled, and emaciated, I lurked in the woods a mile from Fenham. So far I had eluded my pursuers, yet I dared not show myself, for I knew that the alarm must have been sent broadcast. I vaguely hoped I had thrown them off the trail. After that first frenetic night I had heard no sound of alien voices, no crashing of heavy bodies through the underbrush. Perhaps they had concluded that my body lay hidden in some stagnant pool or had vanished forever in the tenacious quagmire.

Hunger gnawed at my vitals with poignant pangs, thirst left my throat parched and dry. Yet far worse was the unbearable hunger of my starving soul for the stimulus I found only in the nearness of the dead. My nostrils quivered in sweet recollection. No longer could I delude myself with the thought that this desire was a mere whim of the heated imagination. I knew now that it was an integral part of life itself; that without it I should burn out like an empty lamp. I summoned all my remaining energy to fit me for the task of satisfying my accursed appetite. Despite the peril attending my move I set out to reconnoiter, skirting the sheltering shadows like an obscene wraith.

Once more I felt that strange sensation of being led by some unseen satellite of Satan. Yet even my sin-steeped soul revolted for a moment when I found myself before my native abode, the scene of my youthful hermitage.

Then these disquieting memories faded. In their place came over-whelming lustful desire. Behind the rotting walls of this old house lay my prey. A moment later I had raised one of the shattered windows and clambered over the sill. I listened for a moment, every sense alert, every muscle tensed for action. The silence reassured me. With cat-like tread I stole through the familiar rooms until stertorous snores indicated the place where I was to find surcease from my sufferings. I allowed myself a sigh of anticipated ecstasy as I pushed open the door of the bedchamber. Panther-like I made my way to the supine form stretched out in drunken stupor. The wife and child — where were they — well, they could wait. My clutching fingers groped for his throat.

Hours later I was — again the fugitive, but a new-found stolen strength was mine. Three silent forms slept to wake no more. It was not until the garish light of day penetrated my hiding-place that I visualized the certain consequences of my rashly purchased relief. By this time the bodies must have been discovered. Even the most obtuse of the rural police must surely link the tragedy with my flight from the nearby city. Besides, for the first time I had been careless enough to leave some tangible proof of my identity-my fingerprints on the throats of the newly dead. All day I shivered in nervous apprehension. The mere crackling of a dry twig beneath my feet conjured mental images that appalled me. That night, under cover of the protecting darkness, I skirted Fenham and made for the woods that lay beyond. Before dawn came the first definite hint of renewed pursuit — the distant baying of hounds.

Through the long night I pressed on, but by morning I could feel my artificial strength ebbing. Noon brought once more the insistent call of the contaminating curse, and I knew I must fall by the way unless I could once more experience that exotic intoxication that came only with the proximity of the loved dead. I had traveled in a wide semicircle. If I pushed steadily ahead, midnight would bring me to the cemetery where I had laid away my parents years before. My only hope, I felt certain, lay in reaching this goal before I was over-taken. With a silent prayer to the devils that dominated my destiny I turned leaden feet in the direction of my last stronghold.

God! Can it be that a scant twelve hours have passed since I started for my ghostly sanctuary? I have lived an eternity in each leaden hour. But I have reached a rich reward. The noxious odors of this neglected spot are frankincense to my suffering soul!

The first streaks of dawn are graying the horizon. They are coming! My sharp ears catch the far-off howling of the dogs! It is but a matter of minutes before they find me; and shut me away forever from the rest of the world, to spend my days in ravaging yearnings; till at last I join the dead I love.

They shall not take me! A way of escape is open! A coward's choice, perhaps, but better — far better — than endless months of nameless misery. I will leave this record behind me that some soul may perhaps understand why I make this choice.

The razor! It has nestled forgotten in my pocket since my flight from Bayboro. Its blood stained blade gleams oddly in the waning light of the thin-edged moon. One slashing stroke across my left wrist and deliverance is assured . . .

Warm, fresh blood spatters grotesque patterns on dingy, decrepit slabs... phantasmal hordes swarm over the rotting graves... spectral fingers beckon me... ethereal fragments of unwritten melodies rise in celestial crescendo... distant stars dance drunkenly in demoniac accompaniment... a thousand tiny hammers beat hideous dissonances on anvils inside my chaotic brain... gray ghosts of slaughtered spirits parade in mocking silence before me... scorching tongues of invisible flame sear the brand of Hell upon my sickened soul...

I can — write — no — more . . .

# WITH WEAPONS of STONE

### A TALE OF THE CAVEMEN

by C.M. Eddy Jr.

THE GREAT CLIFFS teemed with bustle and confusion. From every one of the subterranean chambers that honeycombed the rocky escarpment poured a steady stream of man and women. Tottering age and toddling youth with all the intermittent ages were represented in this stream of humanity that the caverns discharged. They made their way with one accord to the clearing at the foot of the cliffs, for Gra, chieftain of the tribe, had summoned them, and when Gra summoned they must heed his call.

At the far end of the clearing, on a crude throne of huge rocks, sat Gra. His massive frame was clothed in the shaggy coat of the mighty cave bear, and in his hand he bore a gnarled and knotted staff tipped with a monster lance-head of stone. On his right stood Gra, son of Gra, tall, lithe and powerful, a perfect specimen of physical manhood. On his left sat Zo-na, fairest daughter of all the tribe of Gra.

Gra looked down into the semicircle of upturned faces and raised his hand. A hush fell upon the waiting throng. Gra spoke in short, monosyllable sounds, amplified by many eloquent signs and gestures, for the art of speech was young and undeveloped and the primitive mind often groped long in the darkness before it found expression. It could not be accurately transcribed. The nearest one can come to it is to record the ideas, expressed by the combination of sounds, expressions and gestures.

"It has long been a custom with the people of Gra that, when a youth desires to mate with a woman of his people, his desire should be made known before the tribe in the great council.

"Long, too, have we given the woman the right to choose whether or not she would mate with the man who seeks her, for are not the best children borne by the woman who mates with the man of her choice?

"And now Gra, son of Gra, seeks a mate, that his race shall not cease to live upon the earth. And from the women of the people of Gra, now Gra son of Gra, seeks to mate with Zo-na, daughter of Dur, who with his naked hands has slain the mighty cave bear.

Gra's ponderous voice echoed and reverberated as he reached the end of this oration. The crowd broke into excited chattering as he paused, but fell silent again as the girl stood before them at a sign from Gra. Her voice was musical and clear as a bell, and her words were simple and free from all pomp and ceremony. She looked across to where Gra, son of Gra, stood with his eyes fastened intently upon her, before she spoke:

"Zo-na waits the voice of her people."

A lone figure detached himself from the crowd and, crossing the open space to Gra, prostrated himself before the throne of stone. Gra rose, and again his thunderous tones rang forth:

Arise, Ra-nor, stalwart son of the people of Gra, and state your mission."

Ra-nor arose and drew himself erect.

"For many moons, O Gra, has Zo-na found favor in the eyes of Ra-nor. And has not Zo-na smiled upon him in return? So Ra-nor would seek the girl, Zo-na, to mate with him, to keep his watch-fires bright, to care for the trophies he brings from the hunt, and to be the mother of his children.

An intense hush fell upon the assembled throng. Ra-nor was entirely within his rights, according to the tribal customs of the people of Gra. But to think that he dared defy the wishes of Gra, son of Gra, was in effect a daring challenge. The girl must choose, and her choice must be confirmed by the council congregated there. If their verdict did not concur with her own, she must remain a virgin until another should find favor in her eyes, or else flee with the man of her choice and become ostracized forever from the people of Gra. So far had men progressed from the days when the male, by sheer brute force, took the female of his choice to his cave.

Again the girl took her place before the multitude. Every eye was focused upon her, every ear intent on the words she might have to say. Gra, son of Gra, moved uneasily, but his face remained as emotionless as the pictures graven on the walls of his cave.

"Zo-na needs must find it hard to make a choice, for Gra, son of Gra, and Ra-nor both find favor in her eyes. But this is the answer of Zo-na to Ra-nor, and Gra, son of Gra. Many times of late has the voice of Aa, the saber-tooth tiger, been heard in the mighty forest. Already have some of the brave hunters of the people of Gra fallen prey to the great beast. More dangerous is he than Brahg, the woolly mammoth, or even Gur, the shaggy cave bear. To him who will lay before her cave the head of Aa, with this one shall Zo-na mate. Zo-na has spoken."

Now the silent throng found voice and raised a mighty shout of approval at the decision the girl had made. Gra lifted his hand once more for silence.

"Words of wisdom has the fair Zo-na spoken. It is well. Tonight the full moon shines upon the people of Gra. It is a good sign. Tomorrow shall Ra-nor and Gra, son of Gra, set out upon the trail of the great beast, Aa. And until one returns, Zo-na shall wait in the cave of her father, Dur. If neither should return from the great forest . . . "

Gra's massive shoulders moved in a suggestive gesture. With a wave of his huge staff he dismissed the throng.

That night Zo-na's sleep was troubled. She dreamed that she was alone in the great forest and Aa, the sabor-tooth tiger, sprang upon her from the underbrush. But instead of the head of a tiger, the monster in her dreams bore the head Gra, son of Gra. She woke with a startled cry, the name of Ra-nor on her lips, and in her heart a fear that harm might befall this brave lad who dared defy the mighty son of Gra.

Ra-nor, too, dreamed, but his dreams were all of a glorious girl with raven tresses and wonderful sloe-black eyes. And in those eyes gleamed the wonder-light of the great love, and he knew that this woman was his mate as surely as he knew that his only foe would be not only the terrible Aa.

But Gra, son of Gra, did not dream. His heart was filled with a great hate for the one who had dared to interfere with his plans; for Gra, son of Gra, did not wish to hunt the great beast, Aa. Much rather would he remain in the sanctuary of Gra, his father, and bask in the pleasant plaudits of the admiring crowd as he strutted proudly about, garbed in his garment made from the shaggy coat of the mighty cave bear. Far into the night he lay awake, scheming, planning, plotting, seeking some way he might win the girl, Zo-na, and yet not jeopardize his own precious hide.

With the the rising of the sun, Ra-nor slipped quietly away into the great jungle that lay between the Great Cliffs and the sea. But Gra, son of Gra, was not so simply satisfied. He, too, rose with the first rays of the morning light, and made his way to the cave of Na-nor, the flint-maker. From his store he selected the best weapons he could find: a stone ax, a keen-tipped lance, and a long, needle-like dagger of stone that had caused Na-nor many an unsuccessful attempt before he had obtained his objective. Then he breakfasted before the cave of Gra, his father, on the flesh of reindeer, and listened to the many words of council that the old chieftain spoke into his ears. Then, leisurely, conscious of the many eyes that were upon him, Gra, son of Gra, entered the jungle.

And Zo-na, as she watched him take his leave, again experienced the odd sensation of impending disaster, that strange foreboding of danger for the one who had gone on before him into the mighty forest.

## II

The noonday sun shone down upon the lone figure of Ra-nor, as he plodded on into the trackless jungle, searching out the spoor of the great beast, Aa. His eyes scanned every inch of the ground over which he passed, reading the signs as plainly as if it were a printed page; here was where Gur, the shaggy cave bear, had passed; there, where the foliage was crushed and trampled, the woolly mammoth had crashed on its cumbersome way.

On and still on, sometimes going on all fours, his nose close to the ground that his keen sense of smell might detect the presence of Aa, even if his sharp eyes failed to do so. At last the troglodyte came to the spot where the trail of the great cat crossed his own and he pressed on with redoubled speed. The trail led him to where the great, fernlike trees grew on the sides of the cliffs until it came to an end at the mouth of a large, dark cave. The mouth of the cave was littered with clean-picked bones of reindeer, bison, mammoth, even the bones of the cave bear.

Here, indeed, was the lair of Aa, the mighty saber-tooth tiger, who already had robbed the people of Gra of three stalwart sons. Perhaps, thought Ra-nor, their bones, too, were in that gruesome pile. He found a stone about the size of his hand and hurled it into the recesses of the cave. His only answer was the sound of the missile as it struck one of the walls. Evidently Aa was not at home. So much the better. For some time Aa must return, and he would find a warm welcome awaiting him.

Ra-nor climbed into the branches of a tree from which he

could command a view of all the approaches to the cave, and waited until the shadows of the night began to fall, but Aa did not return. Boldly, Ra-nor crept into the very lair of the huge cat and made his bed on the floor of the cave. He knew that no beast other than Aa would disturb him, for all would give a wide berth to the cave of the great beast. All through the long night he kept up his vigil, while not a hundred feet above him, in a cavern that might have been a mate to the one he occupied, slept Gra, son of Gra.

He, too, had traversed the big forest, but little care had he given to the trail of Aa. Instead, he had followed the trail that Ra-nor had blazed. Let Ra-nor track the great beast to his lair; he would follow on at his leisure. Let Ra-nor spend his strength battling with the tawny animal; it was far easier to wrest spoils from a man already spent with a mighty struggle than to risk life and limb in an effort to take for himself the head of Aa. It was far simpler to overpower a fellow man than a monster with the strength of ten men.

He had overtaken Ra-nor as the latter came in sight of the cave of Aa. When Ra-nor had taken up his post in the branches of the big tree, Gra, son of Gra, did a little scouting of his own and found the cave above, where he planned to spend the night. He dared not risk a fire, for the smell of smoke might warn the other of his presence.

Morning found Ra-nor again in his perch among the branches of the tall tree. Beneath the overhanging boughs the life of the jungle passed in an incessant steam. Chattering monkeys swung from limb to limb; huge, hideous, hairy apes, with misshapen bodies and slavering jaws, pushed their way through the underbrush. From the distance came the howling, devilish cry of the hyenas and the answering bellow of the stag. Ra-nor could picture the persecuted animal fighting against overwhelming odds, and the pack of hungry brutes snapping and biting at him from all sides.

Ra-nor became conscious that he was hungry. For two days and a night he had been without food. He heard the challenging growl of Gur, the shaggy cave bear, as he lumbered into sight through the trees. Here was food enough for more than one satisfying meal. Another moment and the animal would be directly beneath his tree. The hungry man steeled himself for the attack.

Then, through the great forest, came an answer to the challenge of Gur — the blood-curdling cry of the great beast, Aa. Never would Gur let the voice of his life-long foe remain unanswered. The bear turned in the direction of the sound, and rumbled defiance to the mighty Aa. Again the voice of Aa echoed through the trees.

Ra-nor drew into the sheltering foliage of the tree until only his eyes were visible. His keen ears could detect not a sound. Over the great forest fell a silence fraught with the expectancy and dread. The cave bear sniffed the air and shook his huge bulk savagely, rearing upon his hind quarters and focusing keen, penetrating eyes upon the surrounding jungle.

A sudden swish, a crashing through the trees, and the mighty body of Aa came hurtling through the air, landing full upon the broad shoulders of Gur. Then the silence was broken with a terrible commixture of sounds as the two beasts battled for supremacy, a snarling, growling tangled mass of flying flesh and fur. At last the curved fangs of the great cat, fully eighteen inches long, sank deep into the throat of Gur, and Ra-nor knew that it was the beginning of the end. Finally the shaggy body of Gur lay still, and through the jungle rang the triumphant cry of Aa. Again a long and intense silence as the victorious animal settled itself to its feasting.

But Aa did not long feast uninterrupted. Noiselessly, moving even more silently than the mighty beast below him, Ra-nor lowered himself to the ground within a few rods of where the tail of Aa switched through the air, and hurled his lance powerfully into the body of the monster, full between the shoulder-blades. With an angry snarl, the great beast turned but quicker yet was the bold hunter as, with the agility of a monkey, he gained the sanctuary of the big tree.

Aa crouched, ready to spring upon his new foe, his tail cutting great arcs through the air. His long fangs dripped blood and his body was cut and bleeding from the struggle with his late antagonist. Aa's huge body swayed from side to side, and with a cry he leaped straight for the branches of the tree where Ra-nor waited. There the great cat met the stone ax of the troglodyte cleaving into its skull, between the eyes.

Again, and yet again, the mighty beast sprang. Each time the man in the tree met his attack with crushing counter-blows. Once the claws of Aa struck the shoulder of the daredevil, ripping his flesh open clean to the bone and nearly dislodging him from his lofty perch.

Now blood streamed from the mouth and nose of the great beast, and Ra-nor knew that his shaft had found a vital spot. Throwing caution to the winds, the man dropped lightly to the ground and closed in upon the spent and wounded Aa. A last terrific effort and the lifeless body of Aa slumped in an inert mass beside the shaggy form of its victim, Gur.

Forgetful of his own wounds, intent only upon making sure of the prize that was to win for him the hand of Zo-na, Ra-nor set about his task of severing the head of Aa from its body.

From his vantage point at the mouth of the upper cave, Gra, son of Gra, had watched the struggle. Now was his opportunity. One well-directed blow and the prize would be his. The story he would tell was plausible enough to pass the dwarfed, childish minds of the people of Gra; how he had come upon Ra-nor struggling with the great beast Aa; how Aa had killed the other man before he, Gra, son of Gra, could lend his aid; and how he had meted out vengeance for the death of his tribal brother by slaying. single handed, the great jungle terror.

Stealthily, he wormed his way through the tangled underbrush until he came near enough to reach out and touch Ra-nor with his hand. From his gee-string he selected the long, sharp needlelike stone dagger that had been the pride of Na-nor the flint-maker. Slowly, deliberately, he gauged the distance between himself and his unsuspecting victim and lifted the dagger of stone high above his head. One blow and Gra, son of Gra, would be mighty among the people of Gra; one blow and the fair Zo-na would be his mate; one blow and the upstart Ra-nor would be forever removed from his path.

## III

Zo-na, in the cave of her father, Dur, waited impatiently for the return of the victor with the head of Aa. Deep in her heart lurked a longing that Ra-nor would be the one to lay the trophy at her feet, but should it be the other... Zo-na had given her word.

All day long she paced to and fro about the confines of the dwellings, like some hunted beast at bay. She could not shake off her evergrowing sense of peril. She almost regretted her attitude toward her suitors the day before. Why should she have concealed her greater love for Ra-nor, even if the other claimant was Gra, son of Gra? Why had she sent the man she loved to face the perils of the vast forest that her vain wish might be gratified? It had all been so unnecessary.

Again she felt that tightening around her heart — a stifling, suffocating fear that threatened to drive her wild. Night came on, and with the darkness her anxiety for the man she loved increased a thousandfold. All night she tossed and turned a futile endeavor to sleep. She wished to set forth into the jungle, that she might in some way protect the daring man who had so fearlessly gone forth to do her bidding. To Gra, son of Gra, she gave but a passing thought. Might the powerful mammoth crush the life from his body, and the lean hyena pick his bones!

In the gray dawn of early morning, Zo-na stole silently from the cave of Dur, her father. Hidden in the folds of her doe-skin garment she bore a keen-edged knife of stone. Though the trail was a day old, the girl picked it up with ease. Alone, undaunted, she sped on, her one thought being to find Ra-nor and beg him to flee with her. What matter if they became out-casts from the people of Gra? Would they not have one another?

She came to the point where the spoor of the great beast, Aa, crossed that of her lover. Once more that strange premonition of danger. Her heart beat wildly as she bent close over the trail and doubled her speed. Then upon the stillness of the forest came the challenge of Gur and the answering cry of Aa.

Unheard, unseen, the girl came to a point where she could watch this terrific struggle between the enraged beasts. She watched until the body of the shaggy cave bear lay silent at the feet of the giant cat. Then, her terror-widened eyes following every move, she watched her lover as he battled with the great beast, Aa. She barely repressed a cry as the claws of the tiger ripped open his shoulder. She saw the last great conflict, saw the tiger roll lifeless at the feet of her lover, and watched while he set about severing his trophy from the body of Aa. She would watch him, she told herself, until he had finished his task and then she would make her way back as she had come — alone. For soon he would return and lay at her cave the prize she had seen him wrest from the jaws of death itself.

But suddenly her sharp ears caught the sound of a snapping twig. Her keen eyes saw the form of a man through the tangled underbrush, saw his arm raise high above his head, and saw the stone dagger as it poised in mid-air.

As quick as thought, her hand flew to her bosom, where lay her own keen blade. Straight and true as an arrow from a bow she flung it from her with all the strength she could command.

The man's form crumpled and fell, and the body of Gra, son of Gra, rolled into the clearing straight to the feet of Ra-nor, his heart pierced with the girl's weapon of stone.

Zo-na turned and, with the speed of a deer, flew over the trail that led back to the cave of Dur, her father, to watch and wait the few short hours until her lover returned, to lay at her feet the head of the great beast, Aa.

# Red Cap of the Mara

INSOMNIA MAY BE attributed to various causes. Billy Bascom's frequent attacks of the malady could be traced to one fundamental source: his unremitting quest for Romance. Perhaps it was not so much the quest itself as the utter lack of success attending his efforts that accounted for his many sleepless nights.

It was not due to any lack of prospective flames. Billy always made it a point to keep his calling list well supplied with choice, fluffy femineity. And it was not due to any lack of knowledge of the finer points of up-to-the-minute love-making. If practice makes for perfection. Billy was never more than a step behind. Yet this one step proved a gap that even Bill's seven-league-boots of desire were unable to bridge.

He had just returned from the intriguing presence of a dainty damsel who, by virtue of her seductive wiles, had lured him to a point that seemed to him propitious for a consummation of his most passionate desires; but who had then with the elusiveness of an elf, slipped through his fingers.

He bit savagely at the end of his cigar, mentally berating himself for his habitual trick of making the wrong move at the right time. If only he had had sense enough not to force the issue. Better to be in doubt than faced with the cold fact of irretrievable loss. He spat out his sentiments at the same time as the end of his cigar.

"I seem to be getting more of a damn fool every day! Somebody ought to draft another Amendment prohibiting..." He stopped, struck a match, lighted his cigar and crossed to the center table. "I ought to be fed up on women for awhile! Still, I suppose the next pretty face I see...."

Another incompleted sentence, punctuated by a puff of smoke. He rummaged among the books and papers on the table. "If I go to bed now. I'll be calling myself names 'till the cock crows. Maybe I can lose my troubles in some yarn before I hit the hay."

He discarded, as unsuited to his mood, current issues of the most popular, spicy magazines, a volume or two of de Maupassant's most peppy tales, and a paper-covered novel bearing the lurid title: THE SISTERHOOD OF SIN. At last he unearthed a red-bound book that held his attention:

WEREWOLVES AND KINDRED SUPERSTITIONS. "Ugh! Where the devil did that come from? Oh, yes, I know! That's the book a swell dame wished on me at the Charity Bazaar. A fool and his money! Werewolves! Pleasant subject for a bedtime tale!" He shrugged his shoulders. "Oh well it can't make me any more wakeful than I am already. Here goes!"

He dropped into a chair and turned the pages aimlessly, his mind still far from the printed pages in his hand. A chapter-heading caught his eye.

" 'Maras and Swan-Maidens.' " His inherent interest in woman-kind asserted itself. A moment more and he was reading it with avid interest:

"In the person of the Mara, the werewolf finds a suitable superstitious sister. She is commonly known as a malicious tormenting spirit, who, assuming the form of a beautiful naked woman, sits astride the body of her victim while he is sleeping causing him nightmares and even stopping respiration.

"But the Mara sometimes appears in less revolting form, and becomes the mistress or even wife of some mortal man. In nearly all these legendary accounts, however, the Apsaras or cloud maiden has a dress of swan's feathers, which replaces the cape or girdle of the werewolf. If you could capture and burn a werewolf's sack, a permanent cure was effected. By the same rule, the swan-maiden keeps her human form as long as she is deprived of her garment of feathers.

"The story is told of a man travelling along a little used road. He passes a lake where several beautiful nude girls are bathing, he stealthily steals one of the dresses. When the girls are finished bathing they come in for their clothes and swim away as swans. But the one whose dress is stolen must stay on the shore and marry the thief.

"However, it is not always a shirt of feathers.

The mermaid's cap has given its share to the superstitious beliefs of witchcraft. It is rated as quite a common thing on the coasts of Ireland for young sea-fairies to get human husbands in this way. The bold, brazen creatures even come ashore on purpose, leaving their red caps behind for young men to pick up; but it behooves the husband to guard the red cap with care if he would not see his wife disappear to join her swan-maiden sisters."

Billy Bascom read the chapter, replete with illustrative examples of these hoydenish sprites, through to its close. He tossed the book to the table, parked his cigar in the ash-tray, and headed for the bedroom. His unpleasant thoughts of the earlier evening were virtually buried beneath the mental pictures conjured up by the article he had just read. Still a trace of his rancor lingered as his head hit the pillow.

"No wonder they call 'em nightmares." he mused, "if a woman's got anything to do with it. Still," dreamily. "I don't know's I'd be so terribly adverse to meeting up with one of those swan-maidens!"

## II

Billy Bascom had about reached the conclusion that there was not one iota of truth in the tantalizing tales to be found in his favorite brand of frothy fiction. At all events, the girls of his acquaintance did not seem to hold love so lightly as the frisky females his most-read authors created.

He jumped at the suggestion made by a trio of bachelor friends that he share a summer cottage with them at the seashore. Perhaps, away from the environment of the sweltering city, he would find relief for his ever-recurrent attacks of insomnia. Besides, the hot weather had already driven his newer young lady friends to cooler climes, and he lacked the temerity to hunt up his older flames after the decisive throw-down each had tendered his ardently amorous attentions.

On the eve of his departure, Billy should have been busy packing his luggage. Instead, the lure of a jazz palace proved too strong, and he spent three perspiring albeit enjoyable hours piloting several fair partners through the intricacies of some of the newer dance steps. One in particular held his attention. She was one of these ultra-modern, bobbed-haired flappers, with a dare in her eyes that Billy refused to permit to go unchallenged. It required but little urging to persuade her to shake the girls who were with her, and allow him to accompany her home. With his usual impetuosity, Billy forced the issue.

Her scathing denunciation was still burning his ears when he threw his grips into the machine, the next day, and started for the beach. His companions did their level best to prod him into some semblance of good-nature, but he maintained an attitude of sullen, morose taciturnity that was, to say the least, a disquieting harbinger of pleasant vacation.

"Leave him alone," one of the trio finally advised. "He'll come out of it after awhile. He always does. When he gets a line on some of the dolls dotting the silvery sand, he'll forget his troubles!"

The allusion to the female of the species  brought a bark of protest from Billy.

"You go to the devil! I wouldn't give the best of 'em the once-over, let alone taking a second look! I'm not going on this trip to chase chickens; I'm going to forget them. I'm through with women!"

The colony which proved to be their goal comprised nearly thirty cottages, grouped in a half moon around a natural beach that rivaled the best anywhere. A few of the buildings were occupied the year round by families seeking surcease from the high rentals and congestion of the city. For the most part, however, they were leased for the short summer season by groups, either of fellow or girls, who used them as headquarters for week-end outings and annual business-vacation trips, while the remainder were occupied, as the one Billy and his pals had chosen, for the best part of the season.

There is a certain freemasonry about a colony of this kind; opportunities are offered and grasped for social intermingling that would be banned by the stricter conventionalities of the cities.

Billy's friends threw themselves into the spirit of the occasion with unrestricted zeal. By the evening of the first day acquaintances had already been made, and discussions were in order as to the mapping out of an intensive campaign of pleasures. Billy announced his ultimatum with an air of finality.

"It's no use trying to count me in on anything where the girls are concerned. I'm done! I told you that on the way down! If you fellows want to fool around with a bunch of bathing beauties, that's your business. I can have a better time keeping myself company. As far as women are concerned, I'm like milk that's been left out in the sun too long. I'm soured!"

He clung to his decision with a very un-Billy-like obstinacy. For a week he stuck close to the cottage, nursing his grouch, and not even so much as donning a bathing-suit. He stood the jibes of his living-mates with a surprisingly stoical calm. Indeed, he might as well have been a recluse, so far as fraternizing was concerned.

A baking-hot, sultry midsummer's day will go a long way toward breaking down a man's most stolid resolves. It was Saturday, and all day long the beach was black with a cheerful, good-natured throng, each one seeking relief from the humidity in the cooling waters of the bay. Billy Bascom sweltered in the insufficient shade  of the piazza of the cottage, face black as a thundercloud, and watched the happy-go-lucky mermaids and mermen disporting themselves in the foaming breakers. It was even too hot to smoke, with any degree of enjoyment. Still, Billy clung to his new-born attitude of stubbornness and refused to yield to the urge to join the care-free crowd.

Night came at last, and with it a breeze that brought alleviation from the suffocating heat of the day. Billy's companions were soon snoring lustily, but he tossed and turned, as he mentally reviewed for the thousandth time, each disheartening failure in his search for the object of his passionate desires.

The soft lapping of the waves against the shore, the gentle breeze that wafted through the opened windows, soothed him. He wondered if a dip into the friendly billows would not have an equally soothing quality. A sudden reversion to his old-time impetuousness, and the decision was made. A few moments later, clad in his bathing togs, he stepped out upon the still-warm sands. A moment later he stopped short, blinked, rubbed his eyes, and frankly stared at the vision that had caught this attention.

Silhouetted against the background of one of the other cottages, clad only in bathing trunks, every curve of her lithe, sinuous body clearly outlined in the light of the full moon, the girl descended the steps and made her way towards him across the sands, apparently oblivious of his admiring gaze.

He drew into the shadows of his own cottage and watched the boyish, supple figure as it moved closer to his hiding place. He caught a flash of white, well-shaped legs.

"What the devil is she doing, out at this hour?" he asked himself. "If it ain't well after midnight, I'll eat my trunks! Gosh she's a stunner! Billy Bascom, you never were cut out for a hermit. Wine, women and song is the life; and seeing you can't sing, the only thing I can see left for you is women!"

She was almost abreast of him now. He wondered why she had not gone into the water as soon as she had left the cottage. Oh, yes he remembered now. One of the boys had spoken of a tiny cove a little beyond the colony, where the waters of the bay had been trapped into what was almost the equivalent of a placid pool. She must be going there. The beach was almost as light as day. He could even catch the gleam of her golden hair; a radiant glowing gold, as though her tresses had caught the rays of the moon and held them there. And atop her head, was poised a bathing cap as red as sin.

It may have been Fate; it may have been coincidence; or it may only have been that Nature was feeling particularly prankish that evening. As she passed Billy's place of concealment, almost close enough for him to reach out and touch her with his hand, an errant breeze, stronger than any that had gone before, lifted the cap from her head and dropped it almost at the feet of the hidden man.

She turned in his direction to retrieve it, and stopped with a startled cry as Billy stepped from the shadow, red cap in hand.

"My, how you frightened me! I thought everyone was fast asleep in bed!"

She extended her hand.

"The same to you," Billy returned, thrusting the cap behind him. "Suppose I keep the cap as a penalty for venturing out in a costume that would hardly pass the censors?"

The red crept up into the girl's cheeks. She dug a bare toe into the sands. Then, with a sudden burst of frankness:

"You see, I'm just down for over the week-end.," she confided. "I didn't discover until after I'd arrived that , I'd forgotten to pack — my — my — bra. I couldn't, as you say, go in this way with so many here, this afternoon, and it's been so hot today, I couldn't go home without taking a dip. Of course, "she conceded, with sisterly candidness, "I could have borrowed one from one of the other girls, but I knew they'd jolly the life out of me if I admitted how thoughtless I'd been, so I pretended the heat had given me a headache, and begged off. But I figured I'd be perfectly safe at this unholy hour."

"I'm harmless," he assured her. " but why call it unholy? Magic would seem to me to be a better word. You were going to the cove?"

She nodded.

"If you return my runaway cap, I still intend to."

Bill's eyes feasted on the pleasing picture she presented. They followed from her shapely shoulders; encompassed her well-rounded contour, every line accentuated by the sung fit of her single garment; studied the dimpled knees, the perfect calves, the trim ankles; and brought them back with an effort to her own. She blushed again, beneath his scrutiny.

"One should not relinquish a gift from the Gods," he bantered. "Suppose, then I keep it as a talisman. I came out for a dip myself. With such charming company, the cove seems to call. You see," he lowered his voice to a mysterious whisper. "I thought perhaps a plunge might drown the thoughts of a too hectic past!"

"I thought you said you were harmless," — as he fell into step beside her.

"Reformed," countered Billy, "you're safer with me than with a church deacon, Miss —."

"Dale. Marilyn Dale. And you?"

Billy told her his name, and they exchanged brief histories as they wended their way along the path through the trees beyond the nest of cottages to the waters of the sheltered cove. Billy thrilled at the nearness of the girl. He clung to the red bathing cap as though it precluded any possibility of her running away.

The magic combination of a moonlight night, a quiet spot,

and two hearts in which smolder the sparks of youthful desire, has never lost its potency. The serene solitude of the cove seemed to shut the pair away from the rest of the world. The silvery sheen of the waters; the winking stars that peeped through the trees; the whispering of the trees themselves as the leaves stirred in the gentle breeze; each a partner in the conspiracy to strengthen the urge of their leashed desires.

The sudden reversal of Billy to his usual mood, after a week of morose broodings, left him particularly impressionable to the enchanting glamour of the scene. His senses reeled as a realization of the potentialities of the situation swept over him, engulfed him. His arm stole around the waist of the girl at his side. He could hear her quickened breathing as he drew her closer to him, but she made no move to remove his tightening arm. He swayed in the intoxication of the moment. The scene swam before his eyes.

All at once the waters of the cove seemed alive, peopled with phantasms of beautiful naked forms. The shore was strewn with downy, fleecy garments of feathers. As if conscious of his intruding gaze they swam rapidly to the shore, donned their clothes and swam away, each one a handsome swan. Only one remained behind, searching futilely for a missing shirt of feathers. Her wet, nude body glistened in the bright rays of the moon, all at once she seemed to spy her observer, and pointed an accusing finger at his free hand. Billy followed the direction of her eyes.

The vision faded and disappeared. Billy found himself staring at the red cap in his hand. A lock of golden hair brushed his cheek. This girl by his side was no apparition, no vague figment of the imagination. She was a real, flesh-and-blood creature that whetted the appetite of his unsatiated passions. The blood raced through his veins at the feel of her warm, pulsating body nestling at his side. He watched the rise and fall of her bosom as she strove to control her pent-up emotions. His voice was husky, his throat parched and dry. He stumbled over his words.

"Marilyn. My swan-maiden. My Mara-girl. You're mine — mine by virtue of this magic token. Mine."

He crushed her soft, yielding body in his strong arms. Two satin-like arms stole about his neck; two warm, red lips met his in reckless abandon.

At last she disentangled herself from his embrace and pulled him down beside her on the sands.

"My Billy-boy," she breathed softly, "I'm half afraid that I shall wake to find this all a dream. But, Billy, what was that name you called me! I've never heard it before."

"My Mara girl."

He told her of the legends he had read, and finished by dangling the red cap before her eyes. "And so you see, Marilyn, you belong to me, and me alone, as long as I keep this magic cap of yours and little sweetheart, I shall keep it forever!"

Once more she yielded herself to his arms.

The sky was graying with the first streaks of approaching dawn when Billy Bascom and Marilyn Dale stole surreptitiously into their respective dwellings. Billy still clutched the red cap tightly in his hand.

Each remaining week of the summer season meant for Billy

Bascom five days of ecstatic anticipation and two days and nights of unalloyed pleasure.

When at last he returned to the city, the red cap accompanied him. At the close of another two months, the night before Marilyn Dale became Mrs. William Bascom, he locked the same red cap in his office safe, as surety that his bride would never be able to sever the bond that joined them.


III


If Billy Bascom had hoped to find a cure for his insomnia in marriage, he was doomed to disappointment. Six months a benedict and he was quite willing to admit that whoever penned the old saw about repentance and hasty marriages knew considerably more about humanity than some of the more modern writers.

His wife seemed to think that her wedding ring was sufficient symbol of her integrity to her husband to permit her to flirt openly with any man, married or single, who happened to find favor in her eyes. With Mara-like hoydenishness, she flaunted her hosts of admirers before the eyes of the world.

In public Billy tolerated her actions with an amused, cynical smile. In the privacy of their own apartments, however, he unbridled his tongue until at times it dripped vitriol.

"I wouldn't give a damn," he concluded one particularly strenuous battle of words, "If you only clothed your 'affairs' in some semblance of decency. But no, the minute you get a new fish nibbling on your line, you have to publish the news so all the gossips from here to Gehenna can wag their tongues over it. I'll bet my last nickel you're the most talked about woman in three states! There are times when I don't wonder at all at your willingness that night in the cove. God knows how many... ."

Marilyn's face crimsoned.

"Billy Bascom, do you dare to insinuate... ."

"It's no worse than I've heard said about you in the clubs since you've taken up with Malcolm DuVerne. Everybody knows what kind of a skunk he is!"

"Billy! Malcolm is..."

Again he interrupted.

"The biggest rogue that ever stepped his foot in this city. He couldn't think a clean thought if he had his mind vacuum cleaned! Women stand for but one thing to a man of his type — as you damn soon will learn, if you keep fooling around. My advice to you is to drop him as you would a red hot coal."

He caught himself up, with a shrug of his shoulders. "Aw, the devil, it's a waste of breath talking to you. You'll do as you darn please anyway!"

"Quite right, Billy. When I get to the point where I can't steer my own ship of destiny it's time I went on the rocks. I think you've said about enough for one session. All in all, I've had a strenuous day. Nighty-night," as she strode savagely toward the door of her boudoir, "pleasant dreams!"

Tell a woman that she mustn't do a particular thing, and it's a hundred to one shot that she'll move Heaven and Earth, if necessary, to do the very thing forbidden. It's a trait handed down to them from Eve.

The inference is clear. Marilyn Bascom redoubled her efforts to enmesh Malcolm DuVerne in her coils.

Billy had not over-rated DuVerne's pernicious moral degeneracy. Few women would take up with him at all, and the ones that did were soon listed in the well-known birds-of-a-feather category. Whether she realized it or not, Marilyn was skirting perilously close to the edge of a moral precipice when she so much as countenanced his overtures, to say nothing of her recklessness in planning a deliberate campaign to charm a man whose whole career had been an endless chain of one woman after another.

It was not long before the huntress found herself in the position of the hunted. As a love-maker, as a builder of air-castles, as a painter of illusive pictures of future filled with passion, love, and endless devotion, DuVerne had Billy hopelessly outclassed. At last came the inevitable proposition. And Marilyn, her mind slowly, systematically poisoned by his insistent, intriguing innuendo, acceded to his demands.

Billy found the note waiting for him when he came home from the theatre, where he had spent a thoroughly enjoyable evening in the company of one of his older flames. He was not surprised; he had foreseen the outcome, yet much as one feels on the death of a dear one, who has lingered close to the door of the Great Beyond for a long time, his grief was no less poignant, no less real.

He tried to tell himself that he washed his hands of her

completely. Yet, in his heart of hearts, his love for her was as strong as on the first night he had held her in his arms. Should she ever come back to him those same arms would be willing to welcome her. But he knew Marilyn well enough to know that she would never return, that when DuVerne tired of her and cast her aside for newer passion, she would follow the path she had chosen to the very doors of Hell before she would come back to him.

His eyes caught a glimpse of a red-bound volume on the center table. He did not need to touch it to know its title: WEREWOLVES AND KINDRED SUPERSTITIONS. He had read the chapter on Maras often, the last few weeks in an effort to bolster his faltering faith in the potency of his fetish. Now he crossed to the table, seized the book with a muttered curse, and flung it with unerring aim into the open grate across the room.

"Damn superstitions, and the fools that believe in them! As if the bathing cap of a bathing beauty is worth a tinker's damn against the wiles of a he-wolf like Duverne! Six slugs of hot lead would have been a darned sight more practical safeguard. Take it from me, when I get to the office in the morning, one red rubber bathing cap is going to be the makings for a hell of a bon-fire."

But, at the office next morning, Billy Bascom was met with a staggering surprise. The door of the safe yawned open, hanging by one twisted hinge. Papers were strewn about the floor in chaotic disarray. Cash, bonds, securities had been cleared. Billy searched frantically in the debris, his mind as chaotic as the scene which met his eyes. It was impossible, and yet... .

A sentence from the book he had burned stood out in bold relief before his eyes. He knew it by rote, he had read and reread it so often:

" ... it behooves the husband to guard the red cap with care if he would not see his wife disappear to join her swan-maiden sisters."

For the red cap of the Mara was gone!

# An Arbiter of Destiny

THE ELDERLY PASSENGER closed his magazine with a bang. "Tommy-rot!" he exploded. "Pure unadulterated bunk!"

His seat-mate smiled silent acquiescence, and he turned with a snort to peer out at the swiftly changing panorama.

The shadows of early evening were already obscuring the great out-of-doors, and he fell to studying his companion: the wan face, the deep-set eyes, and the long, scrawny arms and hands.

For hours they had ridden side by side. Several times Congdon had tried to engage in conversation, only to receive that maddening, indulgent smile. His nervous fingers ruffled the pages of the magazine with spiteful vehemence. At last he nerved himself a final attempt to break the monotony of the ride.

"I tell you, it's absolute foolishness." He thrust the magazine before the silent stranger's eyes, "the writer of that delirious nonsense must have been drunk when he wrote it — or crazy! It's the most absurd story I ever read!"

"Why?" There was something soothing in the tonal quality of the monosyllable. He liked the voice exceedingly well — it quieted his jangling nerves.

"It's one of those absurd 'Jekyll and Hyde' affairs. This dual personality idea makes me sick! I don't take any stock in it, and never did. Some of these present day writers with a fevered imagination make a lot out of it because some fool student who thinks he's a scientist  writes a book or two trying to make somebody believe his trash!"

The taciturn gentleman smiled.

"Beware," he warned, "or you'll find yourself treading on someone's pet corns. That idea that a man has two personalities — or more — struggling constantly for possession of his physical being is one of my favorite premises."

He was stumped for a moment. Finally he determined that a casual acquaintance should never have the satisfaction of talking him out of his convictions. He began on another tack, seeking to draw the stranger on, then to squelch him emphatically.

"We-e-ll," he half assented, "there may be some truth in it, but nobody's been able to convince me. What makes you so sure it's so? You must have some kind of proof to offer."

I've seen it work out so many times, seen it in action, so to speak, that I'm sure it's equally true of all of us."

"Huh!" Then doubtfully, "What do you mean by having 'seen it in action?' What's your line, if I'm not too inquisitive?"

"My card."

He glanced at the pasteboard and snorted in apparent disgust.

## PROF. SONPYH
### Hypnotist

The speaker's smile broadened as he continued: " I should judge you have little faith in the science?"

"Of course I don't believe in it!" exploded the older man.

"The only time hypnotism ever works is on the stage where the subjects are paid to do what's 'suggested' before the performance begins. That's just as impossible as your pet theory."

"And just as possible. I'll grant your criticism anent public performances for comedy purposes. If the hypnotist could succeed in getting anyone upon the stage — and that's tough enough in the average theatre – and then ridiculed him to the same extent as the paid 'plants' he'd be tied up in damage suits that would put him in jail for life. I'm speaking from the scientific angle. The medical profession, you know, recognized it some years ago and counts it a great aid in treating and getting at the source of various mental diseases."

"I'm a doctor, myself. Name's Congdon, Chester Congdon. All the same, it would have to be proved to me beyond the shadow of a doubt before I'd believe either one of the fool ideas."

"Then given conclusive proof, you would believe?"

The brakeman interrupted with the half-intelligible announcement of the next station. Both men reached for hat, coat, and suit-case.

"Say," continued the hypnotist, as if struck by a sudden idea, "if you're in no particular rush, why not come up to the hotel with me for dinner? After we eat, you can come up to my room and give me a chance to prove there is something in hypnotism, after all. Perhaps I can get you to see this dual personality thing, too. What do you say? What kind of sport are you?"

Congdon reflected. It couldn't do any particular harm. If he didn't go, the hypnotist would think he was afraid to stand in back of his own convictions. If he went, perhaps he could catch this smart-alec at his own game.

"I'll go. I know it will be a waste of your time, but I'm curious to see what kind of tricks you'll try."

They left the station and walked up the main street of the town to the American House. After a substantial meal, Congdon followed the Professor to his room.

In the center was a large library table with a strong electric light directly above it. A comfortable arm-chair was drawn up beside it. The Professor turned the easy-chair so that its back was toward the light and motioned Congdon to be seated. Then he placed his watch upon the table.

"It's now just three minutes before eight. If I can succeed in placing you under my hypnotic control, and keep you under it for twelve hours or until eight tomorrow morning, would you be convinced that hypnotism was no longer a childish dream?"

Congdon grinned.

"Certainly — if you can perform miracles!"

The hypnotist took a position before his potential subject,

so that the light from the powerful bulb shown directly upon his face. Congdon was still seated with his back to the light, watching his every move.

"Very well, then. No strong-willed man can be satisfactorily put under hypnotic influence or control, if he resolutely wills against it. As I understand it, your contention is that he cannot be hypnotized under any conditions; so give me the benefit of the doubt and an even chance to subject your will to mine. You must agree to no conscious resistance. Relax your muscles, make yourself as comfortable as possible."

Congdon nodded his assent and settled back in the chair.

"Keep your eyes open and fixed on mine. You'd better concentrate your attention on the pupil of my left eye."

Congdon obeyed. He might as well humor this fanatic. It would only be for a short while, then it would be his turn to dominate the situation – to crow over the other's failure. He felt the other's hands upon his shoulders. He could hear his voice in that soothing monotone:

"You feel a sleepy sensation creeping all over your body. You feel a sleepy influence coming all over your head and eyes. You are going sound asleep... sleep... sleep...so sleepy and drowsy... you cannot hold your eyes open any longer."

Congdon's eyelids fluttered, half closed. This fakir was making him nervous with that tiresome sing-song. He tried to draw his gaze from the pupil of the hypnotist's left eye. It was impossible for him to move a muscle. The voice now seemed to come from far away:

"Dead asleep! Down deep! Every breath is a drowsy one, every part of your body is sound asleep... dead asleep!"

Congdon's head fell forward upon his breast, and his regular breathing told that he was fast asleep.

The hypnotist's eyes lighted exultantly. His features twisted in a savage sort of expression and he stepped forward, arms upraised, and fists clenched, as if he would assault the sleeping man.

"No... no... no!" he muttered, "the other way is best; it's safer surer, and it leaves no trail.

At eight o'clock the next morning, Congdon came back to the world to find himself in an unfamiliar setting. It was a small, box-like room, with walls on three sides, while the fourth side was open so that he could look into another similar compartment across a narrow corridor; but it was barricaded by heavy iron bars!

It was his custom, when bewildered, to run nervous fingers through his long, black hair, and to bring his hand down over his face to the point of his beard. His hand found its way to his head but he drew it back as suddenly as though he had burned his fingers, for his head was as closely cropped as a criminal's.

Swiftly he passed his hand down his face. It encountered only smooth shaven cheeks, and beardless chin.

He glanced at his clothes. Instead of the neatly tailored outfit he had been wearing the night before, he was dressed in ancient rags and tatters that sickened him.

He peered through the bars into the room across the way, and gradually growing accustomed to the dim light of the place, made out the figure of a human being. By straining his eyes he could see that the man was dressed in a striped suit of black and gray.

Then he realized — he, Chester Congdon, was in jail! And the strangest thing about it was that he did not know why he was there. He racked his brain for some solution. Try as he might, he could not account for a moment of the time since he had gone to the room in the hotel with the Professor. That was it! Why didn't he think of it before? He was the one to look to for an explanation. He hailed the guard as he passed the cell.

"Do you think you could send a message for me to a friend of mine who's stopping at the American House? I'll make it right with you when I get out. His name is Professor Sonpyh. Just send him word I'd like to see him at once."

The guard was surprised. When he came on duty that morning, he had been warned to "look out for the new guy."

"He's a bad one," the night man had told him. " Took four of us to put him in, an' he cussed like a gutter rat!"

To hear this "bad man" speaking in such a mild, refined tone was enough to surprise even a prison guard.

"You mean that hypnotist fellar that's goin' to show at the op'ra house, tonight, I guess. Don't think he'll do you much good, but if you want to see him, I'll send word. Maybe he'll slip me a coupla passes for the show — you say he's a friend o'yourn."

The guard shuffled off. Congdon paced the cell in growing nervousness and apprehension. Minutes dragged by until a full hour had passed. What if he should refuse to come! What if he could not explain his being there if he did come? It was a full two hours till the Professor stood before his cell, bland and smiling, the watchful guard just out of earshot. Congdon wasted little time in preliminaries.

"I thought you might be able to help me out of my present difficulty. I can remember nothing that has occurred since you so kindly volunteered to put me under your control. I freely admit that I am convinced. I find myself in a cell without even an inkling as to how or why I am here. My head has been shaved, my beard removed, and my clothes exchanged for this ragged, ill-smelling suit. Perhaps you can throw some light on the affair."

" See the morning paper?" inquired the Professor.

"No. Why?"

For reply, he passed it through the bars. The prisoner glanced at it, eagerly.

Page-wide headlines caught his eye.

### JUDGE BRISCOE'S HOME
### SCENE OF ATTEMPTED BURGLARY

---

Assailant Caught Red-Handed by Judge in
Heroic, Hand-to-Hand Encounter, While
Trying to Steal Mrs. Briscoe's Jewels

---

Congdon eyed the Professor quizzically.

"Tough luck for the poor devil. The judge'll give him the limit without a doubt. But what has that to do with my incarceration?"

"More than you dream, Congdon."

"What do you mean?"

"Just what I say. Last night under my hypnotic control, just as I anticipated, I was able to resurrect the personality you have so successfully masked. As a common crook you forced entrance to the home of Judge Briscoe.

Congdon's eyes gleamed with an insane fire. He grasped the iron bars and strained at them with maniacal fury.

"Damn you! I'll kill you for this! If you hadn't hypnotized me it never would have happened!"

The guard stepped forward, but the hypnotist motioned him back to his place. Before his steady gaze. Congdon's anger cooled quickly.

"What a fool I am. With your testimony that I was not responsible for what occurred because of your influence over me, there's no question but what everything will be all right."

The Professor held a pocket mirror before the caged man. "Look here," he requested.

Congdon obeyed, and recoiled in unfeigned terror. He had known the loss of his hair and Van Dyke beard would make a vast difference in his appearance, but he was unprepared for the sight that met his eyes. Across one side of his face, from ear to the corner of his mouth stretched a livid, disfiguring scar! The sheer horror of the vision left him speechless. The hypnotist's voice roused him once more.

"Do you remember Arnold Carpenter?

Congdon reeled as though he had been struck a blow

in the face.

"Can't say that I do. Never heard the name, as far as I know."

"Look at me closely. Surely you remember me now. I am Arnold Carpenter!"

"My God!" cried Congdon. " What have I done that you should come here, now, to torment me?"

"What have you done?" Carpenter's voice oddly combined the qualities of quietude, bitterness, and mockery.

"Nothing at all! Twenty-one years in prison are nothing when the older fellow spends them there. I suppose you could forget a lot in thirty years — a lot — like railroading a man for what you did yourself. That was a damn good way to stop me from sending you and your dirty gang up yourselves. You had a great defense — I'll hand it to you. There wasn't a comeback could spring them. But twenty-one years to think in will teach a lot. I wasn't asleep all the time, depend upon it!"

Congdon started to speak up in protest, but Carpenter went on.

"Your kind of justice gave me plenty of leisure to plan out some justice of my own. That's what you're getting now. I thought I'd even things up a bit with my six dear friends — act as an "arbiter of destinies," as they say in the melodramas. After I got out I had a little luck to make up for the bad luck I had before — I fell in with a hypnotist, the cleverest fellow I ever knew. He was an ex-professor of psychology who had gone into things a little too deep for the mossbacks of his college.

"What I learned from him would made your hair stand on end — but never mind that. I travelled with him till he died, and then went on the road on my own. When I came to get my men I found four dead already — so much for that —they won. Tom Blenden was alive, but somebody else had got him first — he's doing twenty years now. So I'm having to take it all out on you — it's a pity!

"I had to do some tall tracing, but practice made perfect, and when I got wise to your annual trip I knew I could find a way to start things. I'll admit I didn't recognize you in the train. Thirty years have changed you to a remarkable degree. If it hadn't been for our chance converasation, and you telling me your name. I never would have even dreamed that my goal was so near at hand."

Carpenter heaved a deep sigh and continued:

"Now I shall put you once more under my control. From now until sentence is passed upon you, you will be a common house-breaker. When you are at last safely lodged in a cell, I shall release you, and as Chester Congdon you shall spend the most of your remaining years in jail."

The prisoner heard him through in characteristic silence. Then, his voice hardly above a whisper, but so fraught with pent-up passion it seemed to seer the hypnotist's brain, he said:
"You damned, blithering idiot! I'm no more Chester Congdon than you are!

# The Cur

MRS. KING SAT up in bed, blinked, and rubbed her eyes.

The figure of her husband was still hunched over the machine in the corner of the room. The steady click of the keys and the light still burning brightly in the corner told her the story.

"Why, Gerald," she queried, "why didn't you come to bed? Why did you want to sit up all night at that old typewriter?"

At the sound of her voice, King paused and half turned in his chair. His long, black hair was tousled where he had run nervous fingers through it as he tried to catch an elusive idea. His eyes were blood-shot for want of sleep, and there was a strange, new glint in them that Rose King did not understand. He pushed back his chair, crossed the room, and sat on the edge of the bed where his wife lay.

"Rose," he began, "At last I have started the one, big story that will make me famous."

His voice was hoarse, unnatural. That gleam in his eyes

startled her. She sat forward and placed her hands on his shoulders.

"But, Gerald," she protested, "That's what you've said about every manuscript you've written for the past year. Still they all come back, nobody else seems to see any merit in them."

"You don't understand, Rose," he returned, in that same, strange tone, "You *can't* understand. The others were — oh, well, —just stories — but this — this is the one, *big* idea!"

"What is it about, this time, Gerald, dear?"

"It's the same old combination; a man, a woman — and another man. But it's worked up differently. It tells how the man, when he found his wife was infatuated with this other man, went insane; how he proved what a cur he really was, at heart. That's the name of it, Rose, "The Cur". And the things he does, the ways he tortures and torments her, will make my story bigger and better than all the rest of them!"

The woman controlled herself with an effort. Was it possible that her husband suspected? She didn't see any way he could have found out. She had been so careful, so circumspect, so prudent. And Jack was not the kind of man who talked about his affairs. No, Gerald couldn't know, that was all. It was just coincidence that had led him to hit upon this idea.

"I know, Gerald," she went on, her hands still resting on his shoulders, "But think, dear. Don't you remember what the editors have told you so many times! That you should write about the things with which you are familiar, and you know nothing about — "

"But I *shall* know," he interrupted, " I shall be able to write this story as I have never written one before. I shall be able to put into this one the vital spark that has been lacking in all the rest of them, because I am going to *know* — and you are the one from whom I am going to learn!"

He shook himself free from her grasp, and in turn clutched her shoulders, roughly. She shrank before his leering gaze, her own eyes took on a look of fear.

"You don't mean —" her voice faltered, "you wouldn't dare —"

"Dare?" he echoed, his tone wilder than before, "Dare? What wouldn't I dare that I might reach the pinnacles of Fame? What wouldn't I do that I might achieve my greatest desire? There's nothing I would let stand in my way — nothing! I'd even — yes, even kill, if —"

He broke off, abruptly. The weird, insane gleam in his eyes grew more marked. The pupils dilated. They seemed to flash fire with such intensity as to scorch the guilty soul of the woman they looked upon. She opened her lips to scream.

Before a sound passed them, his long, slender fingers closed around her soft, white throat. As she struggled to free herself from his grasp, they tightened. She felt the pressure grow stronger and stronger. Her breath came in short, quick gasps. Her head was throbbing as if it must burst. Then, blackness!

The crazed man watched her struggles with avid interest. As the figure grew limp in his hands he threw back his head and laughed; a long, loud, demonical laugh that seemed to startle even himself.

He listened for a moment to make sure she was still breathing.

"She's all right," he muttered. " I don't want to kill her — yet! Wonder if I can find some rope before she comes to!"

He went downstairs, returning shortly with several yards of old clothes line. Then, stripping the bed-clothes from his still senseless wife, he fastened her ankles together. As the rope cut into her tender flesh, she stirred, uneasily. At this sign of returning consciousness, King forced his handkerchief between her lips, and bound it in place with one of his neckties. Next, he tied her arms behind her back, and paused to inspect this work. Finding it satisfactory, he lifted the inert form, and made his way up the attic stairs.

The attic was divided into two large rooms, but these were so filled with books, magazines and newspapers that he could scarcely find room to move about.

Cursing softly, he dumped his wife unceremoniously on a pile of dusty newspapers in one corner of the room and proceeded to a clear a space by the simple procedure of throwing the rubbish from one room to the other.

At last he had made room enough to suit his purpose, and he returned to his wife, who was regarding him with terror-stricken eyes.

"Woke up, have you!" he leered. He kicked her, brutally, in her unprotected side and laughed wildly as she winced and tried in vain to shrink away. "Stay there, for awhile and see how you like it!"

He descended to the kitchen and brought up one of the chairs. He stopped in the bedroom, on the way, and acquired the remainder of the clothes line. He placed the chair where it could not possibly be seen from out of doors and, as a further precaution, hung an old newspaper over one of the windows. Propping his wife upright upon the chair he wound the clothes line around her — yards and yards of it, knotting it at every turn.

Once more he left her alone.

She could hear his curses as he struggled up the stairs with some heavy burden. He had brought his typewriter, table and all, up into that attic room! She watched him as he placed the table some ten feet in front of her. Her interest grew as he made another trip to the bedroom and came back with a chair.

She noticed that his face was all drawn out of shape. His clean-cut features had assumed a grotesque mask. His lips curled in a repulsive grin that struck terror into her soul. If only she could free herself from this gag long enough to find out if he really knew!

She had never realized, before, how big and strong he was. His collar was off, and his open shirt-front revealed a mass of tensed muscles she had somehow never noticed, before. His giant frame towered above her like a huge monster of prehistoric times.

To her he was no longer the dearly beloved husband she had wed a year before. This crazed creature was as much to be feared as a beast from the jungle. To him she was no longer a beautiful wife, to cherish and protect from all harm; she was his captive, to be tortured and tormented much the same as some South-sea savage would treat the half-civilized being he had brought back from some tribal feud.

She wanted to cry out as he approached her, fist upraised; to plead forgiveness, to beg for mercy, but he had done his work well, and the gag prevented her from making the slightest sound.

The terror in her eyes seemed to satisfy him and he did not strike, but returned to his machine. Then once again, the ominous click- click-click smote upon her ears. She had grown to hate the sound with intensity of feeling that was new to her.

She struggled to loose her bonds, but it was useless. They were tied so tightly she could hardly breathe. The thin, sheer nightdress she wore offered practically no protection, and the strong cords cut deep ridges into the tender flesh of the helpless woman.

All morning, and late into the afternoon, King stayed at the typewriter, grinding out the story that was to bring him fame. Fame at the expense of — God, alone, knew!

Rose King had no idea of the time. The minutes seemed like hours; the hours, like days. When Gerald left the machine and went downstairs, she realized that she was hungry. She was beginning to get thirsty, too. She was fast becoming numb from being kept so long in one position. Her fear grew greater, all the time. What did he intend to do with her? What new form of misery would he devise?

She heard his footsteps on the stairs, and he came into her range of vision bearing a tray, loaded with eatables. Her eyes lit up in pleasant anticipation. Ah! he was going to feed her, after all —

He cleared the table, set the dishes upon it, and sat down to eat his fill. He cleaned up every morsel with evident relish, while

Rose watched him with hungry, pleading eyes. At length, finished, he placed the empty dishes on the tray and sat it upon the floor, replaced the writing materials on the table resumed work on his story — his masterpiece!

All the rest of the afternoon he worked, the pile of closely typed sheets constantly growing; worked until darkness fell and he could no longer see what he was about. Then he took the tray of empty dishes and passed down the stairs, leaving his wife to spend the night in that cramped, torturing position.

Night closed in swiftly around the terrified woman; dark, dense blackness through which her eyes could not penetrate. She imagined all sorts of impossible terrors lurking in the Stygian darkness. Her tortured mind magnified every rattle of a blind or the howl of the wind, outside, 'till it seemed like the hammers on a spirit forge of some ghostly blacksmith or the rush of air from his bellows as he fanned his smoldering embers into flames.

At last her overwrought nerves could bear up no longer. Dame Nature demanded her toll, and Rose King sank into a fitful slumber.

She was awakened by a slight sound, somewhere in the room. The paper had fallen from the window, and the moon lighted one corner of the room.

At first she thought it was her husband, come to inflict some new form of suffering upon her. The sound was behind her and try as she might, she could not turn her head to see. All at once there was a rustle of papers. A shadow flashed across the moon-lit corner. She felt a soft, warm body upon her cold, bare feet for a moment; and she caught sight of it as it scurried across the floor in the direction from which it came.

*Rats!*

A repulsive shudder shook her slight frame as she strained at her bonds like a mad-woman. The only result was to have them cut deeper and deeper into her soft, yielding body, 'till at last she realized the hopelessness of her struggles and gave up with an unuttered sigh of despair.

All the rest of the night she sat there; listening to the pattering of little feet, the rustling of papers, the occasional squeals. She did not close her eyes, again, until the crowing of a rooster foretold the dawning of another day.

She wakened as her husband was mounting a chair in the attic to readjust the temporary curtain at the window. Her thirst had grown to a burning, unquenchable, maddening fire that threatened to drive her out of her senses. Her face showed the effects of her mental anguish in the lines around her eyes. The look of fear in them had become fixed, deep-seated; as though it must stay there for eternity.

Once more she was forced to watch him while he ate, to smell the fragrant aroma of fresh-brewed coffee, the tempting crunching of crisp, brown bacon — she suffered the agonies of Hell!

He gloated over her as he smoked his cigar. He blew puff after puff of smoke into her face and laughed demonically as she grew pale from the effects of it, as it reached her parched, dry throat.

Suddenly a new idea suggested itself to him.

He ripped the nightdress away from her neck, and bared her white, soft, well-rounded shoulders. Then he flicked the ashes from his cigar and pressed the glowing end deep into the soft, quivering flesh!

He laughed again; a wild, weird, insane laugh, as her face contracted in pain and, removing the cigar from the seared, scarred shoulder, transferred it to her forehead — full between her eyes!

Mercifully she fainted.

He tossed the butt away from him and, dropping into the seat before the machine, typed a glowing, insane account of his deed — his "masterpiece" — his key to the Hall of Fame.

So intent was he upon his work, he did not notice his half-extinguished butt had fallen among a pile of old newspapers and magazines. He did not see the small, blue flame that curled around the edge of one of them; did not notice how quickly it spread until there was quite a blaze in the corner behind him.

She was the first to see it. When she recovered her senses the flames were merrily eating their way along both sides of the rubbish-littered room, lapping up all before them like a hungry dog. Yet, she was helpless to make a single move to escape from this place, unable in any way to open her husband's unseeing eyes to his — to their — danger.

He was chuckling as he wrote. A low, hideous, terrifying chuckle that began deep down in his throat and rolled ominously off his lips.

At last they were completely surrounded by a seething mass of flames. Great clouds of smoke rolled in around the terror-stricken woman. She coughed and choked and struggled furtively at her bonds. The heat was becoming unbearable. Yet, that crazed, maniacal being at the typewriter remained oblivious of the ever growing danger.

It seemed to Rose King's tortured mind that she had paid enough for her indiscretions, that she must not be burned alive, burned at the stake in this manner. As the flames closed in about her, she pleaded with her God — prayed that he would spare her — yes spare even that thing at the machine that she had called her husband.

With a last, superhuman effort, she strained at her bonds. The chair tipped forward, swayed unsteadily and crashed to the floor, taking its human burden along.

At the crash, something seemed to snap in Gerald King's brain. No longer was he the mad Fame-hunter. His reason came back to him as suddenly as it had left him, and with it a realization of the precarious position they were in.

He saw his wife on the floor. In a moment he was at her side, pocket-knife in hand. He slashed her bonds and helped her to her feet, but she could not stand. She had been bound so tightly and so long her legs were useless, temporarily paralyzed.

He shuddered as he saw the round, red scar between her eyes. Without a word, he gathered her in his arms and looked about, wildly, for some chance of escape. Nearer and nearer the flames were creeping. One tongue of fire reached his hand and left its mark there.

There was but one way out. He must risk a dash for liberty straight through that seething Hell of his own making.

It seemed an invitation to the grim reaper to attempt it, but to stay where he was would be simply to prolong things for a few moments, and the inevitable. If he must die, better die trying to escape than like a rat in a trap.

He crushed the woman in his arms closer to his bosom and with a mighty oath, plunged into the fiery furnace.

The flames closed in around him as if eager to have caught another in their toils. They scorched his face and arms. His clothing caught fire in several places. All around him the smoke rolled up in great billows, choking him, blinding him, hindering his escape.

Once he stumbled, almost fell, but with another man's great curse he struggled on.

At last he reached the door. Here, he knew, he would find the stairs — and safety. But the flames had done their work well. As he staggered through the doorway into the burning hall, the charred floor gave way under his weight, and he plunged down — down — down —

As he fell, his arms locked in one last embrace around the frail creature who was pressed close to his heart. By some, strange intuition his lips met hers and clung to them in one last, long, lingering kiss; pregnant with pent-up passion and new found love —

# The BETTER CHOICE
### by C.M. Eddy Jr.

A. BROSNATCH

TWO MORE HOURS TO LIVE!

The thought of his approaching death did not seem to cause John Castle much concern. Indeed, he fondled almost lovingly the capsule that contained the deadly drug.

To die — and then to live again!

For countless centuries the wisest men of all lands had vainly sought the secret he possessed. He held the world in the hollow of his hand! Yet he was barely thirty. All the years of middle age stretched ahead in which to enjoy his fame.

On the work-bench before him were the two large glass jars containing the chemicals he had mixed with his own hands. In one corner of the laboratory stood the machine which would transform these chemicals into the life-giving vapor. Upon these inanimate, unfeeling properties he must pin his faith; must launch out upon the Great Adventure dependent upon these alone to prove that his logic was not at fault, that he was really master of eternal life.

He realized, of course that there was a possibility of failure, and he had laid his plans accordingly. He was carrying life insurance to the amount of ten thousand dollars. The powerful drug the capsule in his hand contained was another of his own formulae and would leave absolutely no trace that he was a suicide.

The note to Montague White was already written. He knew that he could trust White to carry out his instruction to the letter. He had grown up with "Monty" from knickerbocker days. He held the friendship of this man next only to that of his wife and little ones. Playmates at school; chums in college; pals now. Although the business world had claimed Monty, he still dropped in for an occasional confab with the scientist, and under the latter's tutelage had learned enough of laboratory methods to make Castle feel that he could safely trust the project to him. Besides, the letter explained everything so clearly that it left no loop-hole for any possible error.

Castle glanced once more at the clock upon the mantlepiece. There was still time for one last test before he died. Not that he feared anything might go wrong, but he felt that he needed the added assurance that such an experiment would give him. After all, it was a momentous step he was about to take.

He wheeled the cumbersome machine from its place in the corner and connected it to the socket in the chandelier. He measured a small quantity of each of the chemicals from the glass jars and emptied them into the bag-shaped body of the machine. Then he switched on the current and waited until time enough had elapsed to vaporize the chemicals.

He crossed to a crate at the other end of the room, and from it brought the cold, stark body of a guinea-pig. Two days before, he had put this animal to death by a small portion of the drug the capsule contained. He wheeled the machine up to the work-bench and placed the body of the animal beside it.

Three long rubber tubes dangled from the grotesque machine. John Castle inserted one of these in each of the guinea-pig's nostrils. He gently pried open the little animal's mouth, and placed the end of the third between its teeth. Last of all, he turned the stop-cock that released the vapor, and anxiously watched the result of his experiment.

One minute — two — three — four — five — ah!

His keen eyes detected the scarcely perceptible pulsation of the animal's body as the heart began to beat once more. Stronger and stronger grew the throbbings, till at length, with a tiny frightened squeal, the resurrected guinea-pig jumped from the work-bench and scurried across the floor.

A hundred times in the last few weeks John Castle had performed this miracle — a hundred different animals had been slaughtered by him and then granted a new lease of life. His was not an idle dream. But one step remained, and that step he was now ready to take: to prove that this same new lease of life could be given to man.

Smiling complacently, John Castle locked the door of his laboratory behind him and made his way to his bedroom. Once there he made his usual preparations for retiring, drew the covers snugly about him and, still smiling, placed the capsule of death between his lips and closed his eyes.

## II

John Castle's astral self floated idly over the bed where the lifeless shell that had been his earthly body lay. It was rather an odd sensation, this being freed from the bodily prison one had occupied so long. It was quite an unusual feeling, too, to look at oneself from the viewpoint of an outsider.

So he was dead, at last. He wasn't quite sure that he liked the idea of being dead, after all. Suppose something should go wrong? Suppose the machine should fail to resuscitate him? But then, it could not fail, he assured himself. It was perfect — without a flaw.

He wondered what his wife would do when she awoke, a few hours hence, and found him dead. At the thought of his wife, he found himself transported to her boudoir. As he drifted over the spot where her graceful form lay sleeping, her features lighted with a radiant smile, as if she sensed his presence there.

He sighed as he thought of leaving the children behind, even for a few short hours. Once more the scene changed, this time to the nursery, with its two cribs, where his little boy and girl slept the sweet, innocent, dreamless sleep of childhood.

Locked doors proved no barrier to John Castle in his new form. A sudden desire for one last look at his laboratory , and he was inside. Yes, everything was just as he had left it before embarking on this perilous voyage.

All at once, Castle sensed another occupant of the deserted room, but not a soul could he see. He could feel the presence of someone else by his side. An invisible hand touched his elbow, and a voice spoke into his ear:

"Come, John, it's time we were moving on."

John Castle turned in the direction of the voice. Still he could perceive no one. He felt no fear, only an eery sensation at the novelty of the situation.

"Moving on? Whither? And who are you, to dictate whither I go?"

"Calm yourself, my dear John, the voice returned; "I happen to be appointed to guide you through nebulous infinities to your ultimate eternal goal. You see, John, you no longer direct your own destiny. The physical 'you' has ceased to be."

The newly-dead man felt an irresistible tug at his arm.

He might just as well go along, he reflected; might just as well get the most out of this experience before his invention recalled him to his earthly body. With a last, long, backward glance at the old, familiar surrounding, he drifted through the window-pane and out into the night, the pressure of the invisible hand guiding him as they floated along.

Far up above the earth they made their way, high up into the azure of the clear sky where myriad twinkling stars lighted their path.

As they mounted, ever higher, it was if a veil fell from John Castle's eyes. The air swarmed with astral bodies like his own. He could distinguish men and women from all walks of life — clerks, bankers, laborers, artists, all rubbed elbows in the most cosmopolitan fashion. But what impressed John Castle most forcibly, what made him realize that these were creatures different from those of the sphere he had left behind, was that each and all of the passers-by were as transparent as the glass in his laboratory window. He could see them, know that they were there, yet look directly through them!

He fell to speculating as to the sensation he would create when, after being pronounced dead by the physicians, he would live and breathe once more. He wondered whether, when he should tell them of his findings in the land beyond, they would believe, or scoff at him.

His ethereal companion seemed to read his thoughts.

"John Castle, have you entirely discounted the possibility of failure? Have you never stopped to wonder why other scientists have never succeeded in obtaining the power over life and death you assume you control?"

Failure . . . assume . . . slowly, surely, the scientist realized the appalling inference in the specter's words. Was he to fail despite his carefully laid plans? Must he really die and leave behind, forever, all that he loved and cherished? Had he been a fool even to dream of matching his man-made science against the great All-Power who ruled the universe? A wave of bafflement swept over him, a sense of distinct loss, a feeling that he had been cheated. Yes, that was it, exactly — cheated! Just at the moment when fame seemed to be within his grasp, two-score years short of man's allotted span; forced to leave home, wife and children while hundreds, thousands of others with not half his opportunities or interests in life lived to a ripe old age!

THE LOVED DEAD

Again his ghostly guide divined his mood.

"Have you forgotten that your life was taken by your own hand?" However, John, there is no room for discontent in the realm whither we are bound. Just what would you consider fair?"

"I would go back to earth as I had planned and live my life according to my own dictates. No one there would be the wiser — no one knows yet that I have died. Grant me just another twenty years of life, and I would be content to leave the world behind."

John Castle's companion sighed.

"I fear, John, that even then you would not be satisfied. For a good many centuries, now, I have guided souls from earth to eternity, and I have not yet found one who did not protest at severing his connection with the world below. Sometimes we find it necessary to send a soul back to earth for a few more years that he may learn to resign himself to the inevitable. It may be thus with you. But, first of all, you must come with me."

He swerved sharply to the left, and soon they left the hurrying throng of astral wanderers far behind. Both fell silent as they traced their meteoric course, mounting higher and higher till the topmost star gleamed far below them in the vast universe.

John Castle became suddenly conscious of encompassing gloom, an illimitable ocean of inky darkness that engulfed him — a darkness so intense that the blackness hurt his eyes — dark, with the darkness of night; black, with the blackness of purgatory!

A tiny point of light appeared in the center of the black void. Slowly it grew, until it became a bright, spinning ball of golden yellow; larger and larger, till its brightness almost blinded him. The whirling slackened and John Castle discerned figures moving about in the nebulous mass. An unseen, magnetic power drew him into the vortex to join them. As he yielded to this uncontrollable impulse, he heard the voice of the stranger in his ear:

"Behold, John Castle, what Fate holds in store should you return to the land whence you came!"


## III

John Castle, wild-eyed, staring, let the latest message slip from nerveless fingers to the floor, and crumpled into his desk chair.

God! How his head throbbed! The strain of the past few weeks had been nerve-racking, nerve-breaking. And now it was all over. This was the end. Home, money, reputation, everything swept away in one mighty, colossal upheaval, that left him penniless, ruined!

He wished he were dead! Then he thought of the odd nightmare he had had so many years before. He had never forgotten that dream. He remembered how he had pleaded with the ghostly stranger for a new lease of life — let him think: he had asked for twenty extra years. The time must be nearly up. How he wished the dream had been true, that the ethereal visitor would come now to take him out of his misery.

Well he knew who was responsible for his downfall. It was Montague White — damn his soul!

As near as he could remember, that crazy vision of his had

been the beginning of it all.

He had always laid that dream to the effect of the drug he had taken. Somehow he had miscalculated the effect of the poison and it had failed to do its work. Then, he was glad; now, he wished it *had* killed him. Dream, vision, whatever it had been, it had so unnerved him that he had been unable to continue his laboratory experiments. His letter to White, the machine itself, he had destroyed.

Then, at his solicitation, White had taken him into his office. They made an ideal team: Castle, the genius, the brains of the combination; White, the doer, the balance wheel. Together they formed an unusually successful pair. Then came the quarrel. He couldn't even remember what it had been about, but he recollected how he had left the office in a blind rage.

Once alone, he had begun to amass a tremendous fortune. A modern midas, everything he touched turned to gold. But for every dollar he made an enemy. Merciless, showing no quarter, he crushed his victims with as little compunction as a thoughtless boy smashes a tiny ant.

Now the tables were turned. Now he was the fly, his enemies the spiders who lay in the far corner of the web they had spun for him, waiting until he became enmeshed in their toils. Not a single stone was left unturned; his failure was sure as the sound of Gabriel's horn. And he knew that Montague White was behind it all. An insane demoniac light glittered in his bloodshot eyes.

He opened his desk drawer, and the bright barrel of a thirty-two gleamed in the sunlight. He snapped open the chambers and looked them through, all the while fondling the weapon as if it were a child, talking to it in low, soothing tones. He loaded the revolver and dropped it into the pocket of his coat. Then, donning his hat, he set out upon his appointed mission— to find White and beg enough from him to insure his rehabilitation. Falling in that — he shrugged his shoulders and his hand sought the weapon in his pocket.

He found Montague White in his office, alone. The interview was brief and decisive. The sound of the shot brought a hundred people to the scene, and they found the half-crazed man standing above the body of his victim, the smoking revolver still in his hand. Strong arms gripped him from behind; firm hands took the smoldering weapon from his grasp.

In the solitude of the lone, dreary cell, the brainstorm passed, and to John Castle came realization of the enormity of his crime.

He clenched his fists until his nails bit deep into the flesh. His brow was furrowed with a thousand wrinkles and the veins stood out in bold relief against his white, set face.

He thought of his son, now grown to young manhood. How proud he was of the boy, his first born. "A true son of his father," everyone had said. He had pictured a wonderful future for the lad. Now...

His daughter was one of the season's most popular debutantes. The eligible males in her set were fairly falling over each other in their frantic endeavors to find favor in her eyes. But now he had killed...

His wife, the woman who had borne and cared for his

children; the woman he loved with all his heart and with all his soul! Now by this one rash deed he had stolen everything from her — home, happiness, reputation — all must go because Montague White was dead, and his own hands had done the killing!

Would to God that it were his own body that lay cold and stark instead of his former partner's! Would that he had died twenty years before, when he could have left behind him a spotless name!

Again his dream of years before came back to him with startling vividness. Perhaps it had not been all a dream. If only he could have looked ahead, how willing he would have been to die!

But he had *not* died. Instead he had lived on, each day weaving the chain of circumstances more tightly about him — and now he was here, behind prison bars, a murderer!

All night long John Castle paced the narrow confines of his cell. All night long his tortured mind revolted at the horror, the gruesome reality of it all. At last, worn out with the strain of the ordeal, just as the first rays of the morning sun peeped over the hilltops — the sun whose light was never seen inside the prison's cold, gray walls — he flung himself in sheer exhaustion upon his cot, and dropped off into fitful slumber.

The next few days were fraught with untold agony for John Castle. A hundred times a day he prayed that death might come and release him from his sufferings. But the law — cold, hard, unrelenting — took care that he should live until he had paid in full for the deed he had done, live to expiate his crime.

At last came the trial. The jury made short work of the case. John Castle was not at all surprised at their verdict. There was nothing else they could have decided: "Guilty of murder in the first degree."

He drew himself erect as the old judge pronounced sentence. At least no one could accuse him of not meeting the situation like a man.

"...hanged by the neck until he is dead."

There was a calendar on the wall of his cell. John Castle ringed the date which the law had set for his execution. As each day dragged by he checked it off upon the calendar, and prayed that the time would pass more swiftly. The nearest he came to breaking down was on the eve of his death, when his wife came to bid him a final farewell.

The next morning, his last on earth, a young priest came and asked a blessing for his sin-steeped soul. Then attendants led him on his last walk, through the narrow corridor lined with cells, out into the morning, out to where the scaffolding reared ghostly and forbidding against the gray walls of the prison. The sun had not risen nor would John Castle see it rise, for with its first beams his life would be snuffed out like a candle.

He walked boldly upright to his place on the platform of death. He marveled at his inward calm as they fitted the black hood over his head and shut out forever the world about him. He felt the weight of the hempen collar as they placed it about his neck; then — waited!

In that last long moment his mind reverted to his weird dream — or was it a dream? He had figured it all out in the loneliness of his cell. It was twenty years to a day! He wondered if the ethereal stranger would be there to meet him and guide him to the seat of judgement... He would not have long to wait before he knew:

The flooring gave way beneath him. His body dropped... a sudden, terrific jolt... then oblivion!


## IV


The blinding effulgence again became a whirling, chaotic jumble. Gradually it diminished, until it was but a tiny revolving point. Then it was gone altogether, leaving intense, impenetrable blackness.

"Come, John," the voice was saying, " the time grows short. Already upon the earth the stars have waned and sun is starting its daily journey. You have seen what the future holds in store, should you choose to return to the life you have left behind. I repeat, there is no place here for the soul that is not content. The decision is yours."

John Castle could not repress an involuntary shudder at the thought of what he had just witnessed. After all, perhaps man was not the best judge of his destiny!

As he hesitated, the ethereal figure of his guide faded out before his eyes. An invisible force gripped him, propelled him at a breath-taking speed toward the earth. He wondered what could exert such a tremendous power. The answer came in a flash. It was morning. They had found his body. White was manipulating the machine!

It seemed hours, yet he knew it could have been but a mere minute before his astral body once more hovered above his inert physical one. His guess had been correct — White was at the machine. He could see his letter of instructions on the table beside the empty jars that had contained the last of his life-giving mixture. His wife and children were there, too, their tear-stained faces watching with prayerful intentness. His comprehensive survey glimpsed the family physician eying the proceedings with a supercilious sneer. He felt the magnetic, irresistible power of his invention drawing his soul back into his body. How wonderful it would be! To die — and then to live again!

Once more came the vision of the scaffold. Once more came memories of long hours fraught with misery, spent behind prison bars...

The watchers in the little room saw John Castle's eyelids twitch feebly. A hand moved. They stared, spellbound, as it described an arc toward his head.

White sprang forward with a sharp cry as the hand closed over the three rubber tubes that connected the man and the machine. Too late! One wrench, with a strength that seemed inconsistent with the wan figure on the bed, and the damage was done. John Castle had made his choice!

As he drifted once more into unconsciousness, he could faintly hear Montague White's hoarse cry of horror:

"Good God! Mrs. Castle! He's broken the machine!"

# Ashes

"HELLO, BRUCE. Haven't seen you in a dog's age. Come in."

I threw open the door, and he followed me into the room. His gaunt, ungainly figure sprawled awkwardly into the chair I indicated, and he twirled his hat between nervous fingers. His deepset eyes wore a worried, hunted look, and he glanced furtively around the room as if searching for a hidden something which might unexpectedly pounce upon him. His face was haggard and colorless. The corners of his mouth twitched spasmodically.

"What's the matter, old man? You look as if you'd seen a ghost. Brace up!" I crossed to the buffet, and poured a small glass of wine from the decanter. "Drink this!"

He downed it with a hasty gulp, and took to toying with his hat again.

"Thanks, Prague — I don't feel quite myself tonight."

"You don't look it, either! What's wrong?"

Malcolm Bruce shifted uneasily in his chair.

I eyed him in silence for a moment, wondering what could possibly affect the man so strongly. I knew Bruce as a man of steady nerves and iron will. To find him visibly upset was, in itself, unusual. I passed cigars, and he selected one, automatically.

It was not until the second cigar had been lighted that Bruce broke the silence. His nervousness was apparently gone. Once more he was the dominant self-reliant figure I knew of old.

"Prague," he began, "I've just been through the most devilish, gruesome experience that ever befell a man. I don't know whether I dare tell it or not, for fear you'll think I've gone crazy — and I wouldn't blame you if you did! But it's true, every word of it!"

He paused, dramatically, and blew a few rings of smoke in the air.

I smiled. Many a weird tale I had listened to over that self-same table. There must have been some kink in my personality that inspired confidence, for I had been told stories that some men would have given years of their life to have heard. And yet, despite my love of the bizarre and dangerous, and my longing to explore far reaches of little-known lands, I had been doomed to a life of prosaic, flat, uneventful business.

"Do you happen to have heard of Professor Van Allister?" asked Bruce.

"You don't mean Arthur Van Allister?"

"The same! Then you know him?

"I should say so! Known him for years. Ever since he resigned as Professor of Chemistry at the College so he could have more time for his experiments. Why, I even helped him choose the plans for that sound-proof laboratory of his, on the top floor of his home. Up to a year or so ago, we were pals. Then he got so busy with his confounded experiments he couldn't find time to be chummy!"

"You may recall, Prague, that when we were in college together, I used to dabble quite a bit in chemistry?"

I nodded, and Bruce continued:

"About four months ago I found myself out of a job. Van Allister advertised for an assistant, and I answered. He remembered me from college days, and I managed to convince him I knew enough about chemistry to warrant a trial.

"He had a young lady doing his secretarial work — a Miss Marjorie Purdy. She was one of these strict-attention-to-business types, and as good-looking as she was efficient. She had been helping Van Allister a bit in his laboratory, and I soon discovered she took a genuine interest in puttering around, making experiments of her own. Indeed, she spent nearly all her spare time with us in the laboratory.

"It was only natural that such companionship should result in a close friendship, and it wasn't long before I began to depend on her to help me in difficult experiments when the Professor was busy. I never could seem to stump her. That girl took to chemistry as a duck takes to water!

"About two months ago Van Allister had the laboratory partitioned off, and made a separate workroom for himself. He told us that he was about to enter upon a series of experiments which, if successful, would bring him everlasting fame. He flatly refused to make us his confidants in any way, shape or manner.

"From that time on, Miss Purdy and I were left alone more and more. For days at a time the Professor would retire to the seclusion of his new workshop, sometimes not even appearing for his meals.

"That meant, too, that we had more spare time on our hands. Our friendship ripened. I felt a growing admiration for the trim young woman who seemed perfectly content to fuss around smelly bottles and sticky messes, gowned in white from head to foot, even to the rubber gloves she wore.

"Day before yesterday Van Allister invited us into his workshop.

"At last I have achieved success,' he announced, holding up for our inspection a small bottle containing a colorless liquid. 'I have here what will rank as the greatest chemical discovery ever known. I am going to prove its efficacy right before your eyes. Bruce, will you bring me one of the rabbits, please?'

"I went back into the other room and brought him one of the rabbits we kept, together with guinea pigs, for experimental purposes.

"He put the little animal into a small glass box just large enough to hold it, and closed the cover. Then he set a glass funnel in a hole in the top of the box, and we drew nearer to watch the experiment.

"He uncorked the bottle, and poised it above the rabbit's prison.

" 'Now to prove whether my weeks of effort have resulted in success or failure!'

"Slowly, methodically, he emptied the contents of the bottle into the funnel, and we watched it trickle into the compartment with the frightened animal.

"Miss Purdy uttered a suppressed cry, and I rubbed my eyes to make sure that they had not deceived me. For, in the case where but a moment before there had been a live, terrified rabbit, *there was now nothing but a little pile of soft, white ashes!*"

"Professor Van Allister turned to us with an air of supreme satisfaction. His face radiated ghoulish glee and his eyes were alight with a weird, insane gleam. When he spoke, his voice took on a tone of mastery.

" 'Bruce — and you, too, Miss Purdy — it has been your privilege to witness the first successful trial of a preparation that will revolutionize the world. It will instantaneously reduce to a fine ash anything with which it comes in contact, except glass! Just think what that means. An army equipped with glass bombs filled with my compound could annihilate the world! Wood, metal, stone, brick — *everything* — swept away before them, leaving no more trace than the rabbit I have just experimented upon — just a pile of soft, white ashes!'

"I glanced at Miss Purdy. Her face had gone as white as the apron she wore.

"We watched Van Allister as he transferred all that was left of the bunny to a small bottle, and neatly labeled it. I'll admit that I was suffering a mental chill myself by the time he dismissed us, and we left him alone behind the tightly closed doors of his workshop.

"Once safely outside, Miss Purdy's nerves gave way completely. She reeled, and would have fallen had I not caught her in my arms.

"The feel of her soft, yielding body held close to my own was the last straw. I cast prudence to the winds and crushed her tightly to my breast. Kiss after kiss I pressed upon her full red lips, until her eyes opened and I saw the lovelight reflected in them.

"After a delicious eternity we came back to earth again — long enough to realize that the laboratory was no place for such ardent demonstrations. At any moment Van Allister might come out of this retreat, and if he should discover our love-making — in his present state of mind — we dared not think of what might happen.

"For the rest of the day I was like a man in a dream. It's a wonder to me that I succeeded in accomplishing anything at all. My body was merely an automation, a well-trained machine, going about its appointed tasks, while my mind soared into faraway realms of delightful day-dreaming.

"Marjorie kept busy with her secretarial work for the rest of the day, and not once did I lay eyes upon her until my tasks in the laboratory were completed.

"That night we gave over to the joys of our new-found happiness. Prague, I shall remember that night as long as I live! The happiest moment I have ever known was when Marjorie Purdy promised to become my wife.

"Yesterday was another day of unalloyed bliss. All day long my sweetheart and I worked side by side. Then followed another night of lovemaking. If you've never been in love with the only girl in the world, Prague, you can't understand the delirious joy that comes from the very thought of her! And Marjorie returned my devotion a hundred-fold. She gave herself un-reservedly into my keeping.

"Along about noontime, today, I needed something to complete an experiment, and I stepped over to the drug store for it.

"When I returned I missed Marjorie. I looked for her hat and coat and they were gone. The professor had not shown himself since the experiment upon the rabbit, and was locked in his workshop.

"I asked the servants, but none of them had seen her leave the house, nor had she left any message for me.

"As the afternoon wore on I grew frantic. Evening came, and still no sign of my dear little girl.

"All I thought of work was forgotten. I paced the floor of my room like a caged lion. Every jangle of the 'phone or ring at the door bolstered my faltering hopes of some word from her, but each time I was doomed to disappointment. Each minute seemed an hour; each hour an eternity!

"Good God, Prague! You can't imagine how I suffered! From the heights of sublime love I mentally plunged to the darkest depths of despair. I conjured visions of all sorts of terrible fates overtaking her. Still, not a word did I hear.

"It seemed to me that I had lived a lifetime, but my watch told me it was only half-past seven when the butler told me that Van Allister wanted me in the laboratory.

"I was in no mood for experiments, but while I was under his roof he was my master, and it was for me to obey.

"The Professor was in his workshop, the door slightly ajar. He called to me to close the door of the laboratory and join him in the little room.

"In my state of mind my brain photographed every minute detail of the scene which met my eyes. In the center of the room, on a marble-top table, was a glass case about the shape and size of a coffin. It was filled almost to the brim with that same colorless liquid which the small bottle had contained, two days before.

"At the left, on a glass-top tabourette, was a newly-labeled glass jar. I could not repress an involuntary shudder as I realized that it was filled with soft white ashes. Then I saw something that almost made my heart stop beating!

"On a chair, in a far corner of the workshop, was the hat and coat of the girl who had pledged her life to mine — the girl whom I had vowed to cherish and protect while life should last!

"My senses were numbed, my soul surcharged with horror, as realization flashed over me. There could be but one explanation. *The ashes in that jar were the ashes of Marjorie Purdy!*

"The world stood still for one long, terrible moment, and then I went mad — stark, staring mad!

"The next I can remember, the Professor and I were locked in a desperate struggle. Old as he was, he still possessed a strength nearly equal to mine, and he had the added advantage of calm self-possession.

"Closer and closer he forced me to the glass coffin. A few

moments more and my ashes would join those of the girl I had loved. I stumbled against the tabourette, and my fingers closed over the jar of ashes. With one, last, super-human effort, I raised it high above my head, and brought it down with crushing force upon the skull of my antagonist! His arm relaxed, his limp form dropped in a senseless heap to the floor.

"Still acting upon impulse, I raised the silent form of the Professor and carefully, lest I should spill some of it on the floor, lowered the body into the casket of death!

"A moment, and it was over. Professor and liquid, both, were gone, and in their place was a little pile of soft, white ashes!

"As I gazed at my handiwork the brainstorm passed away, and I came face to face with the cold, hard truth that I had killed a fellow-being. An unnatural calm possessed me. I knew that there was not one single shred of evidence against me, barring the fact that I was the last one known to be alone with the Professor. Nothing remained but ashes!

"I put on my hat and coat, told the butler that the Professor had left word he was not to be disturbed , and that I was going out for the evening. Once outside, all my self-possession vanished. My nerves were shot to pieces. I don't know where I went — only that I wondered aimlessly, here and there, until I found myself outside your apartment, just a little while ago.

"Prague, I felt as if I must talk with someone, that I must unburden my tortured mind. I knew that I could trust you, old pal, so I've told you the entire story. Here I am — do with me as you will. Life holds nothing more for me, now that — Marjorie — is — gone!"

Bruce's voice trembled with emotion and broke as he mentioned the name of the girl he loved.

I leaned across the table, and gazed searchingly into the eyes of the abject figure that slouched dejectedly in the big chair. Then I rose, put on my hat and coat, crossed to Bruce, who had buried his head in his arms and was shaking with silent sobs.

"Bruce!"

Malcolm Bruce raised his eyes.

"Bruce, listen to me. *Are you sure Marjorie Purdy is dead?*"

"Am I sure that —" His eyes widened at the suggestion, and he sat erect with a sudden start.

"Exactly," I went on. " Are you positive that the ashes in that jar were the ashes of Marjorie Purdy?"

"Why — I — see here, Prague! What are you driving at?"

"Then you're *not* sure. You saw the girl's hat and coat in that chair, and in your state of mind you jumped at conclusions. 'The ashes must be those of the missing girl... The Professor must have made away with her...' and all that. Come now, did Van Allister *tell* you anything —"

"I don't know what he said. I tell you I went *berserk* — mad!

"Then you come along with me. If she's not dead, she must be somewhere in that house, and if she *is* there, we're going to find her!"

On the street we hailed a taxi, and in a few moments the butler admitted us to Van Allister's home. Bruce let us into the laboratory with his key. The door of the workshop was still ajar.

My eyes swept the room in a comprehensive survey. At the left, over near the window, was a closed door. I strode across the room and tried the knob, but it refused to yield.

"Where does that lead?"

"Just an anteroom, where the Professor keeps his apparatus."

"All the same, that door's coming open," I returned, grimly. Stepping back a pace or two, I planted a well-directed kick upon the door. Another, and still another, and the frame-work around the lock gave way.

Bruce, with an inarticulate cry, sped across the room to a huge mahogany chest. He selected one of the keys on his ring, inserted it in the lock, and flung back the cover with trembling hands.

"Here she is, Prague — quick! Get her out where there's air!"

Together we bore the limp figure of the girl into the laboratory. Bruce hastily mixed a concoction which he forced between her lips. A second dose, and her eyes slowly opened.

Her bewildered glance traveled around the room, at last resting on Bruce, and her eyes lighted with sudden, happy recognition. Later, after the first few moments of reunion, the girl told us her story:

"After Malcolm went out, this afternoon, the Professor sent word to me to come into the workshop. As he often summoned me to do some errand or other, I thought nothing of it, and to save time, took my hat and coat along. He closed the door of the little room, and, without warning, attacked me from behind. He overpowered me, tied me hand and foot. It was needless to gag me. As you know, the laboratory is absolutely sound-proof.

"Then he produced a huge Newfoundland dog he had secured from somewhere or other, reduced it to ashes before my very eyes, and put the ashes in a glass jar that was on a tabourette in the workshop.

"He went into the anteroom and, from the chest where you found me, took out the glass casket. At least, it seemed a casket to my terror-stricken eyes! He mixed enough of this horrible liquid to fill it almost to the brim.

"Then he told me that but one thing remained. That was — to perform the experiment upon a human being!" She shuddered at the recollection. "He dilated at length upon what a privilege it would be for anyone to sacrifice his life in such a manner, for such a cause. Then he calmly informed me that he had selected you as the subject of his experiment, and that I was to play the role of witness! I fainted.

"The Professor must have feared some sort of intrusion, for the next I remember is waking inside the chest where you discovered me. It was stifling! Every breath I took came harder and harder. I thought of you, Malcolm — thought of the wonderful, happy hours we had spent together the last few days. I wondered what I would do when you were gone! I even prayed that he would kill me, too! My throat grew parched and dry — everything went black before my eyes.

"Next, I opened them to find myself here — with you, Malcolm," her voice sank to a hoarse, nervous whisper. "Where — where is the Professor?"

Bruce silently led her into the workshop. She shivered as the coffin of glass came within her range of vision. Still silently, he crossed directly to the casket, and taking up a handful of the soft white ashes, let them sift slowly through his fingers!

# Eterna

AS I STEPPED OUT of the warm, brilliantly-lighted concert hall into the night, I turned up the collar of my overcoat, and shivered.

The snow was falling faster than ever, and the icy wind whistled around my ears, driving the swirling flakes into my eyes.

Instead of taking one of the waiting taxis, and going directly home, as was my usual custom, I pushed on down the street in search of a café.

All at once I heard steps beside me, and I felt a slight tug at my coat sleeve.

"Please, sir," a voice whined into my ear, "can't you help a poor fellow out a bit?"

It's no unusual occurrence for me to be accosted by a beggar, and I ordinarily ignore them absolutely, but there was something in his voice that commanded my attention, and I turned to see what kind of man with whom I had to deal.

It has been a hobby of mine to make a study of human nature, and I compliment myself on my ability to analyze a person correctly at a single glance.

I could see in his drawn, wan, pallid face, made even more so by the brilliant rays of a huge, near-by electric sign-board, the ravages which misfortune and suffering had wrought on the once clean-cut, refined features he must have possessed.

His clothes, wet with the storm, flapped disconsolately about him as the wind swept the street in great gusts.

One hand was tucked into the pocket of his thin ragged coat, as if for protection against the icy cold, while the other was still clawing at my coat.

"Well, my man," I returned, "What can I do for you?"

"Do?" he echoed, his teeth chattering in a way that made me shiver; his whole frame shaking with the cold, "Do? My God, man! I'm starving!"

The lights of the lunch room were blazing across the street, and yielding to a sudden impulse I invited:

"Come along, friend, I've a little heart left in me. Let's see what we can find across the way."

He followed me without a word, across the street and into the restaurant, dropping into a chair.

The place was one of those arm-chair lunches that are always open; and, because of the storm, was deserted but for the man behind the counter.

I ordered a good substantial meal for the stranger, and a

sandwich for myself.

As he ate, I remembered the winter I had voluntarily spent at the Salvation Army, and my experiences there among all types of men, had taught me lessons I could have learned in no other way.

I knew by the expression in his face, and the pleading look in his eyes, that he was longing to open his soul to some sympathizing listener and pour out his tale of woe.

As he pushed away the last of his empty dishes, he leaned back in his chair and heaved a contented sigh.

"Feel better?" I asked. "Say, how did you ever come to get this way, anyhow? You don't look to me like a regular hobo."

Then he told me his story — a weird, wild, wonderful tale that has haunted me day and night ever since; a tale of which I remember every word just as if it had been seared on my brain with a red-hot iron, and I offer it to you at face value.

Take it or leave it, as you will — but if you could have seen him as he told it (as I can see him, even now, as I am writing) you would have believed him just as I believed, and you would have been awed and silenced by his earnestness and sincerity.

"If I were to tell you my name, " he began, "You would recognize it at once as one which is familiar on both continents. Jack Dunn is the one I'm using now, and it will serve just as well for tonight.

"Like many another young fellow, whose parents are rich, and who has but to sign a slip of paper to have almost the world at his command, I gradually grew into the idea that money would buy everything —everything, you understand?

"My life was a round of clubs, social events, midnight orgies —a regular wine, woman and song affair.

"After a few years of this sort of thing, my nerves gave out under the strain, and at the advice of my physician, I left Paris and came to this country under an assumed name; knowing that if I used my own, society would never give me even a moment's rest.

"After a few weeks in this country, I made friends, among others, with several artists. They persuaded me to call on them at their studios.

"I was delighted with the freedom of their life, and the work fascinated me. It was an easy matter for them to coax me into taking up the study of art with them.

"A year passed, and I had become quite proficient. Indeed, I executed many sketches which surpassed even the efforts of my instructors.

"One night, Tom Borrett invited me to go with him to a masque ball the artists were to have the following evening.

"As I had been to no social event of any consequence since leaving Paris, I gladly accepted.

"Borrett, ever a lover of Coleridge, went as the 'Ancient Mariner,' and I, not to be outdone, accompanied him as the 'Wedding Guest.'

"It was there I met Her —

"She was dressed to represent Kipling's 'Vampire Woman.' Her daring costume was so arranged as to accentuate every physical charm. In all my years in Parisian society I had never seen one quite as beautiful, quite as wonderful, quite as perfect.

"Her perfect features, her ruby red lips and radiant cheeks were framed by a wonderful luxuriant mass of hair, as black as the wing of a raven, forming a picture such as no painter had ever yet been able to portray.

"Her eyes seemed to scintillate with a brilliancy which vied even with the stars in the heavens: two priceless gems, set in a field of royal purple such as the kings of old would have been proud to wear.

"Her arms and hands, with their long, tapering fingers were beautifully rounded, and of a marvelous whiteness.

"She carried herself with a supreme magnificence, well befitting her, and every eye was turned her way.

" 'Who is she, Borrett?' I whispered, as we moved across the floor in her direction.

" 'Don't know,' he returned, 'Never saw her in my life, before. Gad, but she's handsome!'

"We play this game of life of ours without a chance to win. Fate has the cards all stacked against us before we start, and she only waits until the betting is heavy enough to make things interesting before she plays her hand.

"Right there she dealt me a good looking set of cards, and I played right into her clutches.

"As we crossed the room, I noticed that she was listlessly toying with a magnificent, blood-red rose which she had plucked from the cluster at her bodice.

"It happened almost if it were part of a pre-arranged plan, a page from any of the 'best sellers' of the day; for as we passed her, the rose slipped from her fingers and dropped at our feet.

"With trembling, eager fingers, I stooped and picked it up for her.

" 'Pardon me,' I murmured, as I gave it to her, 'Didn't you drop this?'

" 'Why, yes,' she returned, her lily-white fingers closing gently over the stem, 'Thank you, so much.'

"Her lips parted in a bewitching smile that set my heart beating at twice its normal rate.

"At that moment the orchestra struck up a lively tune. I noticed that no one approached to claim her for the dance. A strange, mysterious something prompted me to ask:

" 'May I have this next dance with you?'

"Imagine, if you can, the mystical thrill of intense joy that surged through my heart as she smiled back at me, and replied:

" 'Most certainly, my friend, I would be delighted.'

"We swung out onto the floor and I fell into step with her. Her dancing was a marvelous as her beauty. I danced as I had never danced before.

"I noticed that the floor had cleared before us, the others lining up around the room watching us dance. As the music came to a pause, and we started for our seats, they burst into applause.

"Again and again we danced; one-steps, fox trots, dances of our own making — everything, 'till finally I grew tired.

" 'May I have the pleasure of accompanying you home!' I requested, as the others began to disperse.

" 'I'm sorry,' she replied, 'But I must say no. That is a

privilege I grant to no one.'

" 'But I may see you again?' I begged.

" 'You may,' she assented, 'I shall be at the Dansant next Thursday. I would be pleased to have you for a dancing partner again.'

"The next few days I was like a man in a haze. I was walking on air — dreaming impossible dreams.

"At the Dansant it was just a repetition of her former triumph, her dancing taking the crowd by storm.

" 'You're a wonderful woman,' I told her, before she left me. 'I'd like to beg permission to paint your portrait.'

"Granted, artist-man,' she unexpectedly replied, 'When and where shall we have the first sitting?'

"I gave her a card with the address of my studio.

"Suppose we make it tomorrow morning at ten,' I suggested.

" 'Done.'

" 'And now what is your name?' I entreated.

She laughed, mockingly, glided away from me and disappeared into the crowd.

"Every day for four long months she came and posed. As the picture neared its completion, she told me time and time again:

" 'Painter-man, it's wonderful. I've had my portrait painted by masters all over the world, but something has always been lacking. You've found that something, painter-man. It's a master piece, a painting among paintings.'

" 'The others,' I always told her, 'painted you with brush

and oils, but my whole being is wrapped up in your personality. It's my soul that I've put onto that canvass — my soul — and yours.'

"At this she would always laugh, and tell me I was a foolish boy, that I was too sentimental for this modern, busy world.

"Many times I had tried to follow her home, to find out where she lived, but she always eluded me. Try as I might to find someone who knew her, or to find out her name, I failed.

"As the days rolled by she became more and more tantalizing. She laughed at me, mocked me, tempted me, seemed to dare me to penetrate beyond the veil of conventionality.

"One morning, as I was putting the finishing touches on the painting, she goaded me beyond the powers of my endurance. I could stand it no longer.

" 'You wonderful girl,' I burst out, 'Ever since that first night I met you, I've loved you. For four long months this love has grown bigger, deeper, more real. My whole life has been surcharged with it. Whoever you are, you were made for me; where ever you come from, you must go with me. I must and I will have you all for my own. Do you understand me, oh, Princess of my soul? I love you — love you — love you!'

"Before she could divine my intentions, I had gathered her in my arms and crushed her to me. I could feel her hot breath on my cheek as I drew her nearer —nearer — nearer 'till finally our lips met in one long, lingering kiss that seemed to knit my very soul to hers!

"She lingered in my arms for one, long, delicious moment.

ETERNA

Then a weird, wild look came into her eyes.

"With a mighty wrench, she freed, herself from my embrace. Her hands on my shoulders, she forced me into the chair. Then, her wonderful eyes gazing into the depths of my soul and flashing fire with every word, she spoke:

" 'You fool!' she hissed, 'Must I send you, too, to ruin? Must I drag you down to the very depths of shame, as I have hundreds of others? Must I make life a living Hell for you?

" 'You ask me who I am, and where I came from. You seek to learn what no other man has guessed for over a century. Very well, I shall tell you; and to your dying day you will be sorry that you asked, sorry that you kissed me, sorry that you ever even met me!'

" 'My name is Eterna – that is all – just Eterna. A century ago I was just like other women. I had a life to live in this great world, a chance to do some good before I died. I knew the joys and sorrows that come to every woman, and I had the same desires, the same longings which every woman keeps locked within her heart.

" 'I was called beautiful, as men reckon beauty. My charms were put on canvass. My praises were sung by poets of the time. Men worshiped me, and the host of my admirers disgusted me.

" 'Still I was not satisfied. I longed for Perfection. I wanted to be more beautiful than any human being that had ever walked within the bounds of this earth. I sought to rival even God, Himself.

" 'All my life I had been vastly different from other girls. I loved to dabble in science, mechanics, chemistry and the like. My people were well enough situated so that I had a little laboratory completely fitted out for my experiments. It was my father's last gift to me before he went to join my mother in the Great Beyond, and it was here that I spent most of my leisure hours.

" 'It was here, painter-man, after many, many long weeks of painstaking experiments, that I made the Great Discovery — a scientifically certain way of attaining absolute physical perfection; that is, if my final test proved successful.

" 'Of course, I realized that such an experiment would be fraught with the gravest danger; that, should it prove a failure, it might mean even Death itself, but it was worth every bit of chance that I might have to take. Just think, painter-man, should success crown my efforts I would be the most beautiful woman in the world — and think what my discovery would mean to the rest of the world!

" 'It took many more long, hard days before everything was in readiness for the Great Adventure. Then, with a prayer for success upon my lips, I began the experiment that was to prove my supremacy over the forces of nature, or result in my ruin.

" 'For nearly three weeks I lay shut away from the world, while the forces set in motion by these scientific principles made me over into a new and wonderful being.

" 'Then on the very day that success crowned my efforts, my soul died! Do you understand me, painter-man? My soul became dead!'

"I began to fear I was dealing with a mad woman. Her hands were no longer on my shoulders, and she was toying with a paper cutter on the table, an ivory-handled affair, with a long keen blade. She held me with her hypnotic eyes, seeming to look through me, rather than at me.

"My soul died, painter-man,' she repeated. 'As a punishment for my sacrilege, for my sin — in achieving what God never intended man should attain — absolute perfection — He cursed me with Immortality, and sent me back into the world to live on — and on — and on!

" 'And, as I've lived on down through the years, never changing, never growing old, I've led a life of sin and shame and degradation. I've left behind me a trail of bloodshed and ruin. For I feed upon the souls of man!

" 'My perfect beauty has been the decoy by which His Satanic Majesty has lured every man who has seen me on to his soul's destruction.

" 'Men have died for me, men have been murdered because of me, homes have been broken up by me. I am responsible for the fall of a countless number of young men, struggling to live honestly and uprightly before their God.

" 'But you, painter-man, you who have put your very soul into that wonder-picture of me — for the soul which shines through my eyes is yours — I did not want to drag you down with the rest.

" 'Now you've kissed me — and an unseen power causes me to place my curse upon you, forces me to break your heart like the others; and I must live to know that another soul is on my list to be accounted for at the Judgement Day — the soul of the man I loved!'

"Her whole attitude changed. She seemed to tower feet

above me. Once more she was the Vampire woman, the blood-sucker of souls.

" 'You fool!' she hissed, through her clenched teeth, 'Kiss me again! Kiss me again!'

"A strange power seemed to lift me from my chair and draw me towards her, up — up — up

"Suddenly her whole attitude changed once more. Again she was the penitent, the sorrowful. Her eyes drove me back into my chair.

" 'I've courted death, painter-man,' she went on, 'I've been in the most dangerous chemical laboratories, I've been with the soldiers on the battlefields, I've nursed the worst cases of contagious diseases, but I am immune. See, painter-man, see!"

"Her voice rose to a shriek; and, before I could make a move to prevent it, her fingers had closed over that paper knife, and she had plunged it, up to the hilt, into her bosom.

"I gave a horrified cry, and buried my face in my hands.

" 'See, painter-man, see!' she called again.

"In spite of myself, as though moved by that same, strange mysterious power, I looked at her again.

"She had bared her breast, and the sight of the handle of that knife protruding from her beautiful being struck terror into my heart. Still I could not take my eyes away.

" 'See, painter-man, see!' she chanted.

"Then, grasping the handle of the knife, while it seemed as if my very heart stood still, she drew that four-inch blade slowly from her breast.

"As God is my judge, not a sign of a wound, not even a scratch was visible!

" 'See, painter-man, see!' she mocked, again, and tossed the knife into my lap.

"I fainted dead away —

"When I came to my senses, she was gone.

"I picked up the knife and examined it. It was as clean and as free from any kind of a stain as the day I bought it from the little Japanese store across the way.

"Then my eyes fell upon her portrait. It seemed to smile at me, to mock me, as she had done.

"In an insane fury, I slashed it to shreds, cursing and ranting like a wild man.

"Hastily I packed up all my belongings, and fled from the studio.

"I've been all over the country, begging my way from town to town. Everywhere I go, she haunts me.

" I can see her now, as she sat by the table that day, the ivory-handled knife protruding from her bared bosom, and I can seem to hear her voice in my ear, mocking me, saying:

" 'See, painter-man, see!' "

As he finished the tale, a clock in a near-by tower struck the magic hour of midnight.

Like a man in a dream, I watched him as he turned up the collar of his thin, tattered coat, slunk out into the night, and disappeared in the storm.

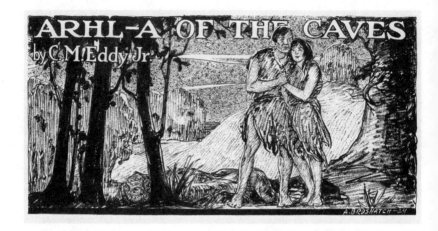

# ARHL-A OF THE CAVES
## by C. M. Eddy, Jr.

WHEN ARHL-A OPENED her eyes, darkness had settled over the universe. The tough cords of reindeer sinews which bound her hands and feet cut deep into her flesh, and her wrists and ankles were raw and bleeding from her futile struggles to free herself from the bonds. The flickering light of the fire at the entrance of the cavern caused the shadows to dance on the limestone walls in a ghostly, ever-changing glow. Silhouetted against the background of the fire loomed the huge body of Zurd, his eyes fastened intently upon her.

Ugh! How she hated him! She spat between her clenched teeth, and her tortured wrists strained anew at their fastenings as her gaze rested upon him. Never would she become his mate of her own free will! Better far that she should bury the keen blade of the stag-handled stone dagger, that lay hidden away beneath her garment of doeskin, clean to the hilt in her bosom than to suffer such insult at the hands of the human monster who had stolen her from her chosen one.

Zurd, the Coward! How well he was named! How different he was from Wagh, the Mighty, the man whom she loved. She could picture him now as she lay there, his tall, lithe, sinewy frame scarred from head to foot by the claws and teeth of the mighty beasts he fought and overpowered. He even wore a necklace made from the very teeth and claws that had inflicted those wounds, trophies she had strung together for him with her own hands and hung about his neck when it was finished. His broad head with its shock of jet-black hair, his powerful hands that could tear apart the jaws of the mighty cave-lion! He was a man, indeed!

She looked again at the squat figure still watching her from the mouth of the cave. His low, receding forehead with its heavy, overhanging brow, his massive jaw, his short grotesque arms and legs, reminded her of the ape people that still roamed the forests and warred against her kind.

Zurd, the Coward! He was even afraid of her, a woman! He had sprung upon her from behind, and even now that he had spirited her many miles away from her own people he dared not loose her bonds. She thought of the day to come, when Wagh should trail Zurd to his hiding place. Then he would take him in his two hands and break him like a stick of wood across his knee.

Zurd rose and crossed the floor of the cavern to the helpless girl, with loping, swinging strides. He did not stand erect, his knees being slightly bent, and his similarity to a huge monkey was more marked than before.

He gave the girl a vicious prod with his foot and spoke to her. His tone was harsh and guttural, not at all like her own — low, liquid and musical. Indeed, he spoke more with his eyes and his gestures than with his lips, for language was then in its infancy and speech a power to conjure with.

"And how likes Arhl-a the fare that Zurd provides for her? A long journey and a longer sleep when was had since last she feasted upon the flesh of the reindeer."

Arhl-a's sloe-black eyes flashed fire.

"And does it aid Arhl-a to digest her food to be slung upon Zurd's back like the carcass of the shaggy cave-bear and be carried thus for miles through forest and field?" she asked. " Does it improve her appetite to lie here bound by thongs of the same creature he would have her eat?"

"Then Arhl-a must needs remain hungry and Zurd will feast alone. For bound she must remain until the fire dies out of her heart and she is tamed — until she will give herself to mate with Zurd."

"Much would Arhl-a prefer to suffer the great hunger and pass into the land of the long sleep," retorted the girl.

Zurd, angered by her taunts, caught up a piece of driftwood from the floor of the cave and raised it high above her head. The girl steeled herself for the blow, but his mood passed, and with an imprecation he flung the stick against the wall of the rock chamber. Satisfying himself with another kick at the defenseless girl, Zurd lumbered out of the cavern and into the night.

Arhl-a knew that he would soon return. When he had gorged himself on reindeer meat he would come back to her, and her night would be filled with nameless terror. For rather would she spend a night in the forest and take her chances with the monsters there. She could hear some of them now as she lay with her eyes half closed; the trumpeting of the elephants as they crashed their way down to the river, the howling cry of the terrible hyena, the bellow of the stag, the roar of the lion, and the growl of the cave-bear.

Her eyes scanned the length of the cavern within her range of vision in search of some way of releasing herself. The dancing light of the fire on the wall was a poor illumination, but fate must have guided her eyes, for they lighted on a ragged point of rock that jutted out a few inches above the floor of the cave.

If only she could reach it before Zurd returned. Should he come back and discover her . . .

Slowly she began her torturing journey toward the jagged rock that must serve as her liberator. At every move the cords cut deeper and deeper into her tender flesh. On, and still on, she rolled; it seemed miles instead of feet, hours instead of seconds. One more twist and she would be within reach of the broken stone. Could she make it? Every muscle, every nerve cried out in protest against the attempt. She gritted her teeth and clenched her fists so tightly that the nails sank deep into her palms. With a supreme effort she made the last turn and paused for the moment, exhausted.

The thought of Zurd roused her from her lethargy. If he discovered her . . .

She bent every energy to the tedious task of sawing through the tough sinews that bound her, until at last they gave way and her wrists were free. The stone dagger in her bosom made short work of her other bonds and Arhl-a gave an articulate sigh of relief when the last cord dropped away.

## II

The sun yet glowed a flaming ball of red in the western sky, when Wagh, the Mighty, paused his way out of the great forest and came in sight of the huge cliffs which had been the dwelling ground of his people. The season was growing cold again, and the larger part of the dwellers had already started on their migratory march to where the warmer breezes would blow upon them. But Wagh, together with a few of the hardier ones, had chosen to linger in the old haunts for a while. Later, by forced marches, they could easily overtake the slower moving older ones and join them in their new camping ground.

The other hunters had not returned from the jungle, and the place was well-nigh deserted. He picked his way over the rocks to his cave and entered, letting his burden of pelts slip from his broad back to the floor. Wagh had a strange premonition that something was wrong; that was why he had left the chase and come home earlier than usual. His keen eyes swept the surroundings in search of that which might either confirm or allay his suspicions. He wondered where Arhl-a could be. Most likely she was with We-na, mate of Ze-ka, the Flint-cutter. He did not see what these two women could find to talk about. They were always together. Still he reflected, he was early. Arhl-a would return in due time.

The patter of sandaled feet fell upon his ear. Ah! But it was not Arhl-a who burst with the speed of the wind into his cave. It was We-na, breathless from the haste with which she had traveled.

"Where is Arhl-a?"

"I have not seen her since early morn. I had thought to find her with you in the cave of Ze-ka. See!"

The girl thrust her hand into her bosom and displayed a broad fillet of tiger hide.

Wagh's eyes dilated as they recognized the object the girl held. He had fashioned this fillet himself for Arhl-a to wear. His strong hand closed about the wrist of the girl in the viselike grip and tightened until she winced beneath the pressure.

"Speak, girl! Where found We-na the head-dress made for the raven locks of Arhl-a?"

"At the edge of the great jungle, where Wagh spends his day hunting the woolly mammoth and saber-tooth tiger who preys upon his people and robs the land of the food that they desire. I thought it might be that Arhl-a had joined Wagh in the chase today, but when I saw him return alone I hastened to show him that which I had found."

"We-na did well to come at once to Wagh with her discovery. Come, take him to the place where she found the fillet of tiger-hide that he might seek for trace of what has become of Arhl-a, woman of Wagh."

"Wait. First shall I take the news to Ze-ka, that he may ask the hunters about her as they return. Then shall I show you where I found the ornament."

At last they set out for the edge of the great jungle, and the girl led Wagh to a spot not far from where he had entered the great forest earlier in the day and indicated the spot where she had found the fillet of Ahrl-a. There in the earth Wagh read the story of the struggle that had occurred. It was all as plain to him as the pictures that decorated the walls of his cave. He saw that it was no jungle creature to whom she had fallen a victim; it was a two-footed beast that had spirited her away. But who had dared to make off with Arhl-a, woman of Wagh, the Mighty? He would track him to his hiding place and beat out his brains against the side of his own habitation!

It was too late, now, to follow the trail, for already the shades of night were falling. He would return to his people and there he would count noses. Soon he would know who had stolen his mate away. Then, on the morrow, he would set out upon the trail, and by the antlers of the great reindeer, one of the two would not return alive!

The hunters were nearly all returned, and already the circle fires had been lighted when Wagh reached the camping grounds. The others straggled in by ones and twos until only one remained unaccounted for — Zurd, the Coward.

## III

Wagh awoke in the morning as the first rays of the the sun were streaking the eastern sky. He selected from the pile of crude weapons in the corner of the cave his favorite lance, the head carved with a likeness of the cave-bear that it might be more effective against him; a stone hatchet which had put the finishing touches to more than one four-footed antagonist; and a long, sharp dagger of stone, with an edge as keen as the finest tempered steel.

Thus armed, the man set out upon his quest. With these simple weapons he would face all the dangers that beset him and make his way to where he knew his Arhl-a must be waiting, an unwilling captive at the mercy of Zurd. With unerring accuracy he read the trail of the fleeing man. Every broken twig or crushed blade of grass bore a message for this man who had learned to interpret their significance. On, and still on, he followed the path so plainly marked for his eyes. At times, when the spoor would not be so clear, he would go along on all fours, his nose close to the ground, sniffing, more like one of the animals of the jungle than man.

He wondered how far the two had gone. He knew that their progress would be slow, for Zurd would be hampered with the burden of the girl — and he knew that Arhl-a would never have gone with him of her own volition.

Well on toward midday he stopped short in his tracks and listened, for the wind had brought to his quivering nostrils the scent of the reindeer, and Wagh realized that he was hungry. Cautiously, silently, he made his way in the direction where he knew the herd must be grazing. He pushed on through the underbrush without making a sound, for man could, if he chose, move more silently than any of the animals that roamed at the edge of a clearing.

The herd were making their way directly toward his hiding place. It could not have been better if he had planned it out for himself. He swung into the overhanging branches of a big tree and waited, until the last of the reindeer passed beneath the tree. Then, swinging lightly from the branches, he dropped to the back of the hindmost animal and plunged his lance clean to the shaft into its shoulder.

The startled animal plunged into the underbrush with its human freight, and Wagh clung to its spreading antlers for support, lest he be brushed off by the branch of some tree and crushed by the flying feet of his wounded steed. The now frantic animal crashed heedlessly on, trying in vain to shake off its unaccustomed burden. Of a sudden, one foot stepped into a deep hole, and the reindeer stumbled and tottered to its knees. With the agility of a monkey, Wagh sprang clean  over its antlers, and before the frightened animal could regain its feet he sank his stone dagger deep into its heart. A last convulsive effort to rise, and the reindeer collapsed and rolled over upon its side, dead!

Regaining his weapons, Wagh proceeded to strip the animal of its pelt. Next he gathered a head of dry leaves and twigs. With a sharp bit of hard wood and hollowed-out piece of soft wood he proceeded to build a fire, twirling the hardwood stick upon the other until a spark caught the dry leaves. He nursed the tiny blaze with care, until he had a fire of the size he desired. Then, cutting a large, juicy steak from the animal he had killed, the proceeded to cook his dinner. Retracing his steps. Wagh finally picked up the trail he had left and once more set out upon his way.

All this had taken time, and it was not until late afternoon when Wagh at last came in sight of the cold, barren, deserted cliffs whither Zurd had borne the helpless girl. Every nerve tense, every sense alert, he drew nearer and nearer to the cave where the single trail led. No sound woke the stillness, save the lapping of the sea-waves upon the beach at the foot of the cliffs. Boldly he entered the cavern, before which the fire had smoldered and died. And there, his body already grown cold, he found Zurd, with Arhl-a's stag-handled stone dagger shaft-deep between his shoulder blades.

But where was Arhl-a?

Once more he took up the trail, harder to follow now, with darkness coming on. Back into the forest Wagh followed the spoor of the woman he loved. Already the moon had risen and flooded the scene with silvery rays. Wagh was desperate. He must find Arhl-a before the animals of the night came out to roam the jungle, else all that he might find would be her bones picked clean!

Suddenly, upon the somber stillness of the night, rang out a piercing cry — the cry of a human voice, a cry fraught with horror and distress.

And in that cry Wagh recognized the voice of Arhl-a!

## IV

Arhl-a, crouching in the shadow, heard the heavy step of Zurd as he approached the cave. Zurd, his belly filled with the savory meat of the reindeer, had turned his thoughts to the helpless girl he had left bound in the far corner of the cavern. Suiting action to impulse, he made his way to where he had left her. The food had warmed his body and blood flowed hot through this veins; he yearned for the solace that only the soft warm body of the girl could give him. His eyes agleam with lust, he entered the cave.

Out of the darkness Arhl-a sprang.

Zurd reeled and lurched forward unsteadily under the impact of the unexpected attack. He tried to shake off the body that clung to him with a grip of steel. He swore a mighty oath, invoking the anger of the gods upon this girl who dared defy him. He felt a sudden biting, stinging sensation as the blade of the girl's dagger was buried deep into his back. His body burned with a feverish fire. Again the stone knife bit his flesh. He could feel the life-blood gushing from the open wound. He staggered drunkenly and pitched face down upon the floor of the cave. The cavern echoed hideously with his mighty groans. At length they grew weaker, until finally they ceased altogether…

Arhl-a breathed a great sigh of relief as the silence of death fell over the cave. Death, sudden and sure, held no terrors for this girl of the cave and the wilderness. It was the living whom she fought and feared. Exhausted with the strenuous experiences of the day and stopping only long enough to replenish the fire, that she might be protected from the chance prowler from the jungle near-by, she curled up into a snug, warm ball and slept — a long, deep, refreshing, dreamless sleep.

When Arhl-a awoke the sun was high in the heavens. With only a passing glance at her lifeless companion she made her way down the side of the cliff to where the sea waves gently lapped the sun-kissed shore. Then, letting her single garment of doeskin slip from her white shoulders, she stepped out into the water and bathed, the little waves playing over her lithe form. At last, tired of her sport, she stretched at full length on the sandy beach and basked in the glorious warmth of the sun.

Donning her doeskin wrap once more, she sought out the remains of the reindeer flesh upon which Zurd had feasted the night before and roasted some of it for her breakfast in the hot embers of the dying fire. Her bodily needs satisfied, Arhl-a became possessed of a desire to be on her way back to her people, and Wagh. But first she must have weapons. She re-entered the cave and stripped the dead body of the weapons it wore, leaving her stag-handled dagger in the body that Wagh, should he be trailing them might know she was safe. Thus armed, she scaled the barren walls of the cliff and plunged into the heart of the great forest.

All through the long day she plunged on, ever on. But Arhl-a possessed not the ability of Wagh to follow unerringly the vaguely defined trail through the jungle. It was not until twilight closed about her that the girl realized that she was lost. Had she known, she had traveled in a gigantic circle and was but a short distance from the cave where she had spent the night before, with the silent form of Zurd her sole companion.

The fast gathering darkness brought with it a disquieting silence — the silence that always preceded the voices of the creatures of the night. Above the tree-tops the white moon shone bright in a clear sky and Arhl-a caught an occasional glimpse of a tiny, twinkling star.

Intent upon finding refuge for the long night ahead, the girl did not see the small, bead-like eyes that peered at her from the underbrush, nor did she hear the catlike tread of the creature that trailed her as she pushed on. She did not know that long, hairy arms reached out to encircle her, until she felt a gigantic paw close upon her shoulder and she wheeled to meet her new-found foe. But when she saw the wicked eyes that burned into her own, the low, slavering jaw and the hairy, misshapen body of the great ape that held her in its grasp, then horror overwhelmed her and she screamed — a shrill, piercing, blood-curdling scream.

In answer, a mighty form came crashing through the forest and stood before them, and Arhl-a's heart leapt with joy as she beheld the one who had come to her aid — Wagh, her mate and her protector.

With a harsh, guttural cry the ape flung the girl from him and turned to give battle to his more formidable antagonist. Another moment and the two were locked in a mighty, death-like embrace, with only the wide-eyed girl to witness the battle supreme for which she was to be the prize.

Silently they fought, the stillness broken only by the snapping of dry twigs beneath their feet or the dull thud as the huge bodies crashed against the trunks of the massive trees.

At last Wagh gained the opening he sought and brought his stone ax down with terrific force upon the head of the beast, cleaving it from skull to chin between the eyes. The hairy bulk tottered for a brief instant and toppled in a inert mass at the feet of the victorious man.

And there in the heart of the jungle, with only the moon looking on, the girl found her place in the outstretched arms of the man and the evening breeze softly kissed the reunited pair.

# The Ghost-Eater

MOON-MADNESS? A touch of fever? I wish I could think so! But when I am alone after dark in the waste places where my wanderings take me, and hear across infinite voids the demon echoes of those screams and snarls, and that detestable crunching of bones, I shudder again at the memory of that eldritch night.

I knew less of woodcraft in those days, though the wilderness called just as strongly to me as it does now. Up to that night I had always been careful to employ a guide, but circumstances now suddenly forced me to a trial of my own skill. It was midsummer in Maine, and, despite my great need to get from Mayfair to Glendale by the next noon, I could find no person willing to pilot me. Unless I took the long route through Potowisset, which would not bring me to my goal in time, there would be dense forests to penetrate; yet whenever I asked for a guide I was met with refusal and evasion.

Stranger that I was, it seemed odd that everyone should have glib excuses. There was too much "important business" on hand for such a sleepy village, and I knew that the natives were lying. But they all had "imperative duties," or said that they had; and would do no more than assure me that the trail through the woods was very plain, running due north, and not in the least difficult for a vigorous young fellow. If I started while the morning was still early, they averred, I could get to Glendale by sundown and avoid a night in the open. Even then I suspected nothing. The prospect seemed good, and I resolved to try it alone, let the lazy villagers hang back as they might. Probably I would have tried it even if I had suspected; for youth is stubborn, and from childhood I had only laughed at superstition and old wives' tales.

So before the sun was high I had started off through the trees at a swinging stride, lunch in my hand, guardian automatic in my pocket, and belt filled with crisp bills of large denominations. From the distances given me and a knowledge of my own speed, I had figured on making Glendale a little after sunset; but I knew that even if detained over night through some miscalculation, I had plenty of camping experience to fall back on. Besides, my presence at my destination was not really necessary till the following noon.

It was the weather that set my plans awry. As the sun rose higher, it scorched through even the thickets of the foliage, and burned up my energy at every step. By noon my clothes were soaking with perspiration, and I felt myself faltering in spite of all my resolution. As I pushed deeper into the woods I found the trail greatly obstructed with underbrush, and at many points nearly effaced. It must have been weeks — perhaps months — since anyone had broken his way through; and I began to wonder if I could, after all, live up to my schedule.

At length, having grown very hungry, I looked for the deepest patch of shade I could find, and proceeded to eat the lunch which the hotel had prepared for me. There were some indifferent sandwiches, a piece of stale pie, and a bottle of very light wine; by no means sumptuous fare, but welcome enough to one in my state of overheated exhaustion.

It was too hot for smoking to be of any solace, so I did not take out my pipe. Instead, I stretched myself at full length under the trees when my meal was done, intent on stealing a few moments' rest before commencing the last lap of my journey. I suppose I was a fool to drink that wine; for, light though it was, it proved just enough to finish the work the sultry, oppressive day had begun. My plan called for the merest momentary relaxation, yet, with scarcely a warning yawn, I dropped off into a sound slumber.

## II

When I opened my eyes twilight was closing in about me. A wind fanned my cheeks, restoring me quickly to full perception; and as I glanced up at the sky I saw with apprehension that black racing clouds were leading on a solid wall of darkness prophetic of violent thunderstorm. I knew now that I could not reach Glendale before morning, but the prospect of a night in the woods — my first night of lone forest camping — became very repugnant under these trying conditions. In a moment I decided to push along for a while at least, in the hope of finding some shelter before the tempest should break.

Darkness spread over the woods like a heavy blanket. The lowering clouds grew more threatening, and the wind increased to a veritable gale. A flash of distant lightning illuminated the sky, followed by an ominous rumble that seemed to hint of malign pursuit. Then I felt a drop of rain on my outstretched hand; and though still walking on automatically, resigned myself to the inevitable. Another moment and I had seen the light; the light of a window through the trees and the darkness. Eager only for shelter, I hastened toward it — would to God I had turned and fled!

There was a sort of imperfect clearing on the farther side of which, with its back against the primeval wood, stood a building. I had expected a shanty or log-cabin, but stopped short in surprise when I beheld a neat and tasteful little house of two stories; some seventy years old by its architecture, yet still in a state of repair betokening the closest and most civilized attention. Through the small panes of one of the lower windows a bright light shone, and toward this — spurred by the impact of another raindrop — I presently hurried across the clearing, rapping loudly on the doors as soon as I gained the steps.

With startling promptness my knock was answered by a deep, pleasant voice which uttered the single syllable, "Come!"

Pushing open the unlocked door, I entered a shadowy hall lighted by an open doorway at the right, beyond which was a book-lined room with the gleaming window. As I closed the outer door behind me I could not help noticing a peculiar odor about the house; a faint, elusive, scarcely definable odor which somehow suggested animals. My host, I surmised, must be a hunter or trapper, with his business conducted on the premises.

The man who had spoken sat in a capacious easy-chair beside a marble topped center table, a long lounging robe of gray swathing his lean form. The light from a powerful argand lamp threw his features into prominence, and as he eyed me curiously I studied him in no less detail. He was strikingly handsome, with thin, clean-shaven face, glossy, flaxen hair neatly brushed, long, regular eyebrows that met in a slanting angle above the nose, shapely ears set low and well back on the head, and large expressive gray eyes almost luminous in their animation. When he smiled a welcome he showed a magnificently even set of firm white teeth, and as he waved me to a chair I was struck by the fineness of his slender hands, with their long, tapering fingers whose ruddy, almond-shaped nails were slightly curved and exquisitely manicured. I could not help wondering why a man of such engaging personality should choose the life of a recluse.

"Sorry to intrude," I ventured, "but I've given up the hope of making Glendale before morning, and there's a storm coming on which sent me looking for cover." As if to corroborate my words, there came at this point a vivid flash, a crashing reverberation, and the first breaking of a torrential downpour that beat maniacally against the windows.

My host seemed oblivious to the elements, and flashed me

another smile when he answered. His voice was soothing and well modulated, and his eyes held a calmness almost hypnotic.

"You're welcome to whatever hospitality I can offer, but I'm afraid it won't be much. I've a game leg, so you'll have to do most of the waiting on yourself. If you're hungry you'll find plenty in the kitchen — plenty of food, if not of ceremony!" It seemed to me that I could detect the slightest trace of a foreign accent in his tone, though his language was fluently correct and idiomatic.

Rising to an impressive height, he headed for the door with long, limping steps, and I noticed the huge hairy arms that hung at his side in such curious contrast with his delicate hands.

"Come," he suggested. "Bring the lamp along with you. I might as well sit in the kitchen as here."

I followed him into the hall and the room across it, and at his direction ransacked the woodpile in the corner and the cupboard on the wall. A few moments later, when the fire was going nicely, I asked him if I might not prepare food for both; but he courteously declined.

"It's too hot to eat," he told me. "Besides, I had a bite before you came."

After washing the dishes left from my lone meal, I sat down for a while, smoking my pipe contentedly. My host asked a few questions about the neighboring villages, but lapsed into sullen taciturnity when he learned I was an outsider. As he brooded there silently I could not help feeling a quality of strangeness in him; some subtle alienage that could hardly be analyzed. I was quite certain, for one thing, that he was tolerating me because of the storm rather than welcoming me with genuine hospitality.

As for the storm, it seemed almost to have spent itself. Outside, it was already growing lighter — for there was a full moon behind the clouds — and the rain had dwindled to a trivial drizzle. Perhaps, I thought, I could now resume my journey after all; an idea which I suggested to my host.

"Better wait till morning," he remarked. "You say you're afoot, and it's a good three hours to Glendale. I've two bedrooms upstairs, and you're welcome to one of them if you care to stay."

There was a sincerity in his invitation which dispelled any doubts I had held regarding his hospitality, and I now concluded that his silences must be the result of long isolation from his fellows in this wilderness. After sitting without a word through three fillings of my pipe, I finally began to yawn.

"It's been rather a strenuous day for me," I admitted, "and I guess I'd better be making tracks for bed. I want to be up at sunrise, you know, and on my way."

My host waved his arm toward the door, through which I could see the hall and the staircase.

"Take the lamp with you," he instructed. "It's the only one I have, but I don't mind sitting in the dark, really. Half the time I don't light it at all when I'm alone. Oil is so hard to get out here, and I go to the village so seldom. Your room is the one on the right, at the head of the stairs. "

Taking the lamp and turning in the hall to say good-night, I could see his eyes glowing almost phosphorescently in the darkened room I had left; and I was half reminded for a moment of the jungle, and the circles of eyes that sometimes glow just beyond the radius of the campfire. Then I started upstairs.

As I reached the second floor I could hear my host limping across the hall to the other room below, and perceived that he moved with owlish sureness despite the darkness. Truly, he had but little need of the lamp. The storm was over, and as I entered the room assigned me I found it bright with the rays of a full moon that streamed on the bed from an uncurtained south window. Blowing out the lamp and leaving the house in darkness but for the moonbeams, I sniffed at the pungent odor that rose above the scent of the kerosene--the quasi-animal odor I had noticed on first entering the place. I crossed to the window and threw it wide, breathing deep of the cool, fresh night air.

When I started to undress I paused almost instantly, recalling my money belt, still in its place about my waist. Possibly, I reflected, it would be well not to be too hasty or unguarded; for I had read of men who seized just such an opportunity to rob and even to murder the stranger within their dwelling. So, arranging the bedclothes to look as if they covered a sleeping figure, I drew the room's only chair into the concealing shadows, filled and lighted my pipe again, and sat down to rest or watch, as the occasion might demand.

## III

I could not have been sitting there long when my sensitive ears caught the sound of footsteps ascending the stairs. All the old lore of robber landlords rushed on me afresh, when another moment revealed that the steps were plain, loud, and careless, with no attempt at concealment; while my host's tread, as I had heard it from the head of the staircase, was a soft limping stride. Shaking the ashes from my pipe, I slipped it in my pocket. Then, seizing and drawing my automatic, I rose from the chair, tiptoed across the room, and crouched tensely in a spot which the opening door would cover.

The door opened, and into the shaft of moonlight stepped a man I had never seen before. Tall, broad-shouldered, and distinguished, his face half hidden by a heavy square-cut beard and his neck buried in a high black stock of a pattern long obsolete in America, he was indubitably a foreigner. How he could have entered the house without my knowledge was quite beyond me, nor could I believe for an instant that he had been concealed in either of the two rooms or the hall below me. As I gazed intently at him in the insidious moonbeams it seemed to me that I could see directly through his sturdy form; but perhaps this was only an illusion that came from my shock of surprise.

Noticing the disarray of the bed, but evidently missing the intended effect of occupancy, the stranger muttered something to himself in a foreign tongue and proceeded to disrobe. Flinging his clothes into the chair I had vacated, he crept into bed, pulled the covers over him, and in a moment or two was breathing with the regular respiration of a sound sleeper.

My first thought was to seek out my host and demand an explanation, but a second later I deemed it better to make sure that the whole incident was not a mere delusive after-effect of my wine-drugged sleep in the woods. I still felt weak and faint, and despite my recent supper was as hungry as if I had not eaten since that noonday lunch.

I crossed to the bed, reached out, and grasped at the shoulder of the sleeping man. Then, barely checking a cry of mad fright and dizzy astonishment, I fell back with pounding pulses and dilated eyes. *For my clutching fingers had passed directly through the sleeping form, and seized only the sheet below!*

A complete analysis of my jarred and jumbled sensations would be futile. The man was intangible, yet I could still see him there, hear his regular breathing, and watch his figure as it half-turned beneath the clothes. And then, as I was quite certain of my own madness or hypnosis, I heard other footsteps on the stairs; soft, padded, doglike, limping footsteps, pattering up, up, up. . . . And again that pungent animal smell, this time in redoubled volume. Dazed and dream-drowsed, I crept once more behind the protecting opened door, shaken to the marrow, but now resigned to any fate known or nameless.

Then into that shaft of eery moonlight stepped the gaunt form of a great gray wolf. Limped, I should have said, for one hind foot was held in the air, as though wounded by some stray shot. The beast turned its head in my direction, and as it did so the pistol dropped from my twitching fingers and clattered unheeded to the floor. The ascending succession of horrors was fast paralyzing my will and consciousness, *for the eyes that now glared toward me from that hellish head were the grey phosphorescent eyes of my host as they had peered at me through the darkness of the kitchen.*

I do not yet know whether it saw me. The eyes turned from my direction to the bed, and gazed gluttonously on the spectral sleeping form there. Then the head tilted back, and from that demon throat came the most shocking ululation I have ever heard; a thick, nauseous, lupine howl that made my heart stand still. The form on the bed stirred, opened his eyes, and shrank from what he saw. The animal crouched quiveringly, and then — as the ethereal figure uttered a shriek of mortal human anguish and terror that no ghost of legend could counterfeit — sprang straight for its victim's throat, its white, firm, even teeth flashing in the moonlight as they closed on the jugular vein of the screaming phantasm. The scream ended in a blood-choked gurgle, and the frightened human eyes turned glassy.

That scream had roused me to action, and in a second I had retrieved my automatic and emptied its entire contents into the wolfish monstrosity before me. *But I heard the unhindered thud of each bullet as it imbedded itself in the opposite wall.*

My nerves gave way. Blind fear hurled me toward the door, and blind fear prompted the one backward glance in which I saw that the wolf had sunk its teeth into the body of its quarry. Then came that culminating sensory impression and the devastating thought to which it gave birth. This was the same body I had thrust my hand *through* a few moments before. . . and yet as I plunged down that black nightmare staircase *I could hear the crunching of bones.*

## IV

How I found the trail to Glendale, or how I managed to traverse it, I suppose I shall never know. I only know that sunrise found me on the hill at the edge of the woods, with the steepled village outspread below me, and the blue thread of the Cataqua sparkling in the distance. Hatless, coatless, ashen-faced, and as soaked with perspiration as if I had spent the night abroad in the storm, I hesitated to enter the village till I had recovered at least some outward semblance of composure. At last I picked my way down hill and through the narrow streets with their flagstone sidewalks and Colonial doorways till I reached the Lafayette House, whose proprietor eyed me askance.

"Where from so early, son? And why the wild look?"

"I've just come through the woods from Mayfair."

"You — came — through — the Devil's Woods — *last night* — and *alone?* The old man stared with a queer look of alternate horror and incredulity.

"Why not?" I countered, "I couldn't have made it in time through Potowisset, and I had to be here not later than this noon."

"And last night was *full moon!*... My Gawd!" He eyed me curiously. "See anything of Vasili Oukranikov or the Count?"

"Say, do I look that simple? What are you trying to do — jolly me?"

But his tone was as grave as a priest's as he replied. "You must be new to these parts, sonny. If you weren't you'd know all about Devil's Woods and the full moon and Vasili and the rest."

I felt anything but flippant, yet knew I must not seem serious after my earlier remarks. "Go on — I know you're dying to tell me. I'm like a donkey — all ears."

Then he told the legend in his dry way, stripping it of vitality and convincingness through lack of colouring, detail, and atmosphere. But for me it needed no vitality or convincingness that any poet could have given. Remember what I had witnessed, and remember that I had never heard of the tale until *after* I had had the experience and fled from the terror of those crunched phantom bones.

"There used to be quite a few Russians scattered betwixt here and Mayfair — they came after one of their nihilist troubles back in Russia. Vasili Oukranikov was one of 'em — a tall, thin, handsome chap with shiny yellow hair and a wonderful manner. They said, though, that he was a servant of the devil — a werewolf and eater of men.

"He built him a house in the woods about a third of the way from here to Mayfair and lived all alone. Every once in a while a traveler would come out of the woods with some pretty strange tale about being chased by a big gray wolf with shining human eyes — like Oukranikov's. One night somebody took a pot shot at the wolf, and the next time the Russian came into Glendale he walked with a limp. That settled it. There wasn't any mere suspicion now, but hard facts.

"Then he sent to Mayfair for the Count — his name was Feodar Tchemevsky and he had bought the old gambrel-roofed Fowler place up State Street — to come out and see him. They all warned the Count, for he was a fine man and a splendid neighbor, but he said he could take care of himself all right. It was the night of the full moon. He was brave as they make'em, and all he did was to tell some men he had around the place to follow him to Vasili's if he didn't show up in decent time. They did — and you tell me, sonny, that you've been through those woods at night?"

"Sure I tell you" — I tried to appear nonchalant — I'm no Count, and here I am to tell the tale! . . . But what did the men find at Oukranikov's house?"

"They found the Count's mangled body, sonny, and a gaunt gray wolf hovering over it with blood-slavering jaws. You can guess who the wolf was. And folks do say that at every full moon — but sonny, didn't you see or hear anything?"

"Not a thing, pop! And say, what became of the wolf — or Vasili Oukranikov?"

"Why, son, they killed it — filled it full of lead and buried it in the house, and then burned the place down — you know all this was sixty years ago when I was a little shaver, but I remember it as if 'twas yesterday."

I turned away with a shrug of my shoulders. It was all so quaint and silly and artificial in the full light of day. But sometimes when I am alone after dark in waste places, and hear the demon echoes of those screams and snarls, and that detestable crunching of bones, I shudder again at the memory of that eldritch night.

# DEAF DUMB and BLIND

## by C.M. Eddy Jr.

A LITTLE AFTER noon on the 28th day of June, 1924, Dr. Morehouse stopped his machine before the Tanner place and four men alighted. The stone building, in perfect repair and freshness, stood near the road, and but for the swamp in the rear it would have possessed no trace of dark suggestion. The spotless white doorway was visible across a trim lawn for some distance down the road; and as the doctor's party approached, it could be seen that the heavy portal yawned wide open. Only the screen door was closed. The close proximity of the house had imposed a kind of nervous silence on the four men, for what lurked therein could only be imagined with vague terror. This terror underwent a marked abatement when the explorers heard distinctly the sound of Richard Blake's typewriter.

Less than an hour before, a grown man had fled from that house, hatless, coatless, and screaming, to fall upon the doorstep of his nearest neighbor, half a mile away, babbling incoherently of "house," "dark," "swamp," and "room." Dr. Morehouse had needed no further spur to excited action when told that a slavering, maddened creature had burst out of the old Tanner home by the edge of the swamp. He had known something would happen when the two men had taken the accursed stone house — the man who had fled; and his master, Richard Blake, the author-poet from Boston, the genius who had gone into the war with every nerve and sense alert and had come out as he was now; still debonair though half a paralytic, still walking with song among the sights and sounds of living fantasy though shut forever from the physical world, deaf, dumb, and blind.

Blake had reveled in the weird traditions and shuddering hints about the house and its former tenants. Such eldritch lore was an imaginative asset from whose enjoyment his physical state might not bar him. He had smiled at the prognostications of the superstitious natives. Now, with his sole companion fled in a mad ecstasy of panic fright, and himself left helpless with whatever had caused that fright, Blake might have less occasion to revel and smile! This, at least, was Dr. Morehouse's reflection as he had faced the problem of the fugitive and called on the puzzled cottager to help him track the matter down. The Morehouses were an old Fenham family, and the doctor's grand- father had been one of those who burned the hermit Simeon Tanner's body in 1819. Not even at this distance could the trained physician escape a spinal tingle at what was recorded of that burning — at the naive inferences drawn by ignorant countrymen from a slight and meaningless conformation of the deceased. That tingle he knew to be foolish, for trifling bony protuberances on the fore part of the skull are of no significance, and often observable in bald-headed men.

Among the four men who ultimately set resolute faces toward that abhorrent house in the doctor's car, there occurred a singularly awed exchange of vague legends and half-furtive scraps of gossip handed down from curious grandmothers — legends and hints seldom repeated and almost never systematically compared. They extended as far back as 1692, when a Tanner had perished on Gallows Hill in Salem after a witchcraft trial, but did not grow intimate till the time the house was built — 1747, though the ell was more recent. Not even then were the tales very numerous, for queer though the Tanners all were, it was only the last of them, old Simeon, whom people desperately feared. He added to what he had inherited — added horribly, everyone whispered — and bricked up the windows of the southeast room, whose east wall gave on the swamp. That was his study and library, and it had a door of double thickness with braces. It had been chopped through with axes that terrible winter night in 1819 when the stinking smoke had poured from the chimney and they found Tanner's body in there — with that expression on its face. It was because of that expression — not because of the two bony protuberances beneath the bushy white hair — that they had burned the body and the books and manuscripts it had had in that room. However, the short distance to the Tanner place was covered before much important historical matter could be correlated.

As the doctor, at the head of the party, opened the screen

door and entered the arched hallway, it was noticed that the sound of type-writing had suddenly ceased. At this point two of the men also thought they noticed a faint effusion of cold air strangely out of keeping with the great heat of the day, though they afterward refused to swear to this. The hall was in perfect order, as were the various rooms entered in quest of the study where Blake was presumably to be found. The author had furnished his home in exquisite Colonial taste; and though having no help but the one manservant, he had succeeded in maintaining it in a state of commendable neatness.

Dr. Morehouse led his men from room to room through the wide-open doors and archways, at last finding the library or study which he sought — a fine southerly room on the ground floor adjoining the once-dreaded study of Simeon Tanner, lined with the books which the servant communicated through an ingenious alphabet of touches, and the bulky Braille volumes which the author himself read with sensitive finger-tips. Richard Blake, of course, was there, seated as usual before his typewriter with a draft-scattered stack of newly written pages on the table and floor, and one sheet still in the machine. He had stopped work, it appeared, with some suddenness; perhaps because of a chill which had caused him to draw together the neck of his dressing-gown; and his head was turned toward the doorway of the sunny adjoining room in a manner quite singular for one whose lack of sight and hearing shuts out all sense of the external world.

On drawing nearer and crossing to where he could see the author's face, Dr. Morehouse turned very pale and motioned to the others to stand back. He needed time to steady himself, and to dispel all possibility of hideous illusion. No longer did he need to speculate why they had burned old Simeon Tanner's body on that wintry night because of the *expression* it wore, for here was something only a well-disciplined mind could confront. The late Richard Blake, whose type-writer had ceased its nonchalant clicking only as the men had entered the house, had seen something despite his blindness, and had been affected by it. Humanity had nothing to do with the look that was on his face, or with the glassy morbid vision that blazed in great, blue, bloodshot eyes shut to this world's images for six years. Those eyes were fixed with an ecstasy of clear-sighted horror on the doorway leading to Simeon Tanner's old study, where the sun blazed on walls once shrouded in bricked-up blackness. And Dr. Arlo Morehouse reeled dizzily when he saw that for all the dazzling daylight the inky pupils of those eyes were dilated as cavernously as those of a cat's eyes in the dark.

The doctor closed the staring blind eyes before he let the others view the face of the corpse. Meanwhile he examined the lifeless form with feverish diligence, using scrupulous technical care, despite his throbbing nerves and almost shaking hands. Some of his results he communicated from time to time to the awed and inquisitive trio around him; other results he judiciously withheld, lest they lead to speculations more disquieting than human speculation should be. It was not from any word of his, but from shrewd independent observation, that one of the men muttered about the body's tousled black hair and the way the papers were scattered. This man said it was as if a strong breeze had blown through the open doorway which the dead man faced; whereas, although the once-bricked windows beyond were indeed fully open to the warm June air, there had been scarcely a breath of wind during the entire day.

When one of the men began to gather the sheets of newly-written manuscript as they lay on floor and table, Dr. Morehouse stopped him with an alarmed gesture. He had seen the sheet that remained in the machine, and had hastily removed and pocketed it after a sentence or two blanched his face afresh. This incident prompted him to collect the scattered sheets himself, and stuff them bulkily into an inside pocket without stopping to arrange them. And not even what he had read terrified him half so much as what he now noticed — the subtle difference in touch and heaviness of typing which distinguished the sheets he picked up from the one he had found on the type-writer. This shadowy impression he could not divorce from that other horrible circumstance which he was so zealously concealing from the men who had heard the machine's clicking not ten minutes before — the circumstance he was trying to exclude from even his own mind till he could be alone and resting in the merciful depths of his Morris chair. One may judge of the fear he felt at that circumstance by considering what he braved to keep it suppressed. In more than thirty years of professional practice he had never regarded a medical examiner as one from whom a fact might be withheld; yet through all the formalities which now followed, no man ever knew that when he examined this staring, contorted, blind man's body he had seen at once *that death must have occurred at least half an hour before discovery.*

Dr. Morehouse presently closed the outer door and led the party through every corner of the ancient structure in search of any evidence which might directly illuminate the tragedy. Never was a result more completely negative. He knew that the trap-door of old Simeon Tanner had been removed as soon as that recluse's books and body had been burnt, and that the sub-cellar and the sinuous tunnel under the swamp had been filled up as soon as they were discovered, some thirty-five years later. Now he saw that no fresh abnormalities had come to replace them, and that the whole establishment exhibited only the normal neatness of modern restoration and tasteful care.

Telephoning for the sheriff at Fenham and for the county medical examiner at Bayboro, he awaited the arrival of the former, who, when he came, insisted on swearing in two of the men as deputies until the examiner should arrive. Dr. Morehouse, knowing the mystification and futility confronting the officials, could not help smiling wryly as he left with the villager whose house still sheltered the man who had fled.

They found the patient exceedingly weak, but conscious and fairly composed. Having promised the sheriff to extract and transmit all possible information from the fugitive, Dr. Morehouse began some calm and tactful questioning, which was received in a rational and compliant spirit and baffled only by effacement of memory. Much of the man's quiet must have come from merciful inability to recollect, for all he could now tell was that he had been in the study with his master and had seemed to see the next room suddenly grow dark — the room where sunshine had for more than a hundred years replaced the gloom of bricked-up windows. Even this memory, which indeed he half-doubted, greatly disturbed the unstrung nerves of the patient, and it was with the utmost gentleness and circumspection that Dr. Morehouse told him his master was dead — a natural victim of the cardiac weakness which his terrible wartime injuries must have caused. The man was grieved, for he had been devoted to the crippled author; but he promised to show fortitude in taking the body back to the family in Boston after the close of the medical examiner's formal inquiry.

The physician, after satisfying as vaguely as possible the curiosity of the householder and his wife, and urging them to shelter the patient and keep him from the Tanner house until his departure with the body, next drove home in a growing tremble of excitement. At last he was free to read the typed manuscript of the dead man, and to gain at least an inkling of what hellish thing had defied those shattered senses of sight and sound and penetrated so disastrously to the delicate intelligence that brooded in external darkness and silence. He knew it would be a grotesque and terrible perusal, and he did not hasten to begin it. Instead, he very deliberately put his car in the garage, made himself comfortable in a dressing-gown, and placed a stand of sedative and restorative medicines beside the great chair he was to occupy. Even after that he obviously wasted time as he slowly arranged the numbered sheets, carefully avoiding any comprehensive glance at their text.

What the manuscript did to Dr. Morehouse we all know. It would never have been read by another had his wife not picked it up as he lay inert in his chair an hour later, breathing heavily and unresponsive to a knocking which one would have thought violent enough to arouse a mummied Pharaoh. Terrible as the document is, particularly in the obvious *change of style* near the end, we cannot avoid the belief that to the folklore-wise physician it presented some *added and supreme horror* which no other will ever be so unfortunate as to receive. Certainly, it is the general opinion of Fenham that the doctor's wide familiarity with the mutterings of old people and the tales his grand father told him in youth furnished him some special information, in the light of which Richard Blake's hideous chronicle acquired a new, clear and devastating significance nearly insupportable to the normal human mind. That would explain the slowness of his recovery on that June evening, the reluctance with which he permitted his wife and son to read the manuscript, the singular ill-grace with which he acceded to their determination not to burn a document so darkly remarkable, and most of all, the peculiar rashness with which he hastened to purchase the old Tanner property, destroy the house with dynamite, and cut down the trees of the swamp for a substantial distance from the road. Concerning the whole subject he now maintains an inflexible reticence, and it is certain that there will die with him a knowledge without which the world is better off.

The manuscript, as here appended, was copied through the courtesy of Floyd Morehouse, Esq., son of the physician. A few omissions, indicated by asterisks, have been made in the interest of the public peace of mind; still others have been occasioned by the indefiniteness of the text, where the stricken author's lightning-like touch-typing seems shaken into incoherence or ambiguity. In three places, where lacunae are fairly well elucidated by the context, the task of recension has been attempted. Of the *change in style* near the end it were best to say nothing. Surely it is plausible enough to attribute the phenomenon, as regards both content and physical aspect of typing, to the racked and tottering mind of a victim whose former handicaps had paled to nothing before that which he now faced. Bolder minds are at liberty to supply their own deductions.

Here, then, is the document, written in an accursed house by a brain closed to the world's sights and sounds — a brain left alone and unwarned to the mercies and mockeries of powers that no seeing, hearing man has ever stayed to face. Contradictory as it is to all that we know of the universe through physics, chemistry, and biology, the logical mind will classify it as a singular product of dementia — a dementia communicated in some sympathetic way to the man who burst out of that house in time. And thus, indeed, may it very well be regarded so long as Dr. Arlo Morehouse maintains his silence.

## THE MANUSCRIPT

Vague misgivings of the last quarter hour are now becoming definite fears. To begin with, I am thoroughly convinced that something must have happened to Dobbs. For the first time since we have been together he has failed to answer my summons. When he did not respond to my repeated ringing I decided that the bell must be out of order, but I have pounded on the table with vigor enough to rouse a charge of Charon. At first I thought he might have slipped out of the house for a breath of fresh air, for it has been hot and sultry all the forenoon, but it is not like Dobbs to stay away so long without first making sure that I would want nothing. It is, however, the unusual occurrence of the last few minutes which confirms my suspicion that Dobbs' absence is a matter beyond his control. It is this same happening which prompts me to put my impressions and conjectures on paper in the hope that the mere act of recording them may relieve a certain sinister suggestion of impending tragedy. Try as I will, I cannot free my mind from the legends connected with this old house — mere superstitious fol-de-rol for dwarfed brains to revel in, and on which I would not even waste a thought if Dobbs were here.

Through the years that I have been shut away from the world I used to know, Dobbs has been my sixth sense. Now, for the first time since my incapacitation, I realize the full extent of my impotency. It is Dobbs who has compensated for my sightless eyes, my useless ears, my voiceless throat and my crippled legs. There is a glass of water on my typewriter table. Without Dobbs to fill it when it has been emptied, my plight will be like that of Tantalus. Few have come to this house since we have lived here — there is little in common between garrulous country folk and a paralytic who cannot see, hear or speak to them — it may be days before anyone else appears. Alone . . . with only my thoughts to keep me company; disquieting thoughts which have been in no wise assuaged by the sensations of the last few minutes. I do not like these sensations, either, for more and more they are converting mere village gossip into a fantastic imagery which affects my emotions in a most peculiar and almost unprecedented manner.

It seems hours since I started to write this, but I know it can be only a few minutes, for I have just inserted this fresh page into the machine. The mechanical action of switching the sheets, brief though it was, has given me a fresh grip on myself. Perhaps I can shake off this sense of approaching danger long enough to recount that which has already happened.

At first it was no more than a mere tremor, somewhat similar to the shivering of a cheap tenement block when a heavy truck rumbles close by the curb — but this is no loosely-built frame structure. Perhaps I am supersensitive to such things, and it may be that I am allowing my imagination to play tricks; but it seemed to me that the disturbance was more pronounced directly in front of me — and my chair faces the southeast wing; away from the road, directly in line with the swamp at the rear of the dwelling! Delusion though this may have been, there is no denying what followed. I was reminded of moments when I have felt the ground tremble beneath my feet at the bursting of giant shells; times when I have seen ships tossed like chaff before the fury of a typhoon. The house shook like a Dweurgarian cinder in the sieves of Niflheim. Every timber in the floor beneath my feet quivered like a suffering thing. My typewriter trembled till I could imagine that the keys were chattering of their fear.

A brief moment and it was over. Everything is as calm as before. Altogether too calm! It seems impossible that such a thing could happen and yet leave everything exactly as it was before. No, not exactly — I am thoroughly convinced that something has happened to Dobbs! It is this conviction, added to this unnatural calm, which accentuates the premonitory fear that persists in creeping over me. Fear? Yes — though I am trying to reason sanely with myself that there is nothing of which to be afraid. Critics have both praised and condemned my poetry because of what they term a vivid imagination. As such a time as this I can heartily agree with those who cry "too vivid." Nothing can be very much amiss or . . .

Smoke! Just a faint sulfurous trace, but one which is unmistakable to my keenly attuned nostrils. So faint, indeed, that it is impossible for me to determine whether it comes from some part of the house or drifts through the window of the adjoining room, which opens on the swamp. The impression is rapidly becoming more clearly defined. I am sure, now, that it does not come from outside. Vagrant visions of the past, somber scenes of other days, flash before me in stereoscopic review. A flaming factory . . . hysterical screams of terrified women penned in by walls of fire; a blazing schoolhouse . . . pitiful cries of helpless children trapped by collapsing stairs, a theatre fire . . . frantic babel of panic-stricken people fighting to freedom over blistering floors; and, over all, impenetrable clouds of black, noxious, malicious smoke polluting the peaceful sky. The air of the room is saturated with thick, heavy, stifling waves . . . at any moment I expect to feel hot tongues of flame lick eagerly at my useless legs... my eyes smart . . . my ears throb . . . I cough and choke, to rid my lungs of the Ocypetean fumes . . . smoke such as is associated only with appalling catastrophes . . . acrid, stinking, mephitic smoke permeated with the revolting odor of burning flesh * * *

Once more I am alone with this portentous calm. The welcome breeze that fans my cheeks is fast restoring my vanished courage. Clearly, the house cannot be on fire, for every vestige of the torturous smoke is gone. I cannot detect a single trace of it, though I have been sniffing like a bloodhound. I am beginning to wonder if I am going mad; if the years of solitude have unhinged my mind — but the phenomenon has been too definite to permit me to class it as mere hallucination. Sane or insane, I cannot conceive these things as aught but actualities — and the moment I catalogue them as such I can come to only one logical conclusion. The inference in itself is enough to upset one's mental stability. To concede this is to grant the truth of the superstitious rumors which Dobbs compiled from the villagers and transcribed for my sensitive finger-tips to read — unsubstantial hearsay that my materialistic mind instinctively condemns as asininity!

I wish the throbbing in my ears would stop! It is as if mad spectral players were beating a duet upon the aching drums. I suppose it is merely a reaction to the suffocating sensations I have just experienced. A few more deep drafts of this refreshing air . . .

Something — someone is in the room! I am as sure I am no longer alone as if I could see the presence I sense so infallibly. It is an impression quite similar to one which I have had while elbowing my way through a crowded street — the definite notion that eyes were singling me out from the rest of the throng with a gaze intense enough to arrest my subconscious attention — the same sensation, only magnified a thousandfold. Who — what — can it be? After all, my fears may be groundless, perhaps it means only that Dobbs has returned. No . . . it is not Dobbs. As I anticipated, the tattoo upon my ears has ceased and a low whisper has caught my attention . . . the overwhelming significance of the thing has just registered itself upon my bewildered brain . . . *I can hear!*

It is not a single whispering voice, but many! * * * Lecherous buzzing of bestial blowflies . . . Satanic humming of libidinous bees . . . sibilant hissing of obscene reptiles . . . a whispering chorus no human throat could sing! It is gaining in volume . . . the room rings with demoniacal chanting; tuneless, toneless and grotesquely grim . . . a diabolical choir rehearsing unholy litanies . . . paeans of mephistophelian misery set to music of wailing souls . . . a hideous crescendo of pagan pandemonium * * *

The voices that surround me are drawing closer to my chair. The chanting has come to an abrupt end and the whispering has resolved itself into intelligible sounds. I strain my ears to distinguish the words. Closer . . . and still closer. They are clear, now — too clear! Better had my ears been blocked forever than forced to listen to their hellish mouthings * * *

Impious revelations of soul-sickening Saturnalia * * * ghoulish conceptions of devastating debaucheries * * * profane bribes of Cabirian orgies * * * malevolent threats of unimagined punishments * * *

It is cold. Unseasonably cold! As if inspired by the cacodemoniacal presences that harass me, the breeze that was so friendly a few minutes ago growls angrily about my ears — an icy gale that rushes in from the swamp and chills me to the bone.

If Dobbs has deserted me I do not blame him. I hold no brief for cowardice or craven fear, but there are some things * * * I only hope his fate has been nothing worse than to have departed in time!

My last doubt is swept away. I am doubly glad, now, that I have held to my resolve to write down my impressions . . . not that I expect anyone to understand . . . or believe . . . it has been a relief from the maddening strain of idly waiting for each new manifestation of psychic abnormality. As I see it, there are but three courses that may be taken: to flee from this accursed place and spend the torturous years that lie ahead in trying to forget — but flee I *cannot;* to yield to an abominable alliance with forces so malign that Tartarus to them would seem but an alcove of Paradise, but yield I *will not;* to die — far rather would I have my body torn limb from limb than to contaminate my soul in barbarous barter with such emissaries of Belial * * *

I have had to pause for a moment to blow upon my fingers. The room is cold with the fetid frigor of the tomb . . . a peaceful numbness is creeping over me . . . I must fight off this lassitude; it is undermining my determination to die rather than give in to the insidious importunings . . . I vow, anew, to resist until the end. . . the end that I know cannot be far away * * *

The wind is colder than ever, if such a thing be possible . . . a wind freighted with the stench of dead-alive things . . . 0 merciful God Who took my sight! * * * a wind so cold it burns where it should freeze . . . it has become a blistering sirocco. * * *

Unseen fingers grip me . . . ghost fingers that lack the physical strength to force me from my machine . . . icy fingers that force me into a vile vortex of vice . . . devil-fingers that draw me down into a cesspool of eternal iniquity . . . death fingers that shut off my breath and make my sightless eyes feel they must burst with the pain * * * frozen points press against my temples * * * hard, bony knobs, akin to horns * * * boreal breath of some long-dead thing kisses my fevered lips and sears my hot throat with frozen flame * * * It is dark * * * not the darkness that is part of years of blindness * * * the impenetrable darkness of sin-steeped night * * * the pitch-black darkness of Purgatory * * *

I see * * * *spes mea Christus!* * * * it is the end * * *

*Not for mortal mind is any resisting of force beyond human imagination. Not for immortal spirit is any conquering of that which hath probed the depths and made of immortality a transient moment. The end? Nay! It is but the blissful beginning. . . .*

# Souls & Heels

THE HOUSE PARTY at the summer home of Howard Montgomery began in a blaze of glory and ended in a tragedy. Shortly after eleven, as the syncopated strains of the jazz band died away, and the hot couples wended their way across the ballroom floor to rest for a moment from the strenuous exertions of the dance, Prescott Wayne, junior member of the firm of Montgomery, Fellows and Wayne, turned in response to a slight tug at his shoulder.

It was Watkins, Montgomery's butler.

"Pardon me, Mr. Wayne, but do you know where Mr. Montgomery has gone? There is a telephone call for him, and I can't seem to locate him."

"Let me see, Watkins, he said something to me about going up to his study, earlier in the evening. Come to think of it, I haven't seen him since."

"Thank you, sir, but I tried the door of the study and it was locked. I rapped several times, and called out to him, but no one answered. " There was a shade of anxiety in the butler's voice. "you don't suppose anything might have happened, sir?"

"Nonsense." He turned to the young lady he had been piloting across the floor. "Pardon me for a moment or two, Miss Young. Watkins, here, has an idea someone has kidnapped your guardian, so I'm going up to the study with him and prove that he's wrong."

The girl nodded acquiescence, and the butler glided away in the direction of the study with Wayne at his heels. Outside the door of Montgomery's study they paused, and Watkins rapped lustily upon the panels. Receiving no response, he stepped aside, with: "You try it, Mr. Wayne."

———————

Prescott Wayne did not knock. Instead, he kicked the door, vigorously.

"Montgomery! Howard!" he called, "Open the door; it's Wayne."

Still no reply.

"Are you sure he didn't go out somewhere?"

"I thought of that, sir. If he had, sir, would the door be locked on the inside?"

Wayne dropped to his knees and peered into the keyhole. The butler was right. The key was still in the lock.

"You see; sir —" the butler began.

Wayne interrupted him.

"Watkins, you impress me as being a damned fool, most of the time, but sometimes you're right. You wait here. I'm going down and get Elliott to come up for a few minutes. Good thing he's here. And I'd better get Martin Fellows, too. He should know about this."

He disappeared, and returned shortly with the two men.

Martin Fellows was a thin, wiry man with a balding pate. He handled most of the details of the firm's contracts, while Wayne did most of the saleswork. He stood outside the door, immobile.

Jasper Elliott was not merely a detective. He was a student of crime. His power lay in his ability to survey the scene of a mysterious circumstance through microscopic eyes. And not only was Jasper Elliott a profound student of crime; he was also a dabbler in the occult. Therein lay the supreme reason for his successes where others had failed. For he had at his command forces that to the unimaginative mind seemed well-nigh beyond the ken of human understanding.

His quiet demeanor, his large, clear blue eyes, the few streaks of gray in his dark hair bespoke none of these capabilities, however. He was none of those types which the average man delights to picture so famous a character.

Wayne and the butler outlined the situation, and Elliott nodded, understandingly.

He sent the butler after his bag.

"It is well that I followed my usual custom, and, brought it along," he explained, as he delved into the depths of the big, black bag and produced an instrument. "I never can tell when I am likely to be called on a case, and there is nothing like being prepared."

He inserted the instrument in the lock, gained a grip upon the key, and turned it slowly. The men heard the click of the tumblers as the lock was unfastened, and the butler looked at him in frank admiration.

He turned the knob, slowly, and pushed open the door. The butler checked an involuntary scream. Wayne grasped the edge of the door for support, while Fellows cried," Oh, my God!"

The detective stepped further into the room that he might better observe the sight which met their eyes.

In the center of the room, in a big arm chair that was drawn up before his reading table, sat Howard Montgomery. His eyes were closed, his head sagged forward upon his chest, and his legs sprawled out grotesquely.

On the floor, at the side of the chair nearest the door, lay an empty wine-glass, where it had dropped from the dead man's fingers.

Elliott crossed the room, picked up the glass gingerly, and sniffed it.

"Enough in that glass to kill ten men," he muttered.

His eye caught the white of a paper on the table and he read its contents through. Then he beckoned the two men and the butler to join him.

"Looks to me like suicide," he announced, indicating the note on the table. Read that. But don't touch it. There may be telltale fingerprints on it."

Watkins, Wayne and Fellows scanned the note, avidiously.

> I cannot go on. This being in eternal fear of discovery is maddening me. I have taken for my personal needs practically the entire funds of Montgomery, Fellows and Wayne. It is bound to be discovered, sooner or later. There is but one way out, and I am taking that way. I am leaving this little note in order that no suspicions shall rest upon anyone else. I alone am guilty. May God have mercy on my soul.
>
> Howard Montgomery

"Come," Elliott's voice bore a note of command. "There's nothing we can do here until morning."

"Don't you have to notify the police and the coroner?" Wayne asked.

"That can wait," Fellows said. "Let's see what Elliott can come up with first. We don't want the party-goers unduly alarmed, do we?"

"I guess not," replied Wayne.

"Is there anything you want me to do, sir?" the butler asked.

"No, thanks, Watkins; I'll let you know if I need your help."

They left the room, Elliott locking the door of the study behind him, and pocketing the key.

Wayne had rejoined Leila Young, the ward of the dead man, and her face went ashen at the news. With the inborn instinct of the society-bred woman, she effectually masked her emotions, and received the condolences of Fellows and Watkins with majestic composure.

At her request, Wayne and Elliott agreed to stay until morning, and the butler showed the men to their respective apartments.

Fellows said his wife was home, so he had to leave; but he asked that Elliott keep in touch with him about developments.

———————————

Alone in his room, the great detective pondered over the affair. He had known Howard Montgomery since boyhood, and it was hard for him to believe that this man was a self-confessed thief and a moral coward. Yet, on the face of things, there seemed no other alternative.

"On the face of things."

He turned that phrase over and over in his mind. His lifelong training had taught him that appearances were not always to be trusted. He laughed at his suspicions. If he hadn't known Montgomery so well — but that was just it, he had.

He remembered that he still had the key to the study in his possession. With a sudden determination he decided to look over the scene of the tragedy again. It was a foolish idea, perhaps, but at least it could do no harm.

Armed with his black bag, he stole silently down the hallway to Montgomery's study.

The big house was now as quiet as a tomb. The party-goers had departed, and the presence of Death seemed to permeate the very atmosphere.

Noiselessly, he opened the door of the death-chamber, and stepped inside, locking the door behind him and retaining the key.

The lights were still burning, and the room was as bright as day.

He crossed to the chair where the body of the dead man sat, peacefully. This time his sharp eyes caught something they had missed before. The ash-try had been overturned from the arm of the easy chair, and left a small pile of ashes upon the floor. He could see the tray some feet away where it had raced off, a tiny trail of ashes in its wake.

That, in itself, was nothing extraordinary; but the heap of ashes had been flattened in the center, crushed into the thick carpet that covered the floor, and Elliott's trained eye detected the print of the heel of a man's shoe.

He dropped to his knees and examined the heel-print, minutely. Then he looked at Montgomery's shoes, and permitted himself a low, surprised whistle.

For the heel-print in the ashes had been made by a rubber heel, and the shoes the dead man was wearing were fitted with wide, extension, leather, anatomic heels!

Someone had undoubtedly been in the room with Howard Montgomery shortly before he died!

A few tiny flecks of ashes indicated the direction the unknown man had taken, and the detective followed the trail. It led to the side of the big table where the confession gleamed up at him like an evil eye.

This document next demanded his attention. Without touching it, he brought a powerful, pocket magnifying-glass to bear upon it.

And then Jasper Elliott made a discovery that confirmed his suspicions, that convinced him that here was something deeper than mere suicide, that Howard Montgomery had been murdered, and that this "confession" was spurious, no, a diabolical, damnable lie!

For the paper was absolutely free from finger-prints of any kind!

Murder!

Not only murder, but treachery, intrigue, the attempt to defame the name of one of the most honest, upright men who ever walked on God's green earth!

For a moment, Jasper Elliott, detective, reverted to Jasper Elliott, the man, and his shoulders shook with silent sobs as he gazed upon the stiff, stark body of his boyhood companion.

Then, as Jasper Elliott, detective, he set himself the task of ferreting out this criminal, whoever he might be, and bringing him to Justice.

He ransacked the room for some sort of samples of Montgomery's hand-writing. At last he unearthed an old notebook of the dead man's. With the aid of his magnifying glass, he studied the writing it contained, and compared it with the confession.

Keen student of chirography though he was, it was some time before he was satisfied that the letter was a forgery. Indeed, so cleverly was it executed, that he would have unhesitatingly have pronounced it genuine had his suspicions not been aroused by the absence of finger-marks.

But even the most expert forger could not achieve such perfection unless he had adequate opportunity for access to specimens of Howard Montgomery's penmanship. Working with machine-line precision, the detective made a thorough search of the room. Not an inch of it escaped his hawk-like eyes, but his exploration proved absolutely barren of any sort of clues.

He next turned his attention to the possible means of exit. That the door had been locked from the inside, he was certain. He had unlocked it, himself. There was no other door leading from the study, and there were three windows at one side of the room.

He crossed to these, and peered out into the night. Two of them presented a sheer drop to the ground below. It would have been impossible for anyone to leave by either of them without the aid of a ladder. He tried them both, and found them tightly locked.

But the third window gave promise of being the means of the murderer's get-a-way. This one was unlocked, and just a few feet below was one end of the roof of the long piazza that extended halfway around the big house.

He examined the sash, the window-pane, and the sill with painstaking care, but all to no avail. If anyone had gone through that window he had obliterated all trace of his departure. Again, how could anyone, hanging from the window-sill, close the window behind him?

He opened the window wide, and peered down at the flat roof, below. He had exhausted all the possibilities the room afforded. His last chance lay in whatever he might find, down there.

He tossed his bag to the ground below. Then, armed with his flashlight, he essayed the drop to the roof of the piazza.

He landed, noiselessly, and the pocket flash played a tiny circle of light upon the dust-covered roof upon which he stood.

Just as he thought. There were the footprints of the man who had killed Howard Montgomery!

He moved the light a little to the right, and stared hard at what he saw there.

For, plainly outlined in the inch of dust that covered the roof, paralleling the tracks of the man, were another set of footprints, and the woman who made them wore French-heeled shoes!

A woman in the case!

Frankly, Elliott was puzzled. He could understand the man, but why the woman? And who were this mysterious pair who left no traces behind them except their footprints on a dusty roof? Who was it that had forged that confession so skillfully that detection was barely possible?

Martin Fellows had apparently been at the party alone. He said his wife was home ill. But that might have been a lie. He had the best motive for the murder, since he handled the funds. And he would certainly be familiar with Montgomery's signature.

On the other hand, Prescott Wayne was younger and more

daring. But he couldn't conceive of Lelia Young being in on the scheme against her own guardian. She just didn't seem the type, unless she was forced to do so, somehow, against her will.

An odd thought came to him. The butler? Didn't the butler always do the crime? Not so in this case, he was sure. It was either Fellows or Wayne, and he would have to find out which one of Montgomery's associates murdered him, and why!

Jasper Elliott followed the trails in the dust to the edge of the roof in hopes of finding some further clues. The roof was too high up from the ground to allow the average person to jump. The easiest way was to hang, and drop. In this thick dust, it would be impossible without leaving one's finger-prints behind.

At last the detective found the place where the man and the woman had gripped the edge of the roof before dropping to the ground. But once more he was doomed to disappointment. Instead of the identifying finger-marks he had hope for, he discovered that both the fugitives had been wearing gloves. This, then, accounted for the lack of finger-prints in the room above.

The woman's glove might possibly be traced, but the smooth, outlined imprints of the man's fingers bore mute evidence that he had taken the precaution to protect his hands with closely-fitted gloves of light India-rubber.

Baffled, discouraged, he dropped lightly to the soft turf below; but beyond the faint outlines of two pairs of heels where the criminals had landed, he found nothing.

Rescuing his bag, he started around to the front of the house, wondering how he might get in without arousing anyone.

As he rounded the corner, he stopped abruptly to avoid colliding with the figure of a woman who was coming his way.

"Why, Mr. Elliott, — you? What in the world are you doing out at this hour of the night?"

"Exploring, Miss Young, And might I ask if you are accustomed to indulge in these nocturnal strolls?"

"Goodness, no!" she threw back her head and laughed. Then, sobering suddenly, she went on: "My guardian's death upset me so I just couldn't sleep, so I sought communion with the stars." It was, indeed, a perfect summer night. The moon shone high above in a cloudless sky; the countless, tiny, twinkling stars winked and blinked their lone eyes from the heavens, and the cool breezes from the waters of Narragansett Bay stirred the branches of the tall, towering trees that stood out like ghostly sentinels against the background of the sky.

"Mr. Montgomery's death upset me, too," the detective returned. "I couldn't quite bring myself to believe that he had committed suicide, so I took the liberty to do a little investigating."

The girl's face went white in the moonlight, and she grasped the detective's arm.

"And you found — ?"

"I found, Miss Young, that he had unquestionably been murdered."

She swayed, unsteadily, and would have fallen had he not steadied her.

"Are you sure of what you are saying, Mr. Elliott? How could he have been murdered? He had no enemies. Why, Pressy, —

Mr. Wayne, I mean, told me you said yourself that it was suicide. "

"It has been my experience as a detective," the man responded, "that I quite often find a case where evidence lies. At the present moment I would stake my reputation that your guardian came to his death at the hands of another. By morning, I shall be certain."

By this time they had reached the door of the big house. The girl produced a latch-key and they entered. With a whispered: "Good night," she left him, and he went on up to his room alone.

———————————

Locked in the sanctuary of his apartment, he summarized the problem that confronted him:

Howard Montgomery had been poisoned. Of that, there was no longer any reasonable doubt.

Two persons, a man and a woman, identity unknown, had been locked in the study with Montgomery when he died, making their escape through the window and over the roof of the piazza to the ground.

The man, who must have been an expert forger, had worn rubber gloves, and rubber heels on his shoes. Had it not been for the peculiar, anatomic heels the dead man wore, the print in the ashes might easily have been mistaken for Montgomery's own.

Every trace of the deed inside the room had been effaced with the exception of the forged confession with its absence of finger-marks.

The only connecting clue was the two sets of footprints upon the roof of the piazza.

The only marks left by the woman were the footprints, and the impression of her gloved hands.

And there he found himself up against a blank wall, an impenetrable barrier.

In the morning he would photograph the prints upon the roof, and the one in the ashes in the study.

But now he had other, more important work to do.

Jasper Elliott had been a dabbler in the occult for many years. A trip to the far East in his early days as a criminal investigator had wakened in him a desire to delve deeper into the higher mysteries of life.

Crime was his life work. Mysticism, with its hidden forces, its untold powers, was his hobby.

Hypnotism, mental telepathy, spiritism – he had mastered them all. And, like the true artisian, he had moulded from them tools to serve him in his daily tasks.

Of late he had probed into a higher branch of the sciences, and had been experimenting along the lines of astral projection. Several times he had succeeded in leaving his physical environment, and gone a-voyaging, free from the restrictions that hampered him in the earthly sphere.

With the singleness of purpose that marked the man, his explorations were all to one end. For Jasper Elliott had evolved a theory which he meant to put to a test at the first available opportunity. He believed that the soul of a murdered man could not rest in peace until his murderer had been brought to Justice, or had passed on into the Great Beyond. That, governed, perhaps, by the same impulses which urge a criminal to return to the scene of the crime, the departed spirit of the victim of foul play returned frequently to the scene of the murder, vainly attempting to assist the seeker for Truth to find the light.

If this was true, if he could establish communication with these astral beings, then he would have made a tremendous stride forward in the detection of crime.

This particular case seemed to the detective to present a golden opportunity to put his theory to the acid test. If he could not use this new found power to gain astral connections with the spirit of a man who, living, had been as close to him as a brother, then he had failed — and Jasper Elliott had yet to fail!

Summoning to his command all the vast resources of his will he concentrated all his energies on the task at hand.

He closed his eyes, relaxed his muscles, and with a superhuman mental effort left the inert shell of clay, and floated free.

This new-found sense of freedom prompted him to drift idly in the glory of it all. But there was work to be done.

Distance was annihilated, walls no longer proved a barrier. A slight effort of the will and he might be anywhere he chose — even though it be a hundred thousand miles away.

He thought of the dead man in the study, and immediately found himself drifting in the room above the silent form.

All at once he became conscious of another presence in the

study. He caught a tiny, iridescent gleam of light hovering about Montgomery's body.

"Howard! Howard Montgomery! It's I — Elliott."

The light wavered, started in his direction, and paused.

Again he sent his silent message into the ether:

"Howard — this way — over here!"

The phosporent glow drew nearer. At its approach, a strange warmth encompassed him. He heard nothing, but suddenly a thought, a sentence, impressed itself upon his mind. Just two words, as plainly as if they had been spoken in his ear, two words that droned over and over again into this consciousness:

"Watch Wayne."

That was all. The glow faded, died away, and was gone. Once more Jasper Elliott's astral self was alone in the study with the body of the murdered man.

"Watch Wayne." His whole being pulsated with the rush of thought those words aroused.

Prescott Wayne. Why, it was Wayne who had accompanied the butler to the study and tried to rouse his associate. It was Wayne, again, who had sought out Elliott and asked him to take a hand in the affair.

Yet, why not? As Montgomery's associate, Wayne had had ample opportunity to study his handwriting. Working along these lines, the motive became instantly apparent. Not only was this man a murderer, but a thief as well. That would account for the forged confession – to divert all suspicion from himself to the man whose life he had taken.

He recalled Wayne's elastic, cat-like tread as he had followed him up the stairs to the study, and, wondered if the man wore rubber heels.

But there was the woman. Where did she fit in?

Then, too, one could hardly be convicted of murder just because he was a member of the victim's firm, nor because he wore rubber heels. Neither would a jury of "twelve good men, and true," condemn a fellow-man on testimony from the spirit world.

No, he must have material proof before he could accuse. There was much to be done, and the best time to do it was now.

All thought of sleep banished, his mind keyed up to its highest point of efficiency, Elliott willed himself back to earth again, and his physical body opened its eyes. Once more, Jasper Elliott fared forth upon a nocturnal pilgrimage, and the sky was gray with the approaching dawn when he at last permitted himself to drop off into fitful slumber.

That morning, the detective was up early, but he found Leila Young up before him.

"I informed Mr. Wayne of your suspicions." she told him. "and he thought it best to notify the police. We also sent for the coroner, and he should be here at any time."

"Well done. Miss Young." Elliott rejoined, surrendering the key to the study, "you may assure the coroner that nothing has been disturbed. If you will let me know when he arrives, I will tell him on what I base my suspicions."

The coroner proved to be a sensible, practical-minded man, Elliott showed him the heel-print in the ashes, proved to his satisfaction that the confession was a bogus one, and he agreed that this was something more than suicide.

At the inquest the following afternoon, Miss Young, Prescott Wayne, Martin Fellows and the butler were asked a few perfunctory questions and Elliott expected the verdict that was returned:

"Death, at the hands of some person, or persons. unknown."

If Jasper Elliott had not made his astral journey the night before, and had been advised to "watch Wayne," he would certainly have found Fellows to be more of a likely suspect because of his nervous mannerisms.

However, he had checked on his story, and Fellows' wife was really ill, in fact was an invalid; so that would account for some of his nervousness. Of course he would also have had motive for that reason, because of the mounting doctors' bills. Perhaps Wayne had figured that out, also, in case the clues did point up to murder.

But there was the question of the woman. He must talk to Miss Young.

After the inquest was over, and the house was quiet once more, the detective sought out the ward of the murdered man.

"Miss Young." he began, abruptly, "Just how much do you know about the death of your guardian?"

The girl gripped the arms of her chair, and half arose. Her big black eyes snapped angrily.

"Why, Mr. Elliott, whatever do you mean?"

"Exactly what I say. What were you doing in the study the night of the murder that caused you to leave by the window?"

She brought herself erect, her eyes flashing fire.

"Be careful with your insinuations, Mr. Elliott. One does not talk lightly about such affairs."

"True," he agreed, undisturbed by her attitude, "It was too bad, wasn't it, that the French heel on your pump couldn't stand the little drop from the roof of the piazza without snapping in two?"

The girl crumped up in her chair as if struck down by a club, and the detective went on, relentlessly:

"It was a shame, too, that I had to surprise you on your midnight stroll. If I hadn't, you might have found the other half of the heel. I didn't discover it, myself, until I went over the ground more carefully a second time.

"I am surprised, though, that you didn't destroy those slippers. I found them yesterday morning when I took the liberty of searching your boudoir. They match up exactly with the photographs I took of the footprints in the dust on the roof. I was also fortunate enough to find these."

He tossed a pair of dust-begrimmed, silk gloves into her lap, and the girl stretched out her arms, imploringly.

"Please don't — any more — Mr. Elliott. They're mine. I was in the study, and I did go out of the window," her antagonism showed itself, again. "But what of that? Hadn't I a perfect right to be in my guardian's study?"

Elliott rose, and crossed the room, laying his hand upon her shoulder.

"Miss Young. I arrest you for the murder of Howard Montgomery."

"No — no — no!"

———————————

Unannounced, unheard, unseen, Prescott Wayne had entered the room. He heard the detective's accusation, and at the girl's hysterical protest, called softly:

"Come. Leila."

The girl broke away from Elliott, and ran into Wayne's outstretched arms.

"Oh, Pressy no Pressy." she sobbed.

The young man spent a moment in trying to comfort her. Then he faced the detective who still stood beside the girl's chair.

"I fear you have made a mistake in your accusation, Elliott. I guess I'm the one you want, instead of my wife."

"Your **wife**?"

"Exactly. We were married the afternoon of the house party. Oh, I suppose I might as well make a clean breast of it. Sit down," he waved Elliott to a chair.

The girl returned to the seat she had vacated, and Wayne swung himself up onto a comer of the table.

"You see, it was this way. Ever since I began filching the company's funds some months ago, I knew that sooner or later Montgomery would find me out. It was only a question of time, and when that time came. I was determined to be prepared.

"Many a long, tedious hour I labored over that confession. I don't quite understand even yet how you discovered it was a forgery. I was sure I left it free of any marks of identification."

"That's exactly where you overplayed your hand." Elliott supplemented. "The utter lack of fingerprints, even Montgomery's, was what made me suspicious. Go on."

"I carried that document, together with a tiny vial of poison, in a leather case I made especially for the purpose. I was determined not to use them unless I was forced to it. If my ventures in the stock market turned out successfully, I could return the money and no one would ever be the wiser. I also carried a pair of rubber gloves with me in case of an emergency. I knew from the reading I had done, that these would leave no evidence behind.

"The afternoon of the day set for the house party, Leila and I were secretly married.

"After Montgomery had excused himself, and went off up to the study, my wife and I met in the upper hallway and went in to break the news of the wedding to him.

"He flew into a rage at the news. In his excitement, he upset the ash-tray from the arm of his chair.

"Then he called me a thief, and told me he had known of my actions for some time, but had been waiting for a more opportune time to bring me to account for them.

"He poured out a glass of wine from the decanter on the table, but before drinking it turned upon my wife again, berating her, roundly, for marrying such a scoundrel.

"That was my chance. In a twinkling, I emptied the contents

of the vial into the glass of wine.

"He drained the glass in one savage gulp, and in an instant. he was dead!"

Wayne showed no emotion in the telling of his ghastly deed; but softened a bit as he turned to his wife and continued:

"Leila, here, was panic-stricken. She hadn't the slightest idea he had been poisoned. She laid his death to a stroke brought on by his intense rage. She grasped at my suggestion of flight through the window, like a drowning man at a straw.

"I noticed she had her gloves in her hand, and I told her to put them on to protect her hands. I don't think she even noticed that I donned my rubber gloves before opening the window for her.

"I promised to join her, immediately, and once she was safely on her way, I set the stage as you found it."

As Wayne went on, Elliott thought he seemed to be more angry with himself for neglecting to cover up all his tracks, rather than at the deed he had done.

"I was a damn fool to forget about that pile of ashes on the floor. I must have stepped in it on my way from the window to the table.

"In a moment or two everything was set to my satisfaction, and I followed Leila out of the window. I worried quite a bit over being unable to close it behind me, but something must have jarred it shut before you opened the door of the study.

"I found my wife searching, frantically, for the heel of her pump that had snapped in two when she struck the ground.

"I told her to look for it in the morning, warned her to say nothing about the affair to anyone, and she got up to her room through the servants' quarters without being seen.

"Luckily, no one had missed us, and we joined the gay throng of dancers all unaware of the tragedy that had been enacted above them."

"Of course, when the confession was discovered, Leila's suspicions were aroused, and I was forced to admit to her my part in the affair."

"At first she was horror-stricken, but when a woman loves a man, she will forgive him almost anything, and at last she agreed to shield me if she possibly could do so.

"All the same, Elliott, if you hadn't found Leila's broken heel and gloves, and accused her of the murder, you never would have been able to prove me guilty. As it was, I could hardly sit back and see my wife suffer for a crime of which I was guilty."

Wayne bowed his head, abjectly. Suddenly, something gleamed in his fingers, and his hand flashed to his mouth.

The detective tried to intercept him, but was just a second too late, and a tiny glass vial fell from Wayne's hand to the floor. It was the end. Another moment, and the soul of Prescott Wayne winged its way to stand trial before the Supreme Judge of the Highest Court of all!

# SIGN OF THE DRAGON

## CHAPTER ONE

### AN OATH OF ALLEGIANCE

WHEN MY FATHER WAS stricken one morning in April, Death was the farthest from my thoughts. I looked upon it, as did Mrs. Waynemore, the housekeeper, as a passing illness. But, as he grew steadily worse, Doctor Barnes, who had known me since he helped usher me into this old world, said to me to hope for the best, but to be prepared for the worst. At last came the day when the doctor told the old gentleman that his hours were numbered, that he had done all in his power to stay the onward march of the Grim Reaper. Father listened to the verdict of the physician, and asked that I be summoned. My heart was heavy as I went in and took my place at his bedside.

He was quite calm, but I could detect a suppressed excitement in his eyes as he asked the doctor and the housekeeper to retire. In spite of its sadness my heart beat a little faster as they left the room, and I began to wonder what it could be that he wanted of me — alone. As soon as he was sure that the others were safely out of hearing, he indicated a seat for me by the head of the bed. "Chester," he began, " before I leave this old world I want to tell you a tale out of my life that I have never told you before. I want you to listen without interruption, for my time is short and I want to be sure that it is finished before I pass on."

He paused for a moment, as if doubtful just how to begin.

"I was just a bit older than you are now, and I had seen pretty much of the world, even at that age. But no matter where I roamed, I always came back to Manorport sooner or later. It was the only real home I knew. I had been back from my last trip just a few days. My pockets were well lined, for my last venture had been a profitable one. We all have our hobbies and mine has always been the acquisition of curios in the way of jewelry or trinkets, worthless except for their oddity. I was somehow reminded of a peculiar ring I had marked in a little Chinese shop, on the waterfront in Boston, which I had passed on my way home a few days before. I was possessed of an uncontrollable desire to add it to my collection. The desire for that ring grew upon me all throughout the day, and I spent a sleepless night because of it. The next morning I left Manorport intent only upon acquiring it. The shop I mentioned was in rather an unsavory section of the city, but I knew my Boston well. Many was the oddity I had picked up in this selfsame shop. The Chinaman who ran the place—Len Sang he called himself—knew me for a regular customer. My luck must have been sidetracked somehow. When I reached the shop I found, to my dismay, that the ring was gone from the window. There was no need of 'pidgin' English with Len Sang. I don't know where he learned, but he could speak our language as well as I.

" 'Yes,' he told me, 'I remember well the ring you have in mind. Was it not a silver ring, with a peculiar setting? A Chinese dragon, with eyes of jade?'

" 'That's the one I came all the way back here to get,' I told him. 'Where is it? I want to buy it.'

" 'It is gone, sir. I sold it only last evening.'

" 'Sold it! But I must have it!' The desire for that ring was becoming an obsession.

" 'But yes,' he returned; 'wait but a moment.'

"He disappeared into the back room of the shop. When he returned, he had in his hand what I could have sworn was the self-same ring I had seen in the shop window.

" 'Sly dog! I thought you told me you had sold it,' I accused him.

" 'Aye, sir, and so I did,' he bowed. "This is its mate. There were only two of these rings ever made. The one I sold last evening to the customer I mentioned. This ring is its exact duplicate.'

"That rather savored of mystery, and I asked him if by chance the rings had a history.

" 'All that I know,' he responded, 'is that a few weeks ago a little old man came into the store with these two rings to sell me.

He told me they had been made especially for two Chinese nobleman, whose names and peculiarities I well knew, and were worn by them until their recent death. He claimed that they were the only rings of their kind ever made. How he came into possession of them, or his right to sell them, I did not question. We seldom question such rights here. I was taken by the peculiar character of the rings, so I bought them, almost at my own price. One I put in the window, where it has remained until last night; the other is here.'

He passed it over the counter for my inspection.

"I was rather skeptical about the story he told of the rings and how they came into his possession. It came too readily to his lips to carry any weight with me. From what I knew of Len Sang, he was, like most of the others of his race, secretive and taciturn. To find him loquacious was to make me suspicious that he must have a reason, for being so.

"I did not give him any inkling of my doubts, however, but began haggling with him over the price of the remaining ring. Len Sang was a shrewd business man, and he knew I wanted the ring badly. Finally we came to terms, I forgot just what the ring cost me, but Len Sang was no loser, of that I am certain.

"Len Sang bowed me all the way to the door of the shop, a sleepy, oily, shop-worn smile on his saffron face, thanking me profusely all the while for my custom. I was sorry, of course, that I had not been able to acquire the pair of rings, but I rather congratulated myself on my luck in their being a second one that I might buy. My bargaining had made me rather thirsty, so I made for a nearby grog-shop to quench my thirst and provide myself with an opportunity to examine my purchase more closely.

"I had settled myself with my half-and-half when I spied some one whom I had not seen in an age. It was 'Spike' Burgess; a big hulking brute of a man, but as good-hearted a chap as had ever been my good fortune to meet. Many a wild time we had weathered together and escaped unscathed. He was the only real 'pal' I had ever had, and I'd been lonesome enough, drifting around since I saw him last, two years before. I hailed him, and he came lumbering over to my table.

" 'Peter Brent, by all that's holy! Where have you been keeping yourself? Damn it all, old man, I'm glad to see you!'

"His mighty fist came down upon the table in emphasis of his remark with a crash that nearly splintered the boards of the table itself. I gripped the brawny hand he extended, and we settled down to talk over the things that had happened since we had last seen one another.

"We exchanged confidences freely, for at that hour of the day the saloon was well-nigh deserted. At length I bethought myself of my latest purchase. I slipped it off my finger and held it up for Spike's inspection.

"I was totally unprepared for the effect it had upon him. At the sight of it his eyes dilated, his hands gripped the edges of the table so tightly that the muscles on his arms stood out like whipcords, and the perspiration ran down his face in streams.

" 'Good God, man!' he rasped, his voice hoarse and unnatural, 'where did you get that ring?'

" 'Why the excitement, Spike?' I questioned. 'I bought that

ring at Len Sang's, not more than a couple hours ago.'

"The terror slowly faded from his eyes.

" 'It's all right, Peter, as long as you bought it,' he returned; 'but the last time I saw that ring, or its mate, was in Hong Kong. It was there I heard the legend that goes with it. If you'll satisfy me by putting that ring back in you pocket before some one else sees it, we'll take a little walk and I'll tell you in a few words why I was so upset at the sight of it.'

"Back went the ring into my pocket, and we strolled aimlessly along the waterfront while he told me the tale he heard about the dragon rings.

" 'The rings are nearly as old as the legend itself, Peter' he went on. 'No one knows who made them, or for whom they were made. But they are supposed to possess this peculiar property. To anyone into whose possession they come legitimately, that person will have good luck and protection against all evil. But, should one of them be stolen, the charm is broken. Instead sudden death is in store for the culprit, and grave danger for the owner of the other until the stolen ring has been recovered, or until the thief disposes of it in some way. The last time I saw one of those rings, it was on the finger of a dead Chinese shop-keeper, in Hong Kong. No one knew how he had come to his death, but it was rumored that the ring had come into his possession by questionable means.'

"But why the concern, Spike, at my simply having one of the rings in my possession? You didn't think I had stolen it, did you?'

" 'No, but someone else might. The news is all over the

waterfront that Len Stang's was entered last night, and the mate to that ring stolen from the show-window. It's a wonder you hadn't heard. I'd advise you to keep it out of sight until you get safely away from here.'

"Then I knew the reason for Len Sang's talkative mood of the morning. He knew the legend of the rings, without a doubt; but he was afraid, should I learn it, he would be unable to dispose of the remaining ring, with its attendant danger for the owner.

" 'I've been up home in Manorport the last few days, so I haven't heard any of the news down around here,' I explained. 'I saw the ring in the show-window when I passed the shop on the way home. I came down to Boston today on purpose to buy it.' Then I told him of Len Stang's story of how he acquired the rings, and the sale of the other the night before.

" 'Smooth tongued yellow devil!' Spike commented. Then, as if dismissing the subject, 'Where are you headed, matey?"

" 'I'm going back up to Manorport and rest up for a little while. After that, the Lord only knows. Say Spike,' with a sudden inspiration, 'come along up home and spend the night with me. I'm all alone, you know.

"He thought it over for a while, and not being able to think up any excuse that I would stand for, accepted the invitation.

"Trains weren't as frequent in those days as they are now, Chester, and it was well along towards ten o'clock before we reached Manorport.

"As we made our way along the deserted main street, Spike caught my arm and drew me into the shadow of one of the buildings.

" 'I've a feeling we're being followed,' he told me.

"I laughed at him. 'What's the matter with you, anyhow, today, Spike? You're as nervous as an old woman. Just a while ago I thought your eyes would pop out of your head at the mere sight of a ring, and now —'

"He swung me out of harm's way just in time. I could feel the swish as the keen blade of a knife fanned my cheek, slashing through the air at the exact spot I had been but a moment before.

"In a flash, Spike was on my assailant. Silently they locked together in a struggle for the possession of that keen, gleaming, ugly blade.

"Back and forth they struggled, neither uttering a sound. I was helpless to take any active part in the fray, lest I dislodge Spike's grip upon the man's wrist. If that happened, one of was as good as dead.

"At last Spike's tremendous weight began to tell. Inch by inch he forced my assailant back over his knee, till they were bent double. Suddenly the knife flashed free, as Spike aimed it at the body of the man who attacked us. He sank to the pavement without a sound.

"We rolled the man over to see who was responsible for our adventure, and looked down into the yellow face of the Chinaman who used to work around Len Sang's.

"And there, on the finger of the hand that had sought to take my life, gleamed the mate to the ring that reposed in my pocket. The legend of the ring had once more worked itself out completely.

"I took from his finger the ring which had been the cause of the trouble. We reached my home at last, and safe in the rooms I occupied, we examined the rings closely. They were just as much alike as two peas in a pod. Far into the night we sat up talking over old times, but always our conversation would revert to the subject of the rings on the table before us. They seemed to hold a strange fascination, somehow. The jade eyes gleamed up at us with a hint of mystery, and power, that enthralled us. At last I was imbued with a big idea.

" 'Spike,' I announced, 'you have saved my life tonight. Many's the close shave you and I have had together; many's the time when our necks have been in danger; but tonight, had it not been for you, it would be I who lies dead out there upon the street instead of that Chinaman. I owe you a debt of gratitude. Take one of these rings. If ever you — or should you settle down some day, any of your family after you — need any assistance of any kind, even at the risk of life itself, the sign of the dragon, the symbol of this ring, will bring that assistance from me or mine.'

"He protested at first, but finally, over the table, in the early morning hours, we took a solemn oath of allegiance before God, to be handed down, if necessary, to the next generation, that Brent or Burgess, whichever the case might be, would respond to the 'Sign of the Dragon' and render assistance to the limit of his ability and power.

"The next morning he left me, and from that day to this I have never seen him. I heard, a few years later, that he had married and settled down, just as I had done, but in all those years I have had no word from him. That night, over the table, with the dragon eyes of the ring gleaming oddly in the lamplight, is just as vivid in my memory as if it had happened yesterday. I want your promise Chester, that, should occasion ever arise, you will keep the oath I swore that night, and lend all assistance in your power, even at the risk of your life."

As he finished his story, father reached beneath his pillow and passed me the most peculiar ring I had ever seen. It was a heavy silver band, with a wonderfully wrought dragon embossed upon it, and worked in green gold. Its eyes were of jade.

"This is the ring, Chester. Somewhere is the mate to it, an exact duplicate, the only other one like it in existence. You have heard my story. Can I depend upon you to take up the promise and live it out to the letter? It is my last wish, Chester."

I felt enthralled with the weirdness of it all. It was the adventure I had longed for, prayed for, all my life. How could I do otherwise than assent to his wishes?

"Dad," I told him, "as God is my judge, I swear to respond to the sign of this dragon ring if it should ever call to me."

"Chester," he returned, "the word of a Brent is good as gold. I can die happy in the knowledge that my trust will be safely carried out. I knew I could depend upon you, boy of mine."

I kissed his hot brow and slipped the mysterious ring into my pocket as the old doctor clamored for admittance once more. That night my father passed out into the Great Beyond. He had gone forth upon his last Adventure.

## CHAPTER TWO

## THE SIGN OF THE DRAGON

Three uneventful years had rolled by since the death of my father. Not so very long before he died, on my twenty-first birthday, to be specific, he had taken me into the business with him as junior partner, and the firm had changed from the widely known "Peter Brent" to "Brent & Son." Therefore, upon his demise, the supervision of the business came into my hands.

In order to be nearer my work I had disposed of the old place in Manorport, and taken apartments in Boston. Here I lived the life of a recluse. The ordinary social life of the city bored me tremendously. I still yearned for some outstanding adventure that I might look back upon in later years, and point to as having lifted me out of the rut of humdrum, everyday life. I had about come to the conclusion that adventure, as I interpreted the word, was dead. At any rate, I felt convinced it was not to be found outside the covers of some lurid fiction magazine. Adventure, however, is somewhat like a German submarine. She lurks in some unexpected quarter, waiting a chance to torpedo her victims without warning, and leaves them to sink or swim as best they may.

I had almost forgotten the dragon ring, which rested snugly at home in a corner of my desk drawer. The tale which had seemed so vivid at my father's telling, was losing its grip as they passed by. In fact, had it not been for an occasional "cleaning up" process, when I would always come across the odd ring he had given me,

I think I would have forgotten the episode entirely.

At such time I would think over the whole story as he told it to me. I often wondered if the sign of the dragon would ever call upon me to keep the pledge my father made those long years before, and that I had sworn to observe.

I would always dismiss the matter with a laugh, and tuck the ring away once more, to be forgotten until the next time I "cleaned house." Of course, nothing would ever come of it! I was a fool to fritter away my time dreaming over such idle fancies. I was living in an age of science and system. Adventure was dead!

My longing for some sort of unusual happening made me weave romances around every odd character I passed upon the street. I built air-castles of adventure from the most trivial incidents. Somewhere I had read that each life was only one of a million "passing tales," that hidden in each life was some unsuspected incident that might furnish the material for a yarn such as few could spin. I wasted many idle moments in a futile endeavor to fathom the "skeleton in the closet" of my acquaintances and business associates.

Perhaps it was this trick of poking my nose into other people's business that accounted for the bad case of "nerves" I was developing. At twenty-five one ought not to shy at a shadow, as I confess I had been doing of late, especially when he was always prattling of an innate desire for adventure.

For the past few days I had the uncomfortable sensation of being followed. I could "feel" the intentness of a pair of eyes watching the back of my head. Wherever I went I had an uncontrollable desire to suddenly turn and confront whoever was on my trail.

Of course it was all absurd. Nothing more or less than a hallucination, due to my foolish imaginings.

Still, the feeling persisted with such bulldog tenacity I could not rid myself of it.

If any one was shadowing me I'll give them credit for making a good job out of it. Try as I might, I could not catch my shadow unawares. I tried every device I had ever read about for forcing one into revealing himself, but all to no avail.

The persistency of the notion gave me an uneasy feeling I can hardly describe. After a few days of it I decided to take a long postponed vacation. Then something occurred which startled me into a belief that perhaps adventure was still on the job, after all.

The morning mail arrived at my apartment each day just before breakfast, and part of my morning program, religiously adhered to, was the opening of the mail over the coffee cups.

There was always something, a bill from the tailor, an invitation to some function or other which would require a polite note of refusal; in fact, the tenor of my morning mail was quite often responsible for the frame of mind in which I reached the office.

This particular morning brought several letters. I glanced at them automatically before opening any of them, and my attention was arrested by one addressed in a distinctly feminine, yet unfamiliar hand.

I instinctively separated it from the others, and left it to be opened last.

There was the usual monthly statement from my club, and an advertisement or two that were quickly disposed of. With my usual habit of making a mountain out of a molehill, I began building a mystery right away around the unopened letter. Why should a young lady be writing to me? My acquaintances included few of the fair sex, and none who would have any reason for writing to me. (Of course, I imagined my unknown correspondent as young and, perhaps, a wee bit good looking.)

I turned the missive over and over in my hands, even holding it up to the light in a vain effort to get some inkling of the contents before I opened it. It was mine all right; there could be no mistake about that. The address was clear enough:


CHESTER BRENT, Esq.
Cheltingham Apartments, Boston, Mass.


I suppose if I had been anything but a hare-brained young fool, I would have had that letter opened and read two or three times, but as I have said before, I was a worshipper at the shrine of any possible adventure. At last I split the flap of the envelope, and drew out its contents expectantly. But with all my suppositions, I was totally unprepared for what that envelope actually contained. The note itself was unsigned, and was in the same firm, legible hand as the writing on the envelope.

It was short and businesslike in the extreme:

MY DEAR MR. BRENT:

> I am very desirous of seeing you on a matter of importance. I take
> this method of announcing that I shall call at your office some time
> Tuesday, the twelfth, to interview you. As it is imperative that I see you
> in person, I shall identify myself by means of a card such as I have
> enclosed.

The note was puzzling enough, I'll admit, but it was not the note with which I was chiefly concerned. It was the enclosure. An ordinary-sized calling-card, perfectly blank except for a large blotch of red sealing wax in the center. And imprinted in the wax was an ensignia that could only have been made by the mate to the green dragon ring with the jade eyes, that reposed in my desk-drawer!

The sign of the dragon!

The words of my father came back to me as vividly as if he was at the moment speaking them again into my ear:

" . . . that Brent or Burgess, whichever the case might be, would respond to the sign of the dragon and render assistance to the limit of his ability and power."

And I was pledged to carry out this promise to the letter. I rescued my ring from its resting place and fitted it to the dragon seal upon the card. Any doubts that I might have had to its authenticity were immediately dispelled. It fitted as well as if my own ring had been the one to make the impression. My brain was whirling in an attempt to grasp the significance of it all. After all these years the twin rings were again fated to cross each other's paths. What would be the outcome?

I slipped the ring on my finger and gazed at it, fascinated by the gleaming jade eyes of the green and gold dragon. I rather hesitated to wear the ring, for I knew its oddity would invite innumerable questions, but I was resolved that it should accompany me wherever I went until this adventure was at an end. Tuesday the twelfth? That was tomorrow! I was keyed up to the highest pitch of excitement. Adventure was not dead! Without warning I had been plunged into what seemed to me must prove the experience I had wished for so long. A years-old pledge of fealty; twin rings of an oddity that defied adequate description as symbols of that pledge; an unsigned note in a feminine hand — what more could one ask in the way of a mysterious setting? I could have imagined nothing more promising of future thrills than this combination.

I don't exactly know how I got through the day, but I know that evening came at last. My mind was still intent upon the caller of the morrow. What would she be like? Would she be dark or fair, young or old? I pictured myself as the hero of all kinds of impossible adventures, with my mysterious correspondent as the much persecuted heroine. I slept but little that night, I can tell you, and my trip to the office was made with my mind way off somewhere above the clouds. Not another word had I heard. All that I knew was that the sign of the dragon had called to me to aid, and that the call had come in the handwriting of a woman.

## CHAPTER THREE

## ANITA BURGESS

My expected visitor kept me on the anxious seat until well into the afternoon. For fear I might miss her, I pointed to a nearby restaurant and had them send my luncheon to the office. I was beginning to be assailed by doubts and misgivings, when the boy brought me an envelope addressed in the same handwriting as my note of the previous day. I knew before I opened it exactly what I would find inside. An exact duplicate of the card I already carried in my pocket. Just a blotch of red sealing wax, stamped with the sign of the dragon.

"Lady to see you, sir," he announced. "She wouldn't give her name, but she told me to bring you the note, and said you would understand."

"It's all right," I assented: "show her in."

The dragon ring in my pocket seemed to find its way to my finger automatically. At last my mysterious caller had arrived. At last I was to learn what service I could render to the owner of the other ring. I suppose I should have been calm and self-possessed, but my heart was beating at trip-hammer speed. I felt myself growing hot and cold by turns. As I rose to greet my visitor, however, I congratulated myself that outwardly I was as cool as a cucumber. My first impression of her was eminently satisfactory. From the top of her modish hat, set jauntily upon a wealth of auburn hair, to the tip of her natty gray kid boots, she was typical of the modern, self-reliant American woman. She was just the type that to my mind fitted her present role to perfection.

"Mr. Brent?" she inquired, extending her hand. I noticed at once, on the middle finger, a replica of the ring I was wearing.

I nodded in acquiescence, and drew up a chair for her.

"You received my note?"

In reply, I produced the two strange calling cards I had received.

"You have the advantage of me, Miss —"

"Burgess," she supplied. "Anita Burgess. I trust you will pardon the rather mysterious way in which I announced myself, but my business is of such a nature that I preferred my identity to remain unknown until I was sure I had found the right Mr. Brent."

"And you are certain?"

"Oh, yes. The ring on your left hand satisfies me on that score. But, to the business at hand. You are familiar with the pledge associated with the ring you wear?"

"I promised my father, on his death-bed, three years ago, to observe the pledge he made to your namesake, should the occasion ever arise."

"Good enough! I do not come to you through choice, Mr. Brent, but dire necessity. I have a favor to ask of you that may entail the risking of your life. I want you to listen closely to what I have to tell, and think carefully before you decide as to whether you wish to take so great a risk as I must ask of you."

I nodded.

"First of all, Mr. Brent, I want your promise that when

I leave this building you will make no attempt to follow me, or to learn anything more of this affair than I choose to tell you."

"In other words, you are asking me to go into this affair with my eyes shut?"

"It is for your own protection as well as mine, Mr. Brent. From the time your connection with this matter is established, both your safety and mine are doubly menaced. I have exercised the utmost caution to keep my visit here this afternoon from reaching the ears of my — suppose I call them adversaries — and any act of yours that might tend  to arouse their suspicions would set all my scheming at naught. Therefore, before I proceed, I would like your promise to make no move that might embarrass me or make my position more difficult."

"Very well, I shall abide by your wishes in the matter. Just what can I do to assist you?"

"I have in my possession certain documents that were left in my care by my father, who gave me the ring and told me its story at the same time. The nature of these documents I am not at present at liberty to divulge.

"There is a certain crowd that is very desirous of acquiring possession of these documents. The importance in which this other faction holds the acquisition of these papers will be emphasized when I tell you that two attempts have been made upon my life in the past few weeks. It was after the second attempt that I bethought myself of the pledge, connected with the odd ring that I had. I knew it could do no harm to look up the owner and see if he, too, held the pledge as sacred. If not, I would be no worse off than before; if he did, I would try to enlist his aid. My first step was to locate the Brents, whom my father had last heard of as still living in Manorport. I went there, and found that the Brent homestead had been sold, but that a Chester Brent, the son of the man my father knew, had moved to Boston, where he was carrying on his father's business. As I said before, all this information had to be gathered with the utmost caution, lest my opponents suspect I planned to enlist the aid of any one; and this made it doubly hard to procure. Luckily, I had but little difficulty in locating you, and here I am. Now, my plan is simply this: The very nature of these documents I speak of make them valueless unless one has the entire set of them."

Miss Burgess drew a sealed envelope from somewhere about her person, and laid it on the desk in front of me.

"In this envelope, sealed, are just half of the papers I mentioned. I have the other half in a duplicate package in my possession. Will you take charge of this package for me, with the solemn promise to guard it with your life, if necessary, until I send or come for it? Of course, you understand that I trust you to make no attempt to learn the contents. I may find it impossible to call for the package in person. Do not let it leave your possession on any pretext unless the one who demands it is wearing the ring I now wear."

"But suppose I am in doubt as to what move to make? I will not know where to locate you, or —"

"You have a phone at your apartment. I will communicate with you from time to time, when I can safely do so. You have my story, Mr. Brent. Think carefully before you make any decision. Remember that two attempts have already been made upon my life, and that, should your connection with this affair be established, your life, too, would be constantly in danger. It is no mere child's play, this undertaking, or I would not be tempted to enlist outside aid."

I picked up the sealed packet, and turned it idly in my hands. Prompted by some peculiar impulse, probably my inborn longing for adventure, I tucked it snugly away in my inside pocket.

"That is my answer, Miss Burgess. The package is now in my care. Rest assured that it will be ready for you when you desire."

"I fear, Mr. Brent," she went on, "that you underestimate the power of the forces that oppose us."

"I must remind you," I told her, "that you have asked me to help you because of the pledge made between my father and yours. Can I emphasize my seriousness more than by promising that, by the sign of the dragon ring, I shall protect these documents no matter to what risks or dangers I may be exposed?"

"My best wishes to you, Sir Knight of the Dragon," she smiled, rising. "Then I have your promise to make no effort to trace me or to ascertain the contents of that packet until I give you permission?"

"You have my promise," I solemnly returned.

With a last smile, the door closed behind her, and she was gone.

Alone once more, the whole conversation seemed more of a dream than anything else. It couldn't be possible, I told myself, that any such thing could happen here, in Boston, in the twentieth century. Impossible! And yet, the two unique calling cards were still on the desk before me, and I could feel the pressure of the package in my inside pocket to help convince me that it was not by any means a mere figment of my vivid imagination.

## CHAPTER FOUR

### THE EPISODE OF THE MYSTERIOUS STRANGER

Yielding to impulse may some day get me into serious trouble.

When I promised Miss Burgess that I would make no attempt to locate her or learn any more about her than I already knew, I made it all in good faith. I would have undoubtedly kept it inviolate had it not been for a trifling incident that occurred a few evenings later.

I had not been to the theater for several weeks, and was determined to see a much-advertised play that was, according to its press agent, "the talk of the town."

I was rather disappointed in the performance. Not but what it was good enough in its way, but it didn't come up to my expectations, as is quite often the case with these over-advertised productions.

It was during the intermission between the second and last act that I spied her, directly ahead of me, just a few rows away.

There was no mistaking her for anyone else. Anita Burgess was of a distinctive type that one could pick out from among a thousand.

I thrilled at the thought that here was a girl whose life was constantly in danger and who was bold enough to attend a well-filled play-house, and alone! Perhaps, I decided, she was safer here than in her own home. One would scarcely attempt an assault where there were so many onlookers. Yes, her reasoning was correct; she was in no danger during the performance, at any rate.

But how about afterwards? I began to fancy all sorts of dangers besetting her. I wavered between my promise to keep away from her until I was sent for, and an asinine desire to play knight-errant, uninvited, and follow along at her heels to protect her.

The last act of the play was beginning, and I temporarily forgot the subject of Anita Burgess in my endeavors to find some redeeming feature in the play being enacted on the stage.

As soon as the play was ended and the lights flashed on, my mind reverted to the mystery girl and her problems again.

She had already risen, and was making her way along the crowded aisle, toward the foyer.

The idea of playing watch-dog to my lady of the ring must have gained a greater control over my mind than I imagined. For the moment my actions seemed to be regulated by some outside agency. I followed her down the aisle, keeping well in the rear, but always near enough so that I did not lose sight of her.

As she reached the foyer my attention was attracted to a man who detached himself from a small group of friends, broke off his conversation with an attractive olive-skinned young lady, and fell into step behind my quarry.

There was nothing unusual for an incident of this kind to happen in the crowded lobby of a theater, but a strange premonition warned me that this stranger was somehow connected with this affair.

He had every appearance of being a gentleman of the first water, and I could not find any logical reason for my suspicions. Still, I reflected, this affair to date had given me no indications as to whether I was arrayed against might of finance or physique.

We reached the street almost simultaneously, and it was with difficulty that I kept from being observed. Miss Burgess summoned a waiting taxi, and I turned my attention to the man whom I instinctively distrusted. He, too, had called a car. While I was not near enough to overhear his directions, I could gather from his gestures that he was instructing the driver to trail Miss Burgess' car. My impulses were leading me into an adventure with a vengeance. My suspicions regarding the stranger were not without foundation after all.

All my reluctance at the thought of breaking my promise to Miss Burgess fled with the increasing possibility of attendant danger. I was resolved, now, to follow on and see this thing through at all costs. I fretted and fumed as I waited for my machine to arrive. It would be all right, I decided, for me to indulge in this escapade. My chauffeur was discreet and would be willing to lend a hand, should I need him.

"Keep that other car in sight," I instructed, indicating the tail-lights of the receding automobile, "and keep out of sight yourself."

He nodded, and we sped along on the trail of the other machines. I hadn't the slightest idea where we were bound. I was still under the distinct impression that I could be of some service to the one who had summoned me at the call of the dragon ring. That was enough for me, all the incentive I needed to persuade me to follow on, irrespective of where the trail might lead. On we rode, until we had left the lights of Boston well behind. Finally I noticed that we were slowing down.

"The car ahead has stopped just this side of an old house up the line," the chauffeur told me through the tube. "I can see the tail-lights of another machine that's stopped directly in front of the house."

"Drive right on, past them both," I directed, "and when you get a way down the road, stop."

We passed the stranger's machine, which was drawn up at the side of the road. I could see that he was still inside. As we drew up to the house I strained my eyes to get a better view of things. It was well back from the road, and was flanked on either side by a heavy growth of underbrush and trees. I soon discovered the reason for the stranger remaining in his car. On the steps of the old mansion stood the trim figure of Miss Burgess, evidently waiting to be admitted. She must have dismissed her taxi, for the driver had turned and was heading his car towards the city. We drove along until we rounded a bend in the road, and the chauffeur brought the machine to a standstill.

Alighting and directing my man to wait until I returned. I picked my way cautiously back towards the old dwelling. I kept to the shadows as far as possible, as I neared my goal, but in spite of my caution I barely avoided a collision with the man I trailed as he emerged from the bushes just ahead. The auto that had brought him to the scene was no longer in sight. He seemed quite unaware that anyone might be following, and it proved an easy matter to observe his every move.

Fate must have directed my footsteps, for, while the stranger was constantly stepping upon dry, crackling twigs, or stumbling over loose stones, I had so far escaped them. A single misstep on my part would have been fatal.

With an ease born of long experience, the intruder noiselessly raised a window in the rear of the house. Silently he drew himself up, inch by inch, until his body was half over the sill, his legs left dangling awkwardly outside.

It was a case of now or never. Once he reached the inside of the house, I would be helpless to lend any assistance. With a single bound I was upon him. There was a crash and a shower of broken glass, as a flying fist crashed through the half-opened window. He lost his grip upon the sill, and we dropped to the ground together, his huge bulk nearly crushing the wind out of me.

In the moment's respite that followed my breathlessness, his hand darted out behind him and I saw the gleam of cold steel in the moonlight as his revolver flashed before my startled eyes. But I struck his wrist up just in the nick of time. A second later, and I would have been in a far, far distant land. The echo of the shot reverberated with enough volume to arouse the dead.

I had no time to speculate what was going on inside the house. I more than had my hands full with my opponent. He was a great deal heavier than I would have guessed, and lithe and wiry as a panther. As long as I could maintain my grip upon his wrist, the revolver was of no use to him, so I concentrated all my energy upon keeping the weapon out of harm's way. As I have hinted, my lucky star must have been in the ascendancy this night, for as we swayed to and fro, locked in a mighty embrace, he backed into the fallen trunk of a tree. In a twinkling I had thrown him, and in another the revolver was in my possession.

"Now get up!" I ordered peremptorily. "And be careful that you keep your distance. I would have no more compunction about shooting you than I would some mangy dog."

Then came the interruption.

"Just toss away that gun, if you please; then put your hands up above your head, and keep them there!"

It was the voice of Miss Burgess that rang out, authoritatively, behind me. I saw the stranger's hands shoot upwards, and, tossing my weapon in the direction of the voice I followed suit.

"Now, if you gentleman will be so kind as to step into the light, I would be interested to know what this is all about."

I turned, my hands still high above my head, and found myself looking into the muzzle of an efficient-looking thirty-two. It described an unwavering half-circle, covering both of us, and we followed Miss Burgess silently, as she made for the front of the house. As we stepped into the path, the light from the road made the scene as brilliant as if it were mid-day.

"Pray tell me what is the meaning of all this? Why, Mr. Brent, is it really you?" she interrupted. "There's no need for you to keep your hands up any longer. On second thought, you'd better go back and retrieve that revolver I made you throw away. I'll keep this other gentleman quiet until you return."

I did as she bade me, and came back quickly, to find their positions unchanged.

"How came you to get mixed up in this affair tonight, Mr. Brent?" she questioned.

I recounted all that had happened since I had first espied her in the theater.

"I apologize for breaking my agreement in regard to keeping away from you," I concluded, "but I felt that the circumstances justified me in following along."

"You have rendered me a service that quite offsets any rules you may have broken," she avowed. "There has been no harm done. I do not live here. My business at hand simply required that I make this trip tonight; that is all." Then turning: "Marion," she called to someone inside, "have you a few yards of clothes-line that I may use?"

In reply, a middle-aged woman appeared in the doorway, a coil of heavy rope in her hands.

"If you will get that for me, Mr. Brent" – then, as I returned, bearing the cord; to the stranger: "just put your hands behind your back, if you please. Remember, I can shoot as straight as anyone you ever knew, Mr. Man! Now, if you will tie his hands Mr. Brent — Thank you, ever so much. Once more I assure you that the service you rendered tonight is a very great one. I can handle this gentleman very nicely now. Goodnight Mr. Brent, until I see you again."

I took this as a dismissal and started down the path to where my car was waiting. As I turned into the road, I looked back just in time to see the mysterious stranger enter the house under the persuasive influence of Miss Burgess' revolver. She followed him, and the door closed behind them. I felt my newly acquired weapon nestling snugly in my hip pocket, and it was with quite a degree of assurance that I directed my driver to take me home.

## CHAPTER FIVE

### A THREAT AND AN INTRUSION

I had been reckless enough to carry the packet of documents on my person since they had been entrusted to me. After the incident of the night before, I decided that it was quite necessary to procure a safer hiding place for them. The next question was where they could be hidden and yet be safe from prying eyes.

At last I hit upon the following scheme. At one of the places where the wall-paper overlapped, I loosened the paper with painstaking care. Then, even more carefully, I scraped away just enough of the plastering so that the packet would fit without causing the paper to bulge, yet not enough to allow it to slip down. A little flour and water paste, and the job was complete. I inspected the result and concluded that an expert would be unable to tell that anything had been tampered with. The ring remained to be concealed.

I turned a small tabourette upside down, and hollowed out enough of one of its legs to allow the admission of the ring. I fastened this in place with a double-headed tack. It was not as well hidden as the documents, but I was satisfied it was in a place where one would be unlikely to look for it, and I took the further precaution of utilizing the tabourette to hold a large pot of ferns that had adorned my center table. Next I cleared up the debris, and felt much relived, now that my charges were disposed of safely.

Quite naturally I was late in getting down to the office. As a matter of fact, I was barely in time to be on hand to receive an out-of-town buyer who was rated as one of the big customers of the firm. When a man is after big business he can scarcely stand on ceremony as to business hours. When R. F. Fitzgerald himself proposed that I dine with him that evening, I saw no other course open but to accept his invitation. By the time I got around to my routine work it was so far ahead of me it took me the biggest part of the day to get caught up. So it was that closing time came before I hardly realized it could be any later than mid-afternoon.

A hurried trip to my apartments, where I cleaned up a bit and changed my clothes, and I was off to meet Fitzgerald. Randolph Fitzgerald was one of the few really big men whose business required the raw materials that my firm handled. It was decidedly unusual for him to bother with the trade at all, his custom being generally to leave the details with his subordinates. So you see, the very presence of this man spoke of something in the wind. An invitation to dine with R. F. Fitzgerald was something to be coveted by one in my position.

It was a wonderful dinner. From a cocktail to demitasse it left nothing to be desired. R. F. punctuated the meal with an occasional reference to my father, whom he had known quite well, but for the most part the conversation was confined to commonplace.

It was not until the last of the dishes were cleared away and we were entrenched behind two big, black cigars that we settled down to business.

I put forth the best efforts of which I was capable, and before we had finished our first cigars I had written up an order so tremendously large that it staggered me. I knew it was by far the largest single order that had ever been written for the firm. At his suggestion we had gone up to his suite of rooms, and I was just about to light up my second cigar, when he rather jolted my visions of hooking the biggest fish I had had on my line.

"Brent," he purred, "before we consider this order as closed, there is a little matter I would like to discuss with you."

His attitude reminded me of a sleek, well-fed cat, who toys with a mouse she has captured just for the sake of seeing it struggle. I don't know just how I gained that impression, but I couldn't seem to banish the comparison from my mind.

"If it is a question of price, Mr. Fitzgerald, I assure you —"

"Tut-tut, my boy; you couldn't do better by me on price. No; it's something altogether different. You might say that it had no direct bearing on the business we have been discussing, but as the entire order hinges on it, I feel I can safely class it as part of the proposition."

I confess I was becoming sorely puzzled.

"I don't understand to what you refer."

"You will in a minute, Mr. Brent, if you'll give me a chance to explain. Listen to me. I know that you have in your possession a packet of papers that are absolutely worthless to you. I represent interests to whom those documents are all-important. We are prepared to leave no stone unturned in our efforts to acquire them, but first I wanted to give you an opportunity to turn them over to us of your own accord. My proposition is simply this: if you will turn that packet of documents over to me within the next twenty-four hours, the order that I have given you stands. Otherwise I will not only cancel it, but promise that I will use whatever influence I may have to turn trade in some other direction."

I was well-nigh stunned by this revelation. Truly, Miss Burgess had been right when she assured me that I greatly underestimated the forces against which I had pitted myself. I was stung to the quick by the offer that had just been made. It was nothing more or less than out-and-out bribery, and he had not even the grace to attempt to camouflage it in any way, shape or manner.

I might be tricked, but I was beyond the temptation of a bribe, alluring though the prize might be. I fully realized the effect on my business, should this man wield his tremendous power against me, but I was pledged by the sign of the dragon ring, and I would be loyal to my trust at any cost.

"What under the sun are you driving at? All this talk of mysterious papers and documents savors some movie serial plot. You sound like the villain in 'Bertha, the Cloak Model,' or some such tommy-rot."

"It's no use for you to pretend ignorance of the affair, I can tell you, we know that you have those papers in your care."

I rose with as much dignity as I could assume.

"You will pardon me for suggesting it, Mr. Fitzgerald, but I fear the wine you had with your dinner must have gone to your head. I had better bid you good-evening."

"As you wish, Brent.' His tone hardened noticeably. "My offer still holds. You have twenty-four hours in which to make up your mind. Remember," he added, ominously, "should you choose to match your wits against ours, we have the power to crush you as one might crush an ant beneath his heel, and crush you we will!"

I left the hotel, my mind filled with all sorts of forebodings. My willingness to jump blindly into this affair, my abominable habit of yielding to my impulses, was due to prove more costly that I had ever realized.

Already I had incurred the enmity of one who was directly responsible for ten per cent of our annual business. A man with an influence far-reaching enough to sway another ten per cent whatever way he chose. I realized that his was no idle threat, and I mentally quavered as I pictured the business difficulties he had it in his power to make for me.

Not only that, but I had no way of knowing just what other powers he had lined up on this side. He had said that he represented 'interests' that would use any means, so long as they attained the ends they desired. I fear I shivered, involuntarily, as I tried to figure the magnitude of 'interests' that could use Rudolph Fitzgerald for an errand-boy.

But youth is optimistic, and I had not reached my apartments before this line of reckoning had given way to another. If a mere slip of a girl like Anita Burgess could see no reason why I, a descendent of a long line of pioneers and adventurers, would not be able to hold my own. I had wished for adventure, and now I was getting my wish, where could I find good cause to complain? I had worked myself into a much more cheerful frame of mind by the time I let myself into my apartments. But my none too tranquil nerves were due for yet another shock.

My rooms looked as if they had been visited by a desert sand-storm. They were a prize picture of chaos and disorder. Whoever my nocturnal visitor had been, he had attended to the task of ransacking my things with a thoroughness that bespoke worlds of experience at the job.

The floor around the desk was littered with letters and papers, the table-drawer was half-opened, its contents strewn recklessly over the place. Chairs were overturned, pictures taken from their places on the wall, the bureau-drawers were open and my clothes were scattered in a tangled mess around the bed-room. Every article in the room had come in for its share of attention. The intruder had even gone so far as to slit the mattress on the bed in an attempt to locate what he sought.

In spite of the completeness of the upheaval, the packet of documents was still safely resting in its niche in the wall, and the ring remained unfound. I thanked my lucky stars that I had taken time to dispose of them in this way. A less carefully prepared hiding-place, and the package would surely have been among the missing.

A half-opened window and a convenient fire escape was enough to show how my place had been entered. I silently resolved to have a burglar alarm installed before the next day came to an end. I would take no more chances, rest assured of that, as this business was taking a decidedly serious aspect. It took me well into the night to put the room into any semblance of order, but the events of the evening had driven all thoughts of sleep from my mind.

I was handicapped by the oath of secrecy and I did not dare report this matter to the police because of the publicity that such a proceeding would entail. No, it was to be a battle of wits, and I must fight it alone.

But was I fighting it alone? I had gotten into the tangle to help Miss Burgess in her trouble, so by the same token why couldn't I count her as an ally? Her assistance might prove invaluable before this matter reached its culmination. The thought strengthened and stimulated me. The deeper I got into this matter, the higher my admiration rose for her courage. The incident of the night before commanded my attention, and I wondered what had occurred after I left the scene. What had gone on between the mysterious stranger and his fair captor? The more I puzzled over this affair, the further away I seemed to get from any adequate solution of the mystery that enshrouded the incident.

What was the nature of the documents in the packet in my keeping? Why should men of the caliber of R. F. Fitzgerald and his associates be so anxious to gain possession of it? What influence had drawn Anita Burgess as deeply into the affair? It was as complex as a Chinese puzzle. The dragon ring was leading me into a maze from which it was becoming increasingly difficult to extricate myself.

## Chapter Six

### The Girl with the Dragon Ring

Coincidence was not responsible for a strikingly handsome girl being in the same restaurant as myself on the following day. She accounted for that sensation I had experienced of being followed from my apartments to the café. Of course, I had no suspicion that she had any business with me, until she came over and sat down at my table.

"Mr. Chester Brent?" she interrogated.

I sipped my coffee thoughtfully, and answered with a nod. The girl was an utter stranger, yet I had the distinct impression of having seen her somewhere before. The waiter appeared, and while she was ordering I took the opportunity to study her carefully. I instinctively assumed she was in some way connected with the dragon mystery (as I had begun to classify the chain of events in my own mind) and I waited for her to announce her purpose.

Perhaps she was an emissary from Fitzgerald. I had heard nothing from him all day, and the time allowed for my decision was practically at an end. If she was, I admired his choice. She was a decided brunette, dark-skinned, with carefully moulded features. Indeed, the olive tint of her skin and a slight accent when she addressed me, conveyed the impression that she was of foreign extraction. The waiter hurried off to fill her order, and she directed her attention to me again.

"I have heard of you, Mr. Brent. I came in here to dine to-night, and it is so extremely lonely, dining alone, don't you think so? I saw you, also alone, and took the liberty of joining you. I hope you are not offended?"

"Not in the least," I parried. I knew there was some deeper motive in her action than a mere desire for companionship. I was slightly disappointed that she had not offered some more plausible excuse to defend her move.

Her eyes narrowed, and she eyed me piercingly, as though to determine my seriousness. The scrutiny must have satisfied her, for she went on:

"That is fine. We shall have a delightful dinner together."

"And afterwards?"

"We shall let afterwards shape its own course, shall we not, Mr. Brent?"

She toyed with one of the forks, drumming idly with it on the edge of the table. Was it merely a trick of my imagination, or did that tap-tap-tapping of the fork resolve itself into measured beats and pauses, some sort of pre-arranged signaling? Nonsense; of course not! The sound would not carry twenty feet away, and the adjoining tables were unoccupied.

"As you choose. I only anticipated a pleasurable evening in your company, unless, of course, you have other plans."

She hesitated.

"No, not exactly that. After all, I could spend my evening in much less desirable company."

It was my turn to pause. I gazed at her intently until politeness forced me to remove my eyes from hers, but I could detect nothing except mere banter in either her tones or manner.

"Thank you. With such an unconventional beginning everything certainly seems most propitious for a rather unusual evening."

I don't know whether it was the remark or the arrival of the waiter that silenced her. When she spoke again her attitude had changed.

"Do you know, Mr. Brent, I have heard a great deal about you lately."

"Really? What, pray tell, has been the reason for my sudden popularity? Or is it some sort of notoriety instead?"

"Perhaps neither. It happens, sometimes, that a friend may speak well of one to an equally close friend, you know."

That remark left me rather up in the air.

"And that mutual friend?"

"From what I have heard your circle of those you count as

friends is not so large but what you should easily guess."

I confess she was proving more of a match for me, but I did not dare venture to volunteer too much information until I understood her connection in this tangle.

When I lapsed into silence she regarded me with her lips curling into an amused smile, and the meal continued in absolute silence. I ventured to think that her desire for companionship was easily satisfied, but wisely kept my thoughts to myself and waited for her to make the next move.

"Your attitude during dinner reminds me of a turtle," she told me as the meal drew to a close.

"In what way?"

"Why when a turtle tires of his associates he simply draws up into his shell and stays there."

"My silence you mean?" and she nodded. "It was simply a case of not being able to think of anything that might interest you. By the way, now that dinner is nearly through, what next?"

"I have a somewhat unconventional favor to ask of you."

Now it was coming. I had known all along her flimsy claim of lonesomeness was crude camouflage.

"I make no rash promises."

"It is just this, Mr. Brent. There is a little matter I wish to discuss with you, but I wish to be sure that I am safely sheltered from prying eyes and ears. I wonder if you could take me to your apartments? We would be perfectly safe there."

"Perhaps we would and perhaps we wouldn't. Bachelor apartments are hardly the place to entertain an unchaperoned young lady. It would be a case of smuggle you in and smuggle you out, and should you be discovered there would be the very devil to pay. "

"I am prepared to meet just such a contingency as you mention. I quite agree that a young lady such as myself could hardly expect to visit a gentleman's apartments alone and at night. But a young man — a boy? Surely, there could be no objections to your bringing home a young male friend?"

"Then you mean — "

"You get my idea exactly; I mean that I shall accompany you to your rooms, but dressed as a boy. It is feasible, even though it is a trifle out of the ordinary. There we can talk things over freely."

She marked my reluctance to decide, opened her bag and took out a card, which she dropped on the table in front of me. I looked down upon the now familiar red seal, marked with the insignia of the dragon, and my hesitancy vanished in a flash.

"As you desire," I assented, "if you think the plan can be carried out successfully."

"I haven't the slightest doubt of it. First I must trouble you to take me to Boule's. As you are probably aware, he is a costumer — rents fancy costumes for masquerades and such things, you know."

I paid the waiter, summoned a waiting taxi, and in a few minutes we drew up to the front of Boule's.

She asked me to wait in the taxi until she returned, and it seemed scarcely a quarter hour when she was again beside me in the machine. The change was so complete that I hardly knew her myself for the charming young lady who had left me such a short time before. As a boy she was even more prepossessing than she was as a girl, and she had told the truth when she said she was prepared for this move. Everything must have been laid out for her in anticipation of just such a procedure. No one, in the semi-darkness of the evening, could ever have detected that she was not the young man she was supposed to be.

Again that feeling swept over me that I had seen her somewhere before, but I brushed it lightly aside and wondered what message Miss Burgess was sending by this stranger, and why she had been unable to deliver it in person.

"You look great," I told my new-found "gentleman friend."

"You'd pass muster anywhere."

She smiled.

"Many difficulties are easily surmounted, Mr. Brent, when one is prepared to cope with them. It was necessary that I make this trip to your apartments, therefore it was equally necessary that I be prepared to make it in safety."

"But suppose I had refused to countenance your proposition?"

"Then I was prepared to use this leverage to overbalance your objections."

There, gleaming in the palm of her hand, was the dragon ring I had last seen on the finger of Anita Burgess. My friend was not lacking in credentials; first the card, then the ring itself. We arrived at the apartments without incident, and made our way up the stairs.

"You will have to excuse the appearance of the place," I apologized as we entered, "but I had a surreptitious visitor last evening, who nearly wrecked the place, and I haven't had ample opportunity to straighten things out as yet."

"You mean that your rooms were broken into?"

"Exactly." I told her of the condition of the room upon my return the night before, concluding: "But they didn't succeed in finding the articles I have reason to believe was the sole object of the intrusion."

"Then they are still safe?"

"You mean the documents? Yes. As safe as when I first took charge of them."

Under the bright lights of the electric bulbs my "boy" visitor looked doubly attractive. Her well-rounded figure and dark skin and eyes fitted her new role to perfection. I saw her eyes glisten as I mentioned the papers.

"I'm so glad they are safe. I feared, when you spoke of the attempted robbery, that they had succeeded in getting them away from you."

"No; I had them safely hidden. Now, may I ask what business brings you here to-night that could not be transacted outside of my rooms?"

"I came for that package we have just been talking about."

I remembered Miss Burgess' instructions: "I may find it impossible to call you for the package in person. Do not let it leave your possession on any pretext, unless the one who demands it is wearing the ring I now wear," and the claimant had not only produced the ring, but one of those odd cards with which Miss Burgess had twice presented me.

"I don't quite see the necessity of this masquerade. Why not have had me deliver the package to you at some point outside?"

"Because I will not be suspected of acting as intermediary in this affair, whereas, if you attempted to carry it on your person there would be danger of its falling into other hands."

"Do you happen to know what disposal is to be made of it?" I wanted to be absolutely certain that I was doing right before I relinquished it. I couldn't rid myself of that sense that of uncertainty that had swept over me at the idea of giving this girl the packet, although she had the dragon ring, and I could think of no reason for doubting her. Of course, the incident had been out of the ordinary, but, for that matter, so had the whole affair.

"Only that I am to take it directly to headquarters," she replied.

I decided everything must be O.K. I could harbor no further doubts but what Miss Burgess had sent her for the documents. I would deliver them into her keeping, and my visitor watched me interestedly as I loosened the wall-paper and drew the packet from its hiding-place.

"Cleverly done, Mr. Brent," she complimented me. "No wonder your intruder failed to locate them."

"It seemed to baffle him just a little."

The jangle of the telephone in the next room interrupted me. The phone was on a stand near enough to the bed to make it handy if I had any night calls.

I thrust the packet of papers into my pocket.

"If you will pardon me for just a moment?"

"Surely. Run right along."

I vanished into the bed-room and snatched the receiver from the hook, savagely.

As I listened to the voice that came over the wire, my manner changed. I listened breathlessly, intent on catching every word.

"Is Mr. Chester Brent there?"

"This is Mr. Brent speaking."

"This is Miss Burgess, Anita Burgess," the voice went on. "I have been trying to get in touch with you all evening. Do not let those documents get out of your hands one single instant until I can see you again. My dragon ring – the one my father gave me, you know, has been stolen!"


## CHAPTER SEVEN

## INTO THE LION'S DEN

Miss Burgess' conversation came to an abrupt termination when I heard the clink of the receiver as it fell into place at the other end of the wire. The message had so startled me that I stood rooted to the spot, the receiver still held to my ear, until the operator's "Number, please," roused me to action.

The warning had arrived just in time, for a few moments

later damage would have been done. The imposter in the other room would have gained her objective – the documents entrusted to me would have been irretrievably lost. I shuddered as I realized how nearly I had made the fatal mistake of giving her the bundle.

A sudden flash of recognition, and I knew where I had previously encountered the masquerader. She was the young lady with whom my mysterious stranger of two evenings before had been talking when I had first noticed him in the foyer of the theatre.

I mentally cursed myself as several varieties of idiot for not having remembered her at sight. Still it had been only a fleeting glimpse of her, so perhaps I was not altogether to blame. Simultaneously a more sinister thought occupied my attention. The legend connected with the ring came back to me. "Should one of the rings be stolen, the charm gave way to a curse, and sudden death would assuredly be meted out to the perpetrator." I thought of the two incidences in which I knew of the working out of the superstition, and I wondered which one of us was to be the victim. The thought of this dark-haired beauty coming to an untimely end was most disconcerting, even though she was one of the elements of danger I was facing.

Thoughts travel fast, and all this had taken but a mere fraction of the time it takes to tell it. Since the fight at the country home I had carried the revolver that I had then acquired, and the feel of it, as my hand stole intuitively to my pocket, reassured me. I felt myself equal to any situation that might arise. It was evident that the girl's suspicions were not aroused. She was still in the big chair where I had left her, looking over a copy of some magazine she had chosen from the stand. My first precaution was to cross the room, placing myself so as to be between the girl and the door.

"Nothing of any importance," I told her. "Just someone with time to kill and a telephone handy. I pleaded important business, and we rang off."

"Then suppose we get back to the matter at hand," she suggested. "It is getting rather late, and I should be going. If I may have that package —"

She paused abruptly. I had backed to the door, and the sound of the tumblers in the lock as I turned the key, surprised her.

Then she rose, her eyes flashing dangerously.

"Exactly what do you mean by doing that, Mr. Brent?"

I took the key from the lock and put in my pocket before I replied.

"It means, my unknown friend, that it is my turn to do a little dictating. I would thank you to hand over that dragon ring that was stolen earlier in the evening."

She drew herself stiffly erect. Her black eyes narrowed until they were mere slits. Instantly she was on the defensive. There was no trace of fear, no hint of timidity in her manner. I could almost picture, in her stead, a tawny panther at bay, crouched ready for a final spring upon those who sought to destroy her.

"Do you mean to imply that I —"

"I mean to imply nothing; I mean to accuse. The owner of that ring has just informed me of its theft. The ring is in your possession. I can draw but one logical conclusion."

"So that was the nature of your 'unconsequential'

telephone call?"

"Your power of intellect does you credit, my fair friend."

Again her eyes flashed belligerently.

"It is quite possible that I might refuse to comply with your request."

"As a lever, cold steel is often quite effective as a talisman."

She did not even quiver as she found herself looking down the barrel of my weapon, and said cooly:

"Granted. In some cases a more powerful leverage is required than others, Mr. Brent. Are you quite sure your particular lever is equal to the task?"

She was slowly retreating in the direction of the window that opened onto the fire escape.

"I think it would be more conducive to your welfare if you didn't exhibit such a roving tendency. I think you had better be seated. Your familiarity with the exits here leads me to believe that perhaps you may have seen these apartments before."

She took the chair I indicated before she parried:

"It is my turn to congratulate you upon your keenness of intellect."

So here was my intruder of the night before! In spite of the fact that she was aligned against me, I could not help but feel a growing admiration for her prowess and courage.

"It might interest you to know that since your previous visit I have taken the precaution to install the protection of a burglar alarm. Another such attempt would only succeed in arousing the household."

"Since your previous visit," she mimicked, with a tantalizing smile. "My, but don't we take a lot for granted this evening. And aren't we progressive. I should apply to you for lessons in locking the barn door after the horse has been stolen."

Her banter was goading me to distraction. My rising anger must have reflected in my expression, for she laughed heartily.

"But in this case the 'horse' wasn't stolen," I reminded her.

"True enough, although it nearly got out of the stable in spite of your elaborate system of 'alarms.' They didn't succeed in keeping me out after all, you see."

"I still have the package." I inwardly regretted that its hiding place was revealed. Should a future opportunity be afforded for a search of the apartments, I feared I could devise no place of concealment where I would feel it was safely disposed of. "Once more I must ask you to give me that ring."

"Suppose I should scream?" she suggested. "If I remember rightly, it was you who mentioned that bachelor apartments were hardly the place for a young lady to be found, alone, at this hour."

"Then I should be forced to the unpleasant necessity of turning you over to the authorities. Sneak-thieves are not uncommon in apartment houses, and the fact that you are in boy's clothes precludes the possibility of your being able to offer a logical alibi."

I had drawn up a chair, and sat facing her, being careful to keep the drop upon her. Behind her banter I sensed her desperation and I knew that, should the slightest opportunity present itself, she would stake her all in a wild attempt to regain her freedom. It was my turn to take the initiative.

"Might I suggest that all this talk is getting us nowhere? Don't you think you might just as well hand over that ring now? Thank you. I felt sure you would see the wisdom of it sooner or later."

She glared at me vindictively as the ring changed hands.

"What is it pleasure to do with me? It is highly improbable that you intend to detain me here all night."

"Quite true. It is also highly improbable that I shall turn you loose to set Lord only knows how many cut-throats after my life before morning."

"You have your burglar alarms, ironically."

"And just at present I have you, which I consider a hundred-fold more protection than all the burglar alarms in the world."

"May I inquire what use the captor intends to make of the prisoner?"

"You may. I was about to tell you, anyway. I understood you to say that your intentions were to take this package," I tapped my pocket significantly, "direct to headquarters,"

"Those were my instructions."

"Suppose, then that you obey those instructions. I would hate to be the one to stand in the way of so admirable a young lady's execution of the task entrusted to her Of course, it will be wiser if they remain in my possession in transit. You see, my fair unknown, I have rather a strong inclination to find out just where the 'headquarters' you spoke of might be."

"You would dare?"

"Why not? When my own rooms are not safe from intrusion, I figure I will be just as secure elsewhere, and you will agree with me, I am sure, that to do the unexpected always gives one a decided advantage; for example, your visit here this evening. I confess, had it not been for that telephoned warning, you would have accomplished your mission with the utmost ease."

"If you insist, Mr. Brent, I suppose I have no other course to pursue. I warn you, fairly and squarely, that you will regret forcing me into doing this thing."

I suppose I was foolhardy in the extreme to propose such a venture. Walking boldly into the lion's den is by no means likely to prove to be a bed of roses. But I was riled. The gullibility with which I had walked into the trap set for me, and the narrowness of my escape, stung me into a rashness that allowed of no prudence or caution.

"I shall have to ask you to step into the other room with me while I telephone for a taxi."

She silently obeyed. I placed her advantageously in front of me while I called up the taxi-cab office and ordered  a car sent up immediately.

Getting into my top-coat and still maintaining the advantage the revolver afforded me was quite a task. I was painfully awkward about it, but the main thing is that I accomplished it without mishap. Then I concealed the revolver in the outside right-hand pocket of the ulster, but still kept it to bear upon my captive.

"Remember," I cautioned her, "although this revolver is out

of sight, I can shoot as well through the cloth of this coat as if it was not in the way. While I would regret shooting at a woman, if the necessity should arise — "

The significance of the pause was not lost upon her.

"You can threaten rather melodramatically, I am sure, she proclaimed. "What, pray, must I do to avoid the sensation of a bullet in my brain — though my capture leads me to doubt if I have one."

"Simply take me back, or let me take you back, to 'headquarters.' As I suggested before, I am anxious to learn more about your superiors in this matter. You interest me only as a means to that end. It is the men higher up who commend my attention."

I suppose the remark was rather brutal. If looks would kill, the one she flashed me would have sealed my doom. As it was, I dreaded the consequences should she succeed in regaining the upper hand. Wound a woman in body or in soul and chances are equal that you may be forgiven; wound her pride and she will seek vengeance for the rest of her days.

"Bear in mind that if I even so much as suspect you of double-crossing me, your apparent freedom will be at an end."

I had transferred the all-important package to the inside pocket of my suit-coat. I felt that it was as safe there as it would be left unconcealed about the rooms. I had also appropriated several yards of heavy cord on the chance that it might be of some use before the night was over, Then the taxi arrived, and my prisoner in the lead, we descended the stairs.

The address she gave the chauffeur surprised me. It was in

one of the most exclusive sections of the city.

Once inside the machine she lapsed into sullen taciturnity. Night rides, I reflected, were becoming a habit. We drew up in front of an imposing residence which bore all the earmarks of being closed for an indefinite period. The windows were boarded, the lawn was unkempt and neglected, the grounds were shrouded in absolute darkness. The general effect was that of some cold, dead thing. No sign of life was visible. A starless, overcast sky, that gave promise of an approaching storm, lent added solemnity to the scene. I paid the driver, and we watched the lights of the receding machine vanish into the darkness.

"The main task that confronts you, young lady, is to arrange things so that I can see and hear all that goes on without being seen or heard myself. Is this the place?"

She chose to maintain her attitude of silence, and replied with an answering nod.

I felt like a maurader as I followed her into the pitch-black darkness of the grounds. Lest she find some chance to elude me in the darkness, I held to her coat-tails with my free hand much as a blind man would cling to his leader for guidance and protection. The other hand still kept its grip upon the revolver that bulged in my pocket until we reached a side entrance to the dwelling, and the girl produced a key which she fitted to the lock. I drew the weapon from under cover. If I was going into this darkened house I would be prepared for emergencies.

"Follow me closely," she whispered as we stepped into the inky blackness of the hallway. "Perhaps you had best keep hold on my coat."

"I will be right at your heels and so will this." I prodded her with the muzzle of my revolver and trailed her through three or four spacious rooms, lighted only by an occasional moonbeam that found its way through the apertures in the boarded-up windows. She steered me deftly around the dust-laden furniture without bumping against anything. It gave me an eerie feeling, this owl-like ability of hers to see in the dark. My own eyes were becoming used to the dense darkness, and I could begin to distinguish the objects we passed more clearly.

We were making our way towards the center of the mansion. At last a light gleamed from behind drawn portieres. A tug at her coat checked the speed of my leader, but the caution was needless. The room though brilliantly lighted, was empty. I noticed the spick and span cleanliness of the room, in striking contrast to the dusty, musty unused apartments we had passed through in reaching it. Its luxurious furnishings were well in keeping with the house itself; heavy draperies at the windows and doors, thick carpets that rendered our steps noiseless, well appointed furniture. Whoever owned them was not only wealthy, but was possessed of marvelously good taste in his selections. All in all, the room was a study in harmony.

"The man I expected to meet here has evidently not arrived," the girl volunteered, sinking into a comfortable looking rocker.

"Then we shall wait for him," I said, preparing to take my place opposite.

A moment later the sound of a closing door brought me to my feet again.

"That must be him now,' she whispered.

The room opened into another that was as dark as the rest of the house had been, and I drew the heavy draperies across the doorway muttering:

"Behind these curtains I can observe all that is going on. Any inkling that I am here, or any false move on your part will prove your undoing." I retreated to the protection of the draperies as the sound of approaching footsteps fell upon our ears. Nearer and nearer they came until I knew their owner must be directly outside the room where the girl lay idly in her chair.

The curtains at the other end of the room parted, and a man steeped into the light. He was the same one I had first seen her talking with in the theater; the mysterious stranger whose hands I had tied and left at the mercies of Anita Burgess at the house in the country two nights before.

## CHAPTER EIGHT

### THE CURSE OF THE RING

The man swept the room with one comprehensive glance, took in the figure of the erstwhile boy in the rocker, and gave vent to his feelings with a low whistle.

"You're some sketch in that rig, Julia, believe me."

She gave him an icy stare.

" 'Miss Sabastino,' if you please."

" 'As you like it,' as the old bard would say."

I sensed a feeling of animosity between them. It was evident from the man's attitude that he was in a position to give the girl orders, but her whole demeanor spoke of forced obedience. He converted the end of the table into a seat, and one foot beat a soundless tattoo upon the carpeted floor.

"Did you get my instructions this afternoon?"

"I wouldn't otherwise be here in this outlandish get-up," she flared.

"Methodically he opened his cigarette case, selected one with care, lighted it without asking her permission, and blew several rings of blue smoke ceiling ward before he continued:

"Did you meet with any degree of success last evening?"

"Don't talk to me of success," she snapped. "It's bad enough for me to have to do your dirty work without listening to your sarcasms. I waited here till nearly sunrise to report on last night's venture, but you couldn't even let me know you were not going to meet me. Bah!"

He waved his hand in an eloquent gesture.

"My dear lady, if you had been in my predicament last evening, I doubt if even you would have been able to send any communications."

"You interest me. What was the dire calamity that befell you?"

"I had the somewhat doubtful pleasure of spending the

night trussed up like a sack of potatoes. In fact, the night before and all of yesterday as well."

"I am surprised to think that a man of your much vaunted abilities should submit to such ignominious treatment!"

He swung angrily from the table and strode menacingly toward her.

"Damn you! Some day you'll rile me to a point where I shall kill you!"

The girl laughed tauntingly.

"But not so long as you have need of my services, signor. Come, calm yourself. Can't you see I can hardly wait to hear what you have been doing since you ran away from me in the theater?"

I was wondering if she was really so desirous of learning what had happened, or whether she was drawing him out for my benefit. His anger passed as suddenly as it has risen, and he resumed his perch on the corner of the table. Then he sketched for her, briefly, his activities from the time I had left him facing Miss Burgess' revolver in the light from the road.

"Everything would have been as easy as rolling off a log if it hadn't been for the interference of that young pup Brent."

My blood boiled at this insult and my muscles tensed in silent rage, but I controlled myself with an effort, and listened as the girl queried:

"You let the Burgess girl take you inside?"

"I had little choice in the matter. Far be it from me to invite anyone to indulge in target practice, with yours truly as the target. She took me up to an attic room, and between the two women had me hog-tied like a steer. That Burgess girl, the young demon tried to make me talk. You can guess how well she made out. She threatened all kinds of terrible punishments and tortures if I insisted on keeping silent, but that didn't worry me much. When it comes right down to brass tacks a women is too squeamish and chicken-hearted to carry out her threats. So I stoutly refused to talk." His features twisted into a wry smile as he added: "They weren't very merciful about the way they tied me up. I haven't worked all the soreness out of my joints yet."

"But how did you manage to get away?"

"Oh, that part of it was easy enough, once the chance came. I had to eat, you know, and at meal times I had the delightful pleasure of Miss Burgess' companionship plus her revolver, while the other women attended to loosening my hands and tying them up again. Yesterday noon the girl must have been out somewheres, and the old women made the mistake of thinking she could manage me alone. Once my hands were free, the rest was simplicity itself. I overpowered her before she could make a sound. Oh, I didn't harm her," as a look of concern registered on the Italian girl's countenance, "I just tied her up as I had been, and left her there."

"My legs had been tied for so long that it was several minutes before I could use them. Then I went a-searching for whatever I might find. My supposition regarding the girl was a correct one. Except for the old women upstairs the house was deserted. It was my turn to play in luck. On the table in one of the rooms downstairs I made a rare find. My capture must have made Miss Burgess careless in the extreme. She had gone off and left her handbag behind, and in that handbag I found the dragon ring and the cards I sent you."

So the girl was not the thief at all! The curse associated with the theft of the ring came back to me for the second time that night, and with it an inward relief that its working portended evil for someone beside the girl.

"I knew the value of my find, the new power the possession of this talisman gave me. The boss had told me of the significance of the dragon ring. In my hands, my find was useless. Brent knew me now as being lined up against him, so that as far as openly approaching him was concerned, my hands were tied. So I thought of you at once. You were unknown to him. In your hands the ring might be of intrinsic value. My next problem was to get them to you, with some sort of instruction for using them, before their loss was discovered. I set off down the road, bent on finding some town or village where I could communicate with the boss. It couldn't have been more than a mile and a half to the nearest town, but that last half- mile was torture. My muscles rebelled at the task put upon them after their enforced vacation. The boss had a nice, hot, ready-made panning out to give me, but when I told him about finding the ring it sort of sweetened his temper. He told me about you falling down on your job last night, too. I only asked you to see what you'd have to say about it."

"After I'd entirely given you up," said the girl, "I phoned him at the number you gave me. I nearly wrecked the place, too, but not a packet of documents could I find. I'd liked to have seen that fellow's face when he got a look at the place. I certainly messed

THE LOVED DEAD

things up for him."

Beyond a doubt, she had. The man continued:

"The boss told me where I could reach you, but said that I'd better not try to see you in person, lest we be seen together by Brent or the girl. He told me to send you the cards and ring by messenger, and that he would instruct you in your part over the telephone."

As he talked the stranger smoked incessantly. All the windows were tightly closed, and the room was slowly filling with a blue, smoky haze. Gradually the rings of smoke drifted behind the draperies where I was concealed. The smoke alone would not have done it, but, combined as it was with the close, musty atmosphere of the unused room, I felt a growing, irrepressible desire to sneeze. The girl had not moved in her chair, except to draw one knee up between her clasped hands while she gave rapt attention to the stranger's tale.

"Yes, I received both the ring and the instructions. To a certain point they worked to perfection."

"Up 'to a certain point,' " he sneered. "You don't mean to tell me that — "

I could not hold it back any longer. It was more than mere human nature could stand. I made an ineffectual attempt to smother it behind my hand.

"Ca-choo!"

The stranger bounded from the table as if shot from a cannon.

"What was that?" he fired the question at the girl.

Her faced blanched white as snow and she shrank

away from him as though she would like to merge herself with the upholstery of the chair she occupied, and recovered her poise almost instantly, but not before a lurking suspicion crossed his mind.

"How do you suppose I know?"

He gripped her arm and pulled her bodily from the chair.

"Rollo Bassino," she panted, " take your hand off my arm! Let me go at once! Let me go, do you hear?"

She winced as his grip tightened.

"I'll let you go when I get damned good and ready! Are you going to tell me who is hidden in that room or must I find out for myself? Is it some lover you have been meeting secretly, or some spy your treachery has allowed to take his place among us?"

Her face flushed hotly at his accusations.

"Very well then, find out for yourself — if you can. You wouldn't believe me if I told you,"

With an oath he literally flung the girl aside. Under the impetus she staggered drunkenly across the room and brought up against the further wall. The jar dislodged a large hanging mirror, and it tumbled to the floor with a tremendous crash, the glass splintering into a thousand fragments.

He was crossing the room towards my hiding-place with tremendous strides. I steeled myself for the encounter that I knew was inevitable, and it struck me as rather a trick of Fate that I was armed with the same weapon I had taken from him two nights ago. I caught the reflection of light upon the automatic in his hand, and knew he had replaced his loss at the first opportunity.

If it was to be fight, I had every advantage on my side. From my location in the darkened room I could watch his every move, while he only knew somewhere in the dark I was lying await for him. While I knew that he was armed he had no way of knowing whether I was or not. It remained for the girl to discount my superiority. I had forgotten her in my endeavor to keep an eye on the man, whose eyes gleamed insanely in the brilliant light of the room. Unseen, she made her way along the wall of the room. With one quick motion she threw aside the protecting draperies, and I stood revealed.

If I could help it, I didn't want to injure this man. If I could capture him unharmed, I would be in a fair way to gain some information I very much desired. I was quite handy with a revolver, and determined on attempting to shoot the automatic from the hand of the other man. If I should succeed, the rest would be comparatively easy. The girl I knew to be unarmed, and could I manage to disarm the man, I felt that I would be master of the situation. If I failed —

My finger tightened on the trigger as Bassino's gun came up into position. Again the girl changed the entire situation. As the hammer of the pistol shot home, she flung at me a small, half-filled goldfish globe in an effort to deflect my aim. Her move was fatal for the man. The glancing blow, as the globe grazed my shoulder, was just enough to change the course of the bullet, but not enough to save the man who opposed me. Instead of shooting the weapon from his hand, as I intended, the bullet chose a course straight as a die for the breast of the victim.

So quickly was the whole scene enacted, that he did not even have a chance to press the trigger. He stopped in his tracks, his fingers slowly relaxed, the automatic slipping through his nerveless fingers. He clutched at the wound, from which a tiny trickle of blood was already seeping. A few staggering steps forward, and he crumpled in a lifeless heap at my feet. Once more the curse of the dragon had been fulfilled.

## Chapter Nine

### Anita takes a Hand

The realization that I had shot the fellow being at my feet appalled me. True, I had only intended to disarm, at the most disable him; nevertheless, the fact remained that he was dead — that he had come to his death by my hand.

I gazed at the still smoking revolver in my hand; then, down at the inert form of the stranger I had mur — No, no not that! Killed in self-defense was better. I was dazed, overwhelmed with the enormity of my deed. The lethargy into which my self-introspection had plunged me proved my undoing.

Not for a moment had Julia Sabastino lost her self-possession. Bassino's automatic had scarce touched the floor when she thought to procure it. I came out of the stupor to find myself facing a determined looking pistol, behind which was an equally determined girl.

"I think the tables are turned once more," she said. "Just drop that gun before you do some more damage."

Had she but known it, she could have taken it from me without the slightest resistance. I was entirely unnerved. For the moment my longing for adventure had departed absolutely. As a bad, bold, brave adventurer I was worth considerably less than a plugged nickel. Where was all the resourcefulness, the ability to extricate oneself from all sorts of pitfalls, that was supposed to be part and parcel of every hero's make-up? I fear I made a sorry hero. Given long, pointed ears and a tail, I could easily have been mistaken for a jackass. Recent events had followed one another in such bewildering confusion that my power to adjust myself to the kaleidoscopic conditions had been utterly exhausted. And to cap the climax I had killed a man!

For the time being I was an automation, subject to the control of any will stronger than my own. I relinquished the revolver not because of any conscious effort on my part simply because the girl had willed me to drop it. I was in a state of self-imposed hypnosis, my mind dominated by Miss Sabastino's.

"Now, if you will back up a few steps while I obtain that gun. I'm taking no chances this time," the girl went on, coldly.

My action brought me to the edge of the darkened area behind me. Had I been in the possession of normal faculties, I might have risked a dash for liberty into the unused portion of the house, trusting to luck to find some safe means of egress. As it was, I paused while she disposed of my weapon, previously the dead man's (I shuddered at the thought), by tucking it into the pocket of her coat.

"For the last time, Mr. Brent, I will ask you for those documents. I trust you will not have the heart to refuse me.'

I handed them over as submissively as a punished child. In anticipation of her next request I extended the dragon ring.

"No, thank you." Her tone was bittersweet. "I do not need your passport now that I have these." She flaunted the documents tauntingly before my eyes. "That rope you brought with you was a happy thought, indeed. I doubt if I could have located any handy enough to be of any value. Must I ask you for it a second time? Oh, thank you. There is a nice convenient, straight-back chair, Mr. Brent. You must be tired after standing for so long a time. My, my how quickly you gather my meaning. We are getting on famously together, aren't we? Steady just a moment now, while I fasten these knots securely. Well done is twice done, so they say."

She had been deftly tying me to the chair as she talked, and when she finished I could not move a muscle.

"I see no need of adding to your difficulties by gagging you. If you should scream I'm sure the sound would not penetrate to the street. I dislike the thoughts of leaving you all alone, but I fear that I must. If you get lonely, think of me. Your anger may dispel your lonesomeness. Now that he is out of the running" — at the reference to him her voice tinged with bitter scorn — "I suppose I've got to do his work as well and take these to the boss. If you don't liberate yourself before morning I promise to be generous and come back and set you free. Now I must bid you *adieu*."

I heard her receding footsteps and the slam of the door

behind her. It was raining. The storm the cloudy sky had foretold had arrived. I could hear the patter of the raindrops as they beat against the boarded windows, while the wind whistled dismally outside.

A night alone with the dead! I don't think it was intention on her part, but the chair was back to the door by which we had entered the room, and placed at just such an angle that when I looked straight ahead, the grim, stark body of my victim was directly in my line of vision. The storm raging outside suggested my similarity to a ship in a storm at sea, battling with over-powering elements against which it was arrayed. That was it; I was a storm tossed ship upon the bosom of the Sea of Life, and my adversaries were the tempest that was slowly bringing about my destruction.

Already our commercial business was feeling the effects of Fitzgerald's power, as only this afternoon we had received word from two of our oldest customers, who had kept a standing order with us for years, that beginning with the next month their business would be transferred to an opposing concern. And I knew this to be only the beginning.

The storm was gaining in violence, while the rain still beat against the window-boards, but it came in torrents now. I strained at my bonds with a sudden fury, and struggled desperately until the cords cut deep ridges into my wrists and ankles. At last I realized the futility of endeavoring, and gave up in hopeless despair. The slam of the outside door brought me bolt upright in my chair. Had the girl come back for something or other she had forgotten, or was this some new factor in the situation, some new danger that beset me? The click of heels upon the bare floor was distinctly feminine, but the footsteps bore little resemblance to those of the Italian girl.

"Chester! Chester Brent!"

I must be dreaming! Could I believe my ears? If only it was really true!

"Here! This way!" I called into the darkness. "Can you find me?"

"Coming," sang out the voice, cheerily.

My optimism rose several degrees. My old-time confidence was returning by leaps and bounds. I heard the swish of skirts behind my chair, and in another moment Anita Burgess stood before me.

"The right pocket of my inside coat. My knife."

She understood. A few quick slashes, and I was free.

"I saw you when you came in with the girl," she told me, "and I saw the man when he arrived. I thought I heard a pistol shot, and feared for you safety. When the girl came out alone I knew that something out of the ordinary had happened, for they always came out together. I let her get safely out of the way before I dared to leave my hiding-place in the shadows across the way. A skeleton key did the rest, and here I am. The man? Where has he gone?"

"Dead!" I indicated the body at the other end of the room. "I had to do it in self-defense. I didn't intend to kill him."

She shrugged her shoulders.

"Perhaps it is just as well. At least he is one stumbling-block removed from our path."

"But how did you know I was coming here?"

"I didn't; that part of it was a surprise. It was the man I was lying in wait for, for I knew he had stolen my dragon ring. I knew that he met the girl here every night between eleven and twelve, for I had followed him here before. Tonight I anticipated him."

"I have the ring." I took it from my pocket and gave it to her. "But the documents, the girl took them with her."

Miss Burgess wrinkled her brows thoughtfully.

"I think I know where she is bound. There is an even chance that we may be able to overtake her. My machine is waiting just a ways down the road. Are you still armed?"

"No; the girl took my revolver, too."

"I have an extra one in the automobile. Luckily I tossed it in at the last moment, as I feared losing the one I usually carry. Come, let us be off."

There was little need of further caution, so far at this house was concerned, so we wended our way through the maze of empty rooms until at last we stepped out into the night.

The tempest had reached the zenith of its fury, causing jagged flashes of lightening to leap across the sky, relieving, momentarily, the stygian blackness of the heavens. The thunder crashed and rolled in mighty awe-inspiring detonations, like the roar of guns upon battlefields. A thunderstorm of such severity at this season of the year, when the autumnal winds were already making themselves felt and top-coats were appearing with increasing frequency, was extraordinary. In all probability it was the last storm of the season, and the elements seemed allied to give us one that we would be sure to remember.

How it did rain! Blinding sheets of it that bewildered, that one must battle against every step of the way. In spite of my protecting ulster I was soaked to the skin before we reached the runabout that waited only a short block away. I doubt if Miss Burgess, her long raincoat buttoned up under her chin, fared as ill at the hands of the storm as I. No chauffeur was waiting in the little machine at the corner, and Miss Burgess waved me into my seat, started the motor at the first turn of the crank, climbed into her place behind the wheel, put on the gear, and we plunged into the storm.

I fell to marveling at the versatility of the girl beside me. Fearless, cool and collected in an emergency; capable of handling a situation that would deviate stouter hearts from their tasks; her familiarity with firearms; and now the masterful way in which she drove the car over the slippery pavements; one would not look for such a variety of accomplishments in her type. I speculated in what way she might next show her superiority over the majority of the vapid, namby-pamby, doll-like creatures I knew, who set themselves up as typical of American womanhood.

## Chapter Ten

### A Beast at Bay

Miss Burgess applied the brakes with a suddenness that nearly threw me out of my seat; the machine skidded several yards over the wet asphalt under its own momentum before she finally

"There she is now."

My eyes penetrated the gloom until I, too, caught sight of the rain-soaked figure just ahead. She was plodding on through the storm, unheeding the wind that whistled about her ears or the rain that poured down in never ending torrents. Her wet, boyish clothes clung to her well-rounded figure.

We followed along in the machine, keeping at a respectful distance, and I took this opportunity to narrate my experiences in detail to Miss Burgess from the time we had parted at the house in the country until she had rescued me. I told of the attempted robbery at my apartments, my interview with Fitzgerald, and the events of the early evening.

"In spite of all our precautions the package got away from me."

"Don't worry," she assured, "we still have a chance to regain it. If my suppositions are correct, we are still due for experiences before the sun rises again."

The storm was abating, and the torrential downpour had given place to a disagreeable drizzle.

Now that I was myself once more, I yearned for action. This sitting back in an automobile, trailing along at a snail's pace after a girl who had bested me twice in a single night, was galling. Had I had my way, I would have pounced upon that lone figure from behind and wrested the documents away from her by sheer brute force.

Steadily the boyish figure of the Italian girl kept on. We had gained an aristocratic quarter of the city, and at last our quarry mounted the steps on an impressive dwelling. We watched until a light gleamed in the hall, and the door opened to admit the girl. Another light flashed from behind shades where darkness had been before, and we knew then in what part of the house the next act of our little drama was to be staged. The light shone from the window of an upstairs apartment, leaving the downstairs in darkness, except for the front hallway. This setting was admirably suited to our present plans. If the interview had taken place downstairs our chances of discovery in trying to force an entrance would have been trebled. Miss Burgess drove to the end of the block, rounded the corner, and we left the machine just as the storm ceased. The clouds had vanished, and tiny stars were peeping at us from a clear sky.

I wondered if this circumstance was prophetic of our situation, if the events ahead were to clear up the mystery that surrounded us and leave everything as calm and peaceful as before.

Our next task was to find a way to enter the house without being apprehended. First we tried the windows. We had almost completely circled the house before I found one that slid up under the pressure I brought to bear. Cautiously, carefully, I drew myself up and through. Then I gave Miss Burgess a hand. With the agility of a boy she clambered to a place at my side, and we silently closed the window. The extra six-shooter Miss Burgess had so thoughtfully provided nestled close at hand in my coat pocket. I could see the glint of her own weapon as she prepared to locate the stairway leading to the upper floor.

We had the light in the hall to guide our search, so it was only a matter of seconds before we located the stairs. Fearful lest some slight sound might arouse servants, we exercised the utmost care in ascending the stairs. As we reached the top, the hum of voices fell upon our ears, and a lighted room indicated our goal. We doubled our vigilance, and crept along close to the wall until we brought up just outside the half-opened door from which we distinctly heard the girl we trailed saying:

"But I tell you I will have nothing more to do with this affair."

All the color, all the snap and vitality had gone from her voice. She spoke in a dull, droning monotone.

"Miss Sabastino, at the present time I positively cannot allow you to do as you suggest. You are in possession of too much information. I must insist that you stick by your original agreement. Any deviation would be extremely unwise."

The sound of the man's voice was a decided surprise. I had not the least suspicion until then that the "boss" who directed her movements was R. F. Fitzgerald. The fact that my room had been raided while he and I were dining together had rather thrown me off the track. I had imagined that perhaps there were two factions struggling for the possession of that mysterious package. Then he must have known all the while we were together that my rooms were being searched. This new turn of affairs added to my bewilderment. What did that package contain that he had gone to such extremes to get it into his hands?

The time was now ripe for action.

Miss Burgess placed her lips close to my ear, and whispered: "You cover the girl; I'll take care of the man myself."

The two were so engrossed in their conversation that they were all unconscious of our presence in the room until Miss Burgess commanded:

"Just raise your hands well above your heads, my friends."

Obediently two pair of arms shot into the air, and at the sight of me the Italian girl acted as if she had seen a ghost.

"Good evening, " I bantered. "You see, I did not have to wait until morning for your assistance, Miss Sabastino."

She cringed. One could see that her iron will was broken, her dominant spirit gone. Her lips quivered, and she struggled to keep back the tears that even now glistened in her eyes. When she spoke her voice faltered, wavered, almost broken.

"You can count on no more trouble from me, Mr. Brent. I have just informed Mr. Fitzgerald that I was about to sever my connections with this affair. Rollo" — she bit her lip in a supreme effort to control herself as she mentioned the dead man's name — "Rollo was mean to me, at times even cruel — but — but — I loved him! And now he is dead!"

Oblivious of the threat of my leveled revolver, she dropped into a chair and buried her head in her arms, her shoulders shaking with silent sobs. The rain-water trickling in little rivulets from her saturated garments, the heaving of her bosom as she sobbed her heart out in grief for the man she loved, combined to make her a pitiful picture of abject despair. The effect of her collapse on the other occupants of the room was varied in the extreme.

For my own part my conscience twinged with sudden qualms, for I was the instrument by which her sweetheart had come to his sudden end. Fitzgerald's thick, sensuous lips curled into an ugly sneer, expressive of his disgust for the girl's weakness in yielding thus to her emotions, and Miss Burgess darted one quick, sympathetic glance in her direction, then her features resumed their mask of immobility.

"That rather simplifies matters, Mr. Brent. Suppose you go through this man's pockets, while I keep him covered with this toy. If will be perfectly safe. He knows I wouldn't hesitate in the least to shoot him if he made an unnecessary move."

I emptied Fitzgerald's pockets swiftly, and efficiently, and found that he was unarmed. I piled the contents of his pockets on the table.

"Now, Mr. Brent, if you will take care of him while I look over these trinkets," suggested Miss Burgess. "Mr. Fitzgerald may be seated if he desires, as long as he doesn't attempt to lower those hands."

I could hear the click of his teeth as he snapped his jaws together in a rage. Again I was reminded of the cat — or was it the leopard — in his manner, only this time the semblance was that of a cat-beast at bay. He chanced a step forward, but the determination in my eyes, coupled with the unwavering weapon in my hand, checked him. He took Miss Burgess' suggestion and made himself as comfortable as possible in a handy easy-chair. If it had not been such a serious matter, the sight of this potbellied, prosperous-looking business man, with his hands thrust grotesquely above his head, would have been funny.

Miss Burgess sorted the articles of which I had deprived

him, and selected a letter or two, which went into her hand-bag. I caught her humming snatches of a popular air as she began a systematic search of the room. The place was evidently Fitzgerald's sanctuary. At nearly every turn she found something which went into her spacious bag. She uttered a happy little cry as she discovered a small, red, morocco-bound book, and scanned its contents before depositing it in her bag with the rest of her finds. Fitzgerald had half-turned in his chair at her enthusiastic cry, and at the sight of the book she had unearthed, he swore volubly. I feared for a moment he contemplated launching his huge bulk at the girl, but he thought better of it, and settled back into his chair.

Miss Burgess was still humming when she had completed the search, and her bag bulged with the weight of its contents. There was a phone at the end of the room, and to this she next turned her attention.

"Is this the Department of Justice? This is Douglass' operative No. 2291, Anita Burgess. You'd better send some men up to Fitzgerald's — yes, R. F. Fitzgerald's — I've got enough evidence to convict him a hundred times. There's a girl here, too, who, I think, will be invaluable to us as a witness. Yes, I'll wait for them, but send them right along. My prisoner isn't any too docile, and there's many a slip, you know. All right; good-bye."

The receiver clicked into position.

"Douglass' operative No. 2291!" That could mean nothing except the Douglass Detective Agency that had recently been proving of great assistance to the government in hunting out undesirable alien enemies.

"There, that's over. I fear, Mr. Fitzgerald, that you will sleep in a strange bed tonight, but you'll have ample opportunity to get familiar with it. All we can do now, Mr. Brent, is wait for the men the department is sending."

The package the girl had taken from me was lying, still unopened, on the center table, and my glance rested on it for a moment.

"The documents," I reminded her; "what about those?"

"Oh, those?" Her rippling laughter rang musically upon my ears. "You may open it now, if you like, Mr. Brent. I'll take charge of my prisoner while you do so. It's quite likely he is still interested in the contents, too."

At last I was to learn the secret of the package. It took me what seemed an eternity to break the seal. My fingers were all thumbs. Eventually I held the contents in my hands, and spread the pages out, expectantly.

Imagine my chagrin, my mortification, as I realized that the documents I had so carefully guarded, the important papers that Fitzgerald had been so anxious to obtain, were nothing more nor less than several sheets of folded, blank paper!

## CHAPTER ELEVEN

## THE WHOLE TRUTH

Fitzgerald's face grew purple with rage at the revelation, while I was nonplussed for a brief moment. Then, I, too was filled with a sense of outraged dignity. To think that I had been hoodwinked into safeguarding a package that contained nothing but blank paper! I was bewildered, confounded, disheartened, humiliated and abashed in quick succession.

Miss Burgess was quick to notice my changing expression.

"Don't feel badly over it, Mr. Brent, or feel that you've been made a fool of. The package served its purpose — to aid in bringing this treacherous snake to justice. I know it is all a puzzle to you, that with the facts at your disposal you cannot quite fathom it. But it's a long story. The men from the department are due at any moment. It's nearly morning, and I'm pretty well used up after the nervous strain I've been under the last few weeks. Suppose we leave the telling for some future time. If I may suggest it, we might dine together tomorrow night at a quiet place I know; then, I promise, I shall tell you the whole interesting truth of the affair."

Her reasoning was sound. I could ask no fairer arrangement. She told me where she wished to dine; we set the time, and the bargain was sealed.

The police came just then, and an astounded butler, awakened by their vigorous ringing, let them in. A still more astounded butler, wide awake now, watched them handcuff his master to them ignominiously. The girl promised to go along without this indignity, and Miss Burgess vouched for her safety. I realized that my Lady of the Dragon was a keen analyst of character, for my knowledge of her abilities was growing. In spite of the lateness of the hour, Miss Burgess insisted on driving me to my apartments, where she left me with a parting injunction to remember our dinner appointment for the next evening.

Just as if there were any danger of my forgetting! I looked forward to that explanation with the eagerness a small boy looks forward to a fishing trip with dad. The restaurant she had selected was quiet and unobtrusive, ideally adapted for a meeting of this kind.

I reached the place far in advance of the time set for our appointment, and fretted and fumed at my idiocy in being so infernally early as I paced to and fro in front of the place, awaiting her arrival. My wait would have been needless had I been on time, for Miss Burgess was punctual to the minute.

"Mr. Brent," she began, when we were at last comfortably settled at one of the tables, "first I must apologize for several necessary falsehoods I told you, and for the deception in regard to the contents of the package which caused you so much trouble. Fact and fiction are so intermingled in the garbled version you have of the affair, I had better start at the very beginning, and this is all how it came about:

"My father died just after the war broke out. He had met with serious financial reverses just previous to his death, and left my mother and I practically penniless. I shall always feel that worrying over the impending crash hastened his death. After the estate was settled, I knew, if we used the slightest remainder to live upon, it would soon be eaten up, and mother and I would be, figuratively speaking, thrown upon the world. I realized that I must find some sort of work at which I could support the two of us. Opportunity beckoned through an influential friend, and I accepted a position with the Douglass Detective Agency. Once well into the work, I reveled in it. I put my whole heart and soul into every task assigned to me, and gradually I came to be used for more hazardous work. Blind luck, more than anything else, aided me in bringing my first few bigger cases to a successful conclusion.

"A short time ago I received instructions to work under the direction of the Department of Justice for the duration of the war. Fitzgerald had been under the surveillance of the department for several months. They suspected his connection with the Central Powers, but needed some positive proof before they dared make an arrest. He was wary. In spite of all their attempts to force his hand, he bided his time. Whatever moves he made were executed in absolute secrecy. Uncle Sam never gives up. Once the government of the United States sets itself against you, you might as well throw up your hands. The men were unable to procure anything in the way of tangible evidence. Very well, if the men failed, put a woman on the job! I was the woman.

"At the earliest possible moment an introduction between Fitzgerald and me was arranged. I proceeded to cultivate his acquaintance. At the same time rumors were started destined to reach the ears of Fitzgerald. These rumors had it that I was in possession of a formula, made by my father, for an explosive more powerful, more deadly than TNT— which, as you know, is the most powerful explosive the world has ever known. If Fitzgerald was, as we suspected him, in the pay of the German government, he would be desirous of obtaining this formula before the allies had a chance to open negotiations for it.

"In the hours I spent in the company of this man, I purposely avoided all reference to the subject, but the rumors fostered by the department persisted. Finally he began to be interested. Of course, he was too wise to allow me to know that he was interested. My first clue to his interest was when I came home one evening, after a theater party and midnight supper — with Fitzgerald — to surprise some one in the act of searching my room.

"Douglass put him through the third degree, but he might just as well have tried getting blood out of a stone. The ruffian denied all knowledge of any such person as R. F. Fitzgerald, or any other party by that name. No way had yet been devised for forcing a man to tell the truth. The only excuse we had for holding him was on a charge of attempted burglary. Acting upon a suggestion from Douglass, the judge gave the culprit a limit sentence.

"In order that Fitzgerald might not suspect I connected him with the episode, I doubled my attentions towards him. It was then that Bassino came into the affair. He was an adventurer, pure and simple. Although Italian, his love of money was greater than his love of country. You should have been at the department this morning when the girl told how she had been forced to serve his ends against her will. Like many another good woman she had thrown herself away on a worthless scoundrel; and despite the many heartaches and troubles he caused her, she loved him deeply, fiercely. She holds Fitzgerald responsible for her lover's untimely end, and swears vengeance by all the saints. Her willingness to tell what she knows will most likely let her off with a light sentence. But I am straying from the main line.

"Bassino's espionage was worthy of a more deserving cause. Inside a week he had established my connection with the department, and Fitzgerald dropped me as he would a hot coal. I was confronted with the possibility of failure. So far I had proven a match for every task to which I had been assigned, and was resolved that I would not fall down on this problem. I would work out the solution in my own way.

"I cast about for some new method of attack, and analyzed the business of the man, after which I made a list of the people with whom his business brought him into direct contact. In doing so, of course, I included your name. My father had told me the story of the dragon rings, and the oath of fealty connected with them, and had given his ring to me with a request that I respect the vows he had made.

" 'Brent' is not a common name, and the fact that it was the same as the owner of the other ring, commanded my attention. If you were only a descendent of my father's old chum, perhaps I could use the ring to enlist your assistance; that is, if you knew the story of the ring and held sacred the oath your father had taken. It was worth a chance. So I investigated your family history. I went to Manorport, as I told you. I did not do it secretly, however. Far from it. I knew that Bassino, or some one else, was in full knowledge of my every move. That was as I wished. If you became involved in the affair, Fitzgerald would know of it within half an hour. Then I must stake all on the chance of your connection with the matter forcing him to make some unguarded move.

"When I found out you were actually the son of Peter Brent

I began my campaign. The element of mystery which surrounded my anonymous note and the queer card was to stimulate your interest in the affair. I must have some plausible excuse for asking you to help me, so I fixed up the packet of 'documents' and connected the story I told you. I relied upon your knowledge of the ring and your natural impulsiveness to make you willing to 'go it blind.' You see, I had picked up a great deal of information about you in Manorport that proved of great assistance in formulating my plans. The result of our interview exceeded my wildest expectations.

"I don't know where the 'leak' was in your office, but I do know that Fitzgerald was in possession of every detail of that interview within the hour. I could not have asked for more. You can readily see the importance of keeping that package away from him. Had he discovered that it contained only blank paper, my ruse would have been exposed, my last chance of outwitting him, gone. My other requests for secrecy were simply to impress you more thoroughly, to make you realize the importance of the affair without giving you any real information.

"Practically all the rest of the events you know. That morocco-bound book was a code-book that will help in deciphering several important papers which have fallen into our hands. The other things I took away with me were letters and documents that not only absolutely convict Fitzgerald of being a spy in the pay of the German government, but also implicate parties of national reputation whom we never would have in the least suspected."

So that was the answer to the riddle. It was all simple enough now that the facts were laid before me.

"I trust, Mr. Brent," she was saying, "that just because your connection with this matter is at an end, it will not mean a severance of our relations."

I thrilled at the possibilities contained in the thought.

"Your sentiments coincide with mine, Miss Burgess, to the letter."

I helped her into her wrap and we made our way leisurely to the street, where I hailed a taxi.

"Now that the ban of secrecy is lifted, may I have the privilege of seeing you home — Anita?"

Her blue eyes looked full into mine, searchingly, intently. Her eyelids drooped over them, and she turned partly away as she responded:

"I think you may — Chester."

As we bowled along over the cobblestones my mind was a seething caldron of conflicting emotions. Hope and fear, joy and gloom, happiness and despair, played tag with one another around my tired brain.

In an overwhelming flash it came to me. I knew that this girl at my side was the one girl of all girls in the world for me. Fate had crossed threads of our destinies, and I knew that as surely as there were stars in the heavens that some day I would make her my very own, my Lady of the Dragon.